THE WEB OF WAR

THE WEB OF WAR

E. R. Baillie

iUniverse LLC
Bloomington

THE WEB OF WAR

Certain characters in this work are historical figures, and certain events portrayed did take place. However, this is a work of fiction. All of the other characters, names, and events as well as all places, incidents, organizations, and dialogue in this novel are either the products of the author's imagination or are used fictitiously.

iUniverse books may be ordered through booksellers or by contacting:

iUniverse LLC
1663 Liberty Drive
Bloomington, IN 47403
www.iuniverse.com
1-800-Authors (1-800-288-4677)

ISBN: 978-1-4917-2445-3 (sc)
ISBN: 978-1-4917-2447-7 (hc)
ISBN: 978-1-4917-2446-0 (e)

Library of Congress Control Number: 2014902113

Printed in the United States of America.

iUniverse rev. date: 02/21/2014

For my children, Miguel, Edouard and Anita

CHAPTER 1
JULY 1812

▼

Matthew Elliott

Sarah was wantin' me to use the big office in the front of the house and spend less time in the little room off the kitchen, but it suited me here where the table was solid and the chairs were rough; where the back door used by the Indians was close; where merchants came and went carryin' food and gossip; and where sweet fragrances seeped in from the kitchen. Far as I was concerned there couldn't be a better office. Since I married sweet Sarah, I'd run my farm and my Indian trade from that room and become pretty damn rich in the process.

It sure as hell wasn't in my plans for this office to turn into what was fast becomin' a war room.

Alone, I put my feet up on the table, tilted my chair back, sipped my brandy and stared at the blurred vision of myself in the window. There I was, Matthew Elliott, who, not of my own choosin', had become "Lieutenant Commander, Chief of Indian Affairs." 'Twas a glorious title for an Irishman who had just completed his 72nd year, and in spite of not wanting it, didn't it pleasure me to know how it must stick in the craw of every English officer hereabouts? 'Course, I damned well deserved it, havin' devoted the best years of my life to livin' and workin' with the Indians in the Ohio and Upper Canada regions, but I wasn't stupid; I knew that were it not for the threat of war and the need for a man of my talents, the fekin' British would have had me out on my ear before my next piss.

Alexander, my son, disturbed my reverie when he came in with a letter in his hand. "A soldier delivered this to the front door. Looks like it's from Lieutenant Colonel Procter. Should I open it?"

I sighed and nodded my head. "Sure ta hell it's some kind of complaint!"

I watched Alexander as he tore open the letter. This son was my pride—the man who would take the Elliott name from a rough-and-tumble reputation to one that would be looked up to in Canadian society. He was small-like, and like me no beauty, havin' my sharp cheekbones and receding hairline, but his skin was white like mine, which was fortunate. If he'd had the skin colour of his brother, Boy, and his mother, Love, my beautiful Indian first wife, 'twould have damaged the future I'd planned for him.

I had sent him East for many years, first to study and later to become a lawyer, and here he was back, dressed in frock coat and leggings, every bit the gentleman. Now we would have time to get to know each other again.

Alexander read the note slowly. "It is from Procter. There's a covering note: It says, 'Elliott, because you have repeatedly ignored my orders, I'm forced to send this letter to Quebec.'" Alexander put aside the cover letter and read through the several pages of the official missive.

I was in no big hurry to hear.

"Says here that you are suspected of peculation, that you clash with the military authorities and that you are secretive about the affairs of the Indian department and careless about the department's accounting. Quite a damning document, Da!"

I slammed my feet to the floor and started for the door. "Tear the damned thing up! I'm going to see the snot-nosed son of a bitch and tell him how things get done in this part of the world."

Alexander followed me out. "Procter's the man with the gold on his shoulders, Da. We'd best try to smooth things over."

"That son of a bitch is doin' this because he can't stand the sight of me and this is his way of lettin' me know it."

We kept at it while we waited for a servant to bring our horses up. In frustration, Alexander thrust his fingers through his thick mane of black hair. "You have to own that you don't help matters. When he's in the room, you're worse than a hissing cat!"

I mounted my horse. "Can't help it, my boy. The idjit is girdled by the fekin' 'military rules' and can't see that they don't work with the Indians! Are you coming with me?"

We usually went from my farm to Fort Malden by canoe along the Detroit River, but it was a blustery day and the Indians would be paddling against the wind. Anyway, a gallop into the wind best suited my mood.

The soldier guarding the palisade gate waved us through, and we walked our horses directly to Procter's headquarters.

Alexander took the reins of my horse and tied both animals to the hitching post. "Watch your temper please, Da."

He was right, but men like Procter, weak men with a lot of power, were dangerous human beings who always left a man like me growling with helplessness.

Procter did not look up from his paperwork when we were shown in. All we could see was his receding hairline, long nose and drooping jowls. "I deduce you received my note, Elliott." He continued signing papers, moving each one aside after it had received his venerable signature.

"I did that, sir, and am here to ask you to explain yer complaints."

He stopped writing and looked up but kept his pen poised. "There's really no need to go into it all, Elliott, as you'll not be with us much longer, but as long as you're asking I'll tell you. I ordered you to keep weapons out of the hands of the Indians until we were ready to have them fight. You've disobeyed me and not gone by the book. That's enough for a court-martial right there."

I chewed on my anger. Alexander elbowed me lightly. "Soldiers don't understand how the Indian Department has to be run. Jaysus, God almighty!" Alexander cleared his throat to get my attention, but I ignored him. "Indians have never heard of 'the book,' and there's no way in hell I'll be able to keep them happy by doing things your way!"

"I could have you arrested for speaking to your commanding officer like that."

"You, sir, are not my commanding officer. You've given me a title because you need me to keep Tecumseh under wraps until you're ready to have him fight. And I know that to succeed, not only must we feed the Indians, we're going to have to arm him and his men." I leaned on the desk and stared right into the face of the mealy-mouthed bastard. "And do somthin' more concrete than hollow words about our promises of land on this side of the Great Lakes."

He leaned over and opened a drawer, from which he pulled what I figured was the famous document, and then he pushed his bulk out of the chair and waved the document in front of my face, stepping too close to me. "An officer has gone over the financing for Fort Malden, and it shows that your Indian Department is spending far more than can be easily explained. Quebec will be very interested in your peculations."

I did not retreat from his fat face. He was not going to frighten me. "You go right ahead and send it! We'll see whether Quebec values my services enough to ignore your unproven accusations."

His face blossomed in furor, but he did not back off a single inch. "I was born in Ireland; my father was a surgeon in the British army. I know about men like you, Elliott. You can't resist skimming off the top."

Aha! Then I understood! A Brit who grew up in Ireland! 'Twas sure he'd never be able to tolerate the likes of me. "Do as you see fit, Lieutenant Colonel. Just don't forget that I'm the man who can lead a force of Indians, and without them Indians you're banjaxed before you start."

"You're right, I need the Indians, but I don't need you, Elliott." I could smell his rotten breath, he was that close. "I'll do my level best to relieve you of your position and find someone who is willing to do things by the book. I'll hold on to the letter for a month, but if you don't change your attitude, it will go in August."

I turned to leave, saying, "You won't send it. You need me too much. If you do, I guarantee you'll regret it."

The wind had died down by the time we left. We rode side by side in silence, Alexander respectin' my need to rid myself of the stink of Proctor's breath and the words that spouted out of it. I kept blowing air out of my nose to try to rid myself of the rotten sensations.

Halfway home, Alexander looked over at me. "Are you ready to talk, Da?"

I gave a final blow through my nose and nodded my head.

"You've never told me about your life in Ireland. The Lieutenant Colonel seemed to suggest that he was a superior human being because he grew up there."

"'Course he thought that. Why wouldn't he? The British had passed the goddamned penal laws, which said Irish Catholics couldn't go to school, we couldn't serve as apprentices, and we couldn't even practice our religion or do any other damned thing that might raise us up. I was born into a poor Irish family, and like all the other Irish we lived in scrabblin' misery, too hungry and too poor to revolt. To live in Ireland under fekin' British landlords like that man we just left was to live without hope."

Alexander was quiet for a while as he absorbed the story I'd never told. "That's why you left?" he asked finally.

"Aye, but had I stayed in the country, sure ta God I'd have been jailed for some kind of violence against them snotty overlords."

"It must have been hard to leave your family."

I shook my head. "I'll confess something to you, my son. 'Twas not the departure from kin that weighed me down as I leaned on the railing of the ship and watched the Emerald Isle disappear. No, 'twas a whole load guilt at the relief I felt leaving a family I could not entirely love. They were victims who had accepted their lot, and pity soiled my feelings toward them. For me, real love needed to be packaged in respect." I reached over and squeezed his arm. "Like my love for your mother."

'Twas Alexander's turn to be silent. I knew he was thinking of his mother, as was I.

After a few minutes, he leaned into the neck of his horse and stroked its mane. "It's said that before you married Mother, in your years trading with the Indians, you left a lot of 'half-breeds' like us in your tracks." He choked on the word "half-breeds."

I laughed. "I never denied it a'cause it added to my manly reputation, but truth be told, I didn't shoot any fertile bullets until I married your mother when I was 50 years old. I guess my body was waitin' till the real thing came along."

Alexander slowed his horse down to listen. "I hardly remember her."

I reined my horse in to match the pace of his. "I know, and it breaks my heart. She was small, your mother was, but strong, with large hands and a vertical crease between her eyes, which disappeared when she smiled. She could do everything: medicate, cook, plant and love; Jaysus, Mary and Joseph, could she love! That's why I called her Love, because it felt right and her Indian name was too damned long."

My voice choked on the memories. "I suspect that not everyone has been privileged to experience a special moment in life, one so unforgettable that it never leaves you." The rhythm of the ride rocked my memories. "It happened to me when lyin' on my bed of deerskin-covered pine boughs, with you straddled on my stomach and Love lyin' beside me feeding the baby, Matthew. Your delighted giggle, the cooing of Love, the sucking of the baby and the fragrance of cut pine were all isolated and bathed in light, and my mind sang the words, 'I am happy!'"

"But then my mother died."

"She did. Just like a damned river reflection, seems happiness has to have its opposite. I came down with a fever, Love caught it and it killed her. It hurts to think about that time."

"Is that when you moved us to Amherstburg?"

"We might have moved anyway. For the Indians in the Ohio region, 'twas the beginnin' of the end. The Americans were going after their lands and the British had pulled in their wings and retreated further north."

Alexander shook his head. "You didn't give me enough time to make Amherstburg a home. You dragged me across the Erie and Ontario and down the St. Lawrence River and left me there to be schooled."

"I did that and I'd do it again."

"I was only nine years old!" he complained.

I knew it had been difficult for him, but there was anger mixed with my guilt. "You should be grateful. You got the education not allowed me in Ireland, and look at you now."

That shut him up for a few minutes as he mulled over the conversation. Finally he gave me a sad smile. "At least now I understand."

We spurred our horses and headed for home with unwelcome emotions as passengers on both horses.

As we handed the reins of our horses over to the stable boy, I said to Alexander, "We have to get our hands on Procter's letter before it is sent."

I found Sarah in the parlour with my namesake, Matthew (whom we'd nicknamed Boy so there'd be less confusion with names), and with the two babes born to me and Sarah, my second wife. I was sapped dry and exhausted, but the sight of my little family brought a tired smile to my face. The birth of these two little ones when I was 70 and 72 years of age put a polish on my reputation, that was for certain. My wish had been to spend my senior years enjoying my wealth, running my farm and having time to take advantage of the pleasures of my young family. It was all I wanted.

It was I who should have been down on my knees playing with the little ones, but Boy was there instead. "Rest your weary bones, Da," he said without looking away from the babes. "I'm here."

Did I hear a tinge of sarcasm in his voice?

Alexander disturbed the confusing scene. "They've sent news from the fort. The Americans have declared war!"

Sarah's Diary

I heard the juice in their whispers as they sat down behind me at Father's funeral. There was sympathy, I know, but it was spiked with titillations. "They say he was so drunk he sat backward on Old George and that horse just reared up and threw him headfirst into the rocks." I stared hard at the altar pretending I had not heard and clung to the front of the pew imagining listeners shaking their heads in false sympathy while they bit back smiles and other tales about the wild antics of the Irish schoolmaster.

I heard a woman who more than likely was wiping fictitious tears with a dainty handkerchief mutter, "Poor Sarah, they say she'll have to give up the house to pay her father's debts," and another reply, "She can probably take her father's position. He, at least, trained her well for that."

I was damned if I'd let them see how I loved my wild, sad, brilliant father, so I said my private farewells to him, wiped my tears and followed the coffin down the aisle with emotions locked up tight. I kept them that way through the burial and the gathering that followed, not relaxing until I was finally home alone. I collapsed in Father's chair, which would soon go with the house when the bankers confiscated the property.

That night I stood in front of the mirror, let down my auburn hair and attacked my sparkling vanity with harsh brush strokes. I, "Poor Sarah," had no intention of becoming the teacher of little urchins, all of whom were interested only in shooting, shouting and scrapping.

While I brushed out the tangles, Mr. Matthew Elliott's face popped into my head and with it a plan began to take shape. I had been aware of Mr. Elliott for years because he was always on the tip of everyone's tongue: a man who teetered on the fence of legality but, without fail, seemed to survive the richer for each undertaking.

As I smoothed my hair that night and looked at myself in the mirror, I guessed my youth might appeal to him. My reflection and I developed a plan.

Now here I am, "Poor Sarah," mistress of the biggest house in the area, mother of two beautiful babes.

Mr. Matthew's "peter" is as old as he is. Oh, how I wish I'd known how beautiful his son Boy was before committing myself to the senior member of the family! Since my husband can't read, I shall hide you under my pillow, Dear Diary. I would not want Alexander to find it. He already looks at me with suspicion.

In spite of my yearnings, it has been a successful few years, and now all might be ruined by war.

CHAPTER 2
JULY 1812

▼

Daniel

Since I was 7, I'd crossed the river every day to go to school in Mr. Donovan's schoolhouse in Detroit. Everybody knew Mr. Donovan was a drunk, but Papa said he was also the best teacher in the whole area, so even if he missed a day here and there I'd still get a better education than I would at the Sandwich Schoolhouse. Mr. Donovan died when I was 9, but by then I had good friends, so I kept going.

Every year I sat in the desk next to my best friend, Johnnie Jordan. We both had complications at home, which we almost never talked about, but it drew us together. When we weren't studying, we played lacrosse in the schoolyard or escaped to the woods, where we shared secrets and tried to guess what sex was about.

Yesterday I put my lacrosse stick in the canoe and set out on my usual crossing. There was to be a match against another school, and we'd been practicing for weeks. As I paddled toward the dock, I saw the teacher standing there, which was strange as he always waited in the classroom for the students to arrive.

I shelved my paddle and was half out of the canoe when he said, "I'm sorry, Boyo, but you'll have to go back."

"But why, sir? What's wrong?"

"It seems we've declared war on your country, although for the life of me I cannot see why."

I looked over his shoulder at my friends who were standing in a row, not smiling and not acknowledging my waves. Johnnie was coming down to the dock to meet me, but one of the other boys grabbed him and held him back. "But that won't matter to us, will it?"

"I'm afraid it will, Daniel." He pushed the canoe away from the dock. "Off you go now. I'm sure this foolishness won't last long, and then you can come back and finish out the year with your friends."

I paddled home fighting tears. It was crazy.

After pulling up my canoe, I sat on the bank and flung stones in the water—water that had become a border that separated us from the people over there. All of a sudden, friends on the other side weren't friends anymore. How could that be? What happened? What was a *border*, anyway? Was it meant to keep people in or keep people out?

The water was blue and quiet on top, but all I could think of were the dangerous currents below the surface. It seemed to me there were currents everywhere—in the water, in the air, in whispered worries, in dangling silences.

I supposed it was because I was just 11 that I didn't understand everything. Maybe by the time I was 12, I would know more. Meanwhile, I figured I'd go and visit Mr. and Mrs. Wickam. They were too old to worry—that's what Mr. Wickam told me.

I picked up a broken stick lying on the bank and pretended it was a cane as I walked along the road. The air was heavy with the smell of the ripe apples and pears that drooped from trees in the orchards on my left, and the sun, hot on my back, threw my shadow out in front of me. The cowlicks on the crown of my head showed in the shadow; I tried to flatten them down, but the stupid things just popped back up again, so I decided to ignore them. My shadow limped, but just a little.

The Wickams' doorbell had a steel knob on the outside of the door, which, when turned, made a clapper on the inside of the door bang against the steel cup that covered it. I liked turning the knob so I did it a lot more than was necessary, but Mr. Wickam didn't mind.

Mr. Wickam—Mother told me never to call him Jack on account of he's an adult—told me that he'd moved from his farm into Sandwich when his old bones started to scrape together as he walked behind the plow. I thought that maybe his bones creaked because he was so tall. Every time he bent to go through a door, he grunted. It was like his bones needed oil.

Mr. Wickam let me in because Mrs. Wickam—I didn't call her Clementine, either—was pulling bread out of the oven that was built into the brick wall next to the fireplace. She always baked bread on Tuesdays, which made it a good day to visit. I squeezed into the small hot kitchen, most of which was taken up by a large square table and the rest by Mrs. Wickam, who was very fat, and accepted a piece of hot bread smeared with butter. As I ate, I watched Mr. Wickam sharpen his razor by the basin on the washstand in the corner. The old farmer scraped his razor on a leather strap. I didn't understand how the strap could make the razor sharper.

When I was little, I always helped Mr. Wickam shave when I went to visit. Mr. Wickam used to lift me up on to the washstand and hand me a mirror, which I held as still as possible against my chest so that Mr. Wickam could see what he was doing. That was the beginning of my interest in mirrors. I was intrigued that I was standing behind Mr. Wickam's face—it was like I was in his head! "How does your beard grow every day?" I had asked one day as I watched him stir up the soap in the mug.

"Everything that's alive grows—you know that, don't you?"

I had tried to think of something that was alive but didn't grow but had failed, so I went on to something else. I didn't have my whole mind on the subject, because I was busy watching the foam Mr. Wickam was brushing on his face—always so much it looked like a white cloud.

"Hold the mirror steady now," Mr. Wickam said as he picked up the long razor, tilted his head to the side, twisted his mouth and scraped the razor along his cheek. It sounded like a dog scratching on gravel. I tried to twist my mouth like Mr. Wickam's but couldn't do it without letting the mirror tilt, so I stopped.

I remember asking, "Why don't women have beards?"

His answer was throaty because he had stretched his neck back to get the hair under his chin. "A woman with a beard wouldn't do for kissin', now would she?"

His answer had made Mrs. Wickam laugh, and her fat had jiggled up and down like it was happy too.

I used to think Mr. Wickam was pretty brave, because he always bled some but never complained.

This visit, the Wickams were as nice as ever, but I could feel their worry. Mrs. Wickam's laugh stopped too fast and Mr. Wickam wasn't smiling at all. I hoped things would look up when we went out back. "Can we go to the shed?"

In the shed, Mr. Wickam sat down on a bench he had made from a plank held up by two logs. He took out his whittling knife and picked up the piece of wood he was working on.

From the shelf, I took down the box that was filled with carvings he had completed and carried it to the bench, where I put it on my knee and looked at each piece one at a time. There were circles, squares and stars, each about the size of a big person's hand, and inside those shapes Mr. Wickam had carved other things like angels or numbers or stars inside stars or circles inside squares. Each inside shape was cut right through the wood and was attached to the outside shape by thin, thin pieces of wood, almost like strings. It made the pieces look lacy and light as snowflakes.

I dug out a circle that had a star inside and held it up to a sunbeam that had squeezed through the space between the uneven wood slats of the shed's wall. In the carving, there was a whole lot more air than there was wood. "This one makes me think of Mother."

"Why's that?" Mr. Wickam didn't look up from his work.

"When she's happy, she's like a star—you know, one of those faraway ones you can see on really clear nights, the kind that shimmers and is more exciting than closer stars 'cause you're sure that at any minute it might flicker and disappear."

"And how is she right now?"

"She's flickering." I didn't look away from the piece I was holding up.

Mr. Wickam put down his work and leaned on his elbows. "Why's that?"

"She's scared, I think. She's scared of war."

"We're all afraid of war, Daniel."

"It's not the fear; it's what she does with it that I don't like." I twisted the carving in my hands. If the thin bits of wood holding the star to the edge of the circle were to break, the carving would be destroyed. "Why are we at war, Mr. Wickam? What's going to happen?"

The old farmer put his arm around my shoulder. It felt more heavy than reassuring. "Can't give you an answer to that one, my boy. Only thing I know is when you rattle the hive, a lot of innocent people get stung."

"But why do men want war? Why do they want to kill each other?"

"The way I figure it, there's many a stupid man who believes that to fight and die for his country is the one thing between birth and death that will make him feel he's worth somethin'."

"I guess you don't believe that."

12

"Nope, I don't." He tried to flatten my cowlick. "Sometimes war is forced on yah, like now, but no man should march off with a smile and a song on his lips, 'cause by the time it's over and he marches home—if he marches home—I can guarantee yah, there'll be no laughter on his lips, and there won't be no music in his soul neither."

Every visit to the shed, I watched carefully to see what Mr. Wickam planned to make with his collection of carvings, but they just kept piling up in the box. I never asked, because I was quite sure Mr. Wickam didn't want to talk about it with a kid like me. I figured you had to be pretty grown-up before you could understand all about circles inside squares and things like that, but I understood a little. It was like the good times with Mother are tucked inside the circle, but then the bad times that square the circle take over.

We'd been reading our lesson when the schoolhouse door was yanked open and banged against the outer wall, making even the drowsy heads snap up. I kept my head down, not sure whether to smile or cry.

Hair flying, boots covered in mud, Mother barged into the classroom, stomped over to our teacher's desk and whispered loudly, "Daniel has to come with me."

Our teacher, Mr. Flaherty, scowled over his half-glasses. The last time Mother had demanded my freedom, there had been a war of words, which on my mother's side had started low and finished in embarrassing screams. I certainly didn't want to go through that again, and I guess Mr. Flaherty didn't either, because he just nodded his head, swept her out of his vision with the back of his hand and returned to his reading.

I closed my book, took my coat from the hook and walked out fast before the smile inside me exploded onto my face. My mother was crazy and it was not always a fun-crazy, but I could tell by the twitch in her mouth that this was going to be one of the precious days that I would have to tuck into my mind to bring out in the bad times.

Outside, Mother grabbed my hand and skipped around the corner of the schoolhouse to pick up the picnic basket she had hidden in the bushes, and we ran along the path through the woods laughing so hard that, once we were out of sight of the school, we had to stop and catch our sides because of the pain caused by our happiness.

We broke through the bracken and wandered along an ancient Indian path. Mother squeezed my hand three times in our old signal that said I-love-you, and without looking at her, I squeezed back four times saying I-love-you-too. When the path brought us to one of the many little creeks that fed the huge Detroit River, we found a mossy bank and plunked ourselves down. As Mother set up the picnic, she hummed a quiet song. Laying down on my back, I put my hands behind my head and watched the gossiping geese fly in an organized V. "Do you think the geese keep trading positions because it's hard flying out there at the head of the V?"

"Probably," Mother answered. "And it can't be much fun up there where the gossip can't be heard."

I got up on my knees and took a bite from a sandwich. "I think I'd stay at the head of the V where it's more peaceful."

"But more work, too."

That was true. I sat back on my bottom to think about it, but there were too many distractions. As I ate the food, I watched the squirrels storing their plunder, listened to the woodpecker hammering on dead wood, inhaled the fragrance of the pine and enjoyed the sight of my beautiful mother. Times like this were so special to me that if I had been a dog, my tail would have been wagging with pleasure.

"Come," Mother said. "Let's paddle in the creek."

We took our shoes off and, as Mother hiked up her dress, I rolled up my pants. We stepped carefully into the shallow creek and waded upstream through the running water, stopping to pick up interesting stones or just to listen to the water bubbling over rocks.

"It's time for our game," Mother said. She was behind me, so she couldn't see my smile. "I'll start. Hmm, let's see." We continued up the stream while she thought, and then she started:

> *"There once was a boy who never had time*
> *To do all the good he desired.*
> *The day was too short, the sun rose and set*
> *Before finding the time he required!"*

I turned to her and clapped, and then I stared up at the dancing clouds until something came into my head:

> *"'If I only had time,' he sometimes would say*
> *'What wonderful things I might do,*
> *But I've a mother in need and thoughts to take up,*

So I haven't the time, it is true.'"

Mother laughed, threw her arms out and turned in a circle, almost tripping on a submerged stone.

"And then he'd go back to his reading, I'm sure,
And not having one quarter read,
Would fret and would fume when his mother did say,
'I bet you wish I were dead.'"

I had my back to her, so she didn't see my eyes fly open or my face squeeze up in pain. I had to change her lines quickly.

"It was less important to finish the book
Or stop at the very best part
Than to talk to his mom and tell her she'd always
Be the first for him in his heart."

"Very good." Mother climbed a low bank and dangled her feet in the water. She put her elbow on her knee and hand on her chin and smiled.

"But this boy, he had time to be late for his school
And time to get top of his class
And time for playing and time for delaying
And never for working—Alas!"

I scrambled up out of the water, relieved at the change of subject, and sat down beside her. I threw a piece of driftwood across the creek.

"But if he has time, he shall find, when a man,
Which things come first or come next—
To sleep, to wake, to work, or to play.
Was ever a boy so perplexed?"

I ended on a high note, and Mother clapped her hands and then threw herself on me, almost smothering me with a giant hug. "Oh, Daniel! I love you so much."

I stared at the memory inside the circle. A week later, Mother's mood had leaked out of the circle, and she'd screamed at me that I was a lame weakling who didn't have an ounce of intelligence in his head. I threw the carving back in the box and said goodbye to Mr. Wickam.

When I arrived back at Papa's store, I found Joseph sitting on the top step of the porch. His long Indian hair hung loose, as always, but he appeared to have even more sad wrinkles than usual. He was staring out at the river. I sat down beside him and shared his silence, trying to see what my friend saw. The Detroit River was usually busier than any road in the town of Sandwich. Normally, Indians in canoes weaved in and out between merchant ships that brought goods from the East; fishermen in rowboats, their backs bent over their oars, moved back and forth delivering the early-morning catch to merchants on both sides of the river; and sailors in ships of the British Navy patrolled the shores. But this was not a normal day. The river was almost empty, and its ripples whispered frightening gossip.

I blinked, looked away from the river, took my mirror out of my pocket—Mr. Wickam gave it to me when I was 6 so I'd stop asking him questions about reflections and stuff—and looked at myself. Same missing eye tooth, same freckles across the nose, but the boy in the mirror had no worries. Lucky him!

Joseph watched me and shook his head. "Face in mirror just echo; no soul."

I was about to ask him about echoes when I saw him staring at something down by the river: It was Mother, running toward us like she was being chased by a man-eating tiger. "Hull is in Detroit! He may cross tomorrow! There's no time to pack, we have to leave now!"

Joseph and I both stood up quickly, but then we looked at each other and sat down again. There was a note in my beautiful mother's voice that we both recognized. It was like the first crack in the ice, and I knew it would get longer and wider until it was so big people would get hurt.

I squeezed closer to Joseph. We stared out at the river and pretended not to listen to the conversation inside the store.

"It's all right, Margaret." Papa kept his voice low. "I've already made contact. I'm going to join him when he arrives. You and Daniel will be taken across the river to wait out the skirmish. It shouldn't take too long."

"Cross the river! Are you mad, you stupid man? I'm not a traitor! You're the American, not me! You go! *Go!* I'm tired of you anyway!"

Once my mother started, she couldn't seem to stop. I figured that the first crack often loosened all the bad thoughts she had inside her head.

"Be sensible, Margaret!" All Papa ever wanted was peace, something that was pretty rare in our family, that was for sure.

"I *am* being sensible! Play soldier all you want, I'm going to Montreal. You can send Daniel to Detroit; I'm not travelling with the extra weight of a snivelling child."

She didn't really mean it. When she was like that, words flew out before she could close her lips over them. It was not her fault.

"Listen to me, Margaret! This country is little more than a dictatorship run by the British and their Loyalist friends, and many of us are damned tired of it. We need a democracy, and the only way we'll get it is if the Americans take over, so get off your high horse and act with a little intelligence!"

Papa usually ground his teeth and said nothing, but it seemed his mettle was fairly up, which was not a good sign. I figured out long ago that he was afraid of his own temper and that's why he needed life to be calm. He came out on the porch and the half-door slammed behind him. "Even if you want to, you'll never get away to Montreal! Look at the great British defence! It's laughable!"

Joseph and I followed his gaze. Down by the river, all the farmers who shopped at our store were standing at attention in a crooked line, and a British soldier was yelling at them. I knew most of them because they came to Sandwich once a fortnight to practice being soldiers. They were called the militia—which meant they weren't real soldiers. On the days they came to town, I watched them march to the sound of one drum and shoot at targets set up in a field outside the village. They took turns because there was never much ammunition.

My father laughed. It was a mean laugh and it made me sad. "They'll probably take off for home the minute the first shot is fired!"

"At least they aren't traitors!" Mother screamed from inside the store.

"For God's sake, Margaret, look at those men. They came here to farm the free land they received from the government, and they could care less if Upper Canada becomes another American state!" Papa turned toward the door of the store and growled, "And since the Americans are bound to win this war, they would probably be better off if they just welcomed Hull when he crossed the river."

"Well, I'm not staying around to see what happens," Mother screamed.

A terrible bang came from inside. I figured Mother had thrown the trunk down from the loft. "I will not cross that river to join greedy land-grabbers!"

Papa stomped back into the store to make his point. "They're not land-grabbers, they declared war because the British were boarding American ships and stealing our sailors to fight against Napoleon! They declared war because Britain stopped all our ships going to the continent. They declared war because they were tired of Britain not listening to them."

"Listen to what you're saying! They are going to cross borders, kill and slaughter because they can't sell their merchandise to the continent? If you really believe that's why they are crossing the Detroit thousands of miles away from any ocean-going vessel, you're more of an idiot than I thought! Don't you dare tell me that that's why General Hull is planning to invade Canada! He's attacking the British on land because America has no chance against the Royal Navy!"

There was a big open hand that floated inside my chest that I never thought about until mean, horrible words were spoken. When that happened, the hand closed into a fist, and it hurt so bad I felt sick. And it didn't go away. Words were the problem. The boy in the mirror who looked just like me was lucky: he heard no words. I wanted to cover my ears. I looked at Joseph, who was pretending he was not listening, but I knew he was. He listened for the Indians because it was his job. Joseph was Tecumseh's spy—he'd told me so.

A soldier on horseback came tearing down the road and jumped off his horse at the store's horse rail. He was without his stovepipe hat, and his uniform buttons were askew. "Lieutenant Colonel Baby is here!" I yelled at Mother and Papa. That stopped the bad words! They left their fight to go out on the porch.

Perspiration flowed down the Lieutenant Colonel's face. "I'm evacuating the town! We must all move to the fort at Amherstburg."

Mother was over at the house. She had dragged her trunks across the yard one at a time, thumping them down the stairs of the store and then pulling them across the dirt. Her hair was all over her face and she had forgotten to pull up her skirts, so they were very muddy. Papa and I watched. We didn't offer to help. When Mother was "in a state," it was best to steer clear of her.

Instead, we sat on the steps of the store not talking, too busy trying not to imagine what she was doing down at the house, which was a hopeless undertaking because even though we couldn't hear her, we could feel what was going on over there, having seen it many times before. Her anger poured out of her body, from her mouth in horrible hurtful words, from her hands that banged and threw things and from her feet that couldn't stop whirling her body all over the room.

Papa had calmed down. He put his arm around my shoulder, pulled me in tight and ran his chin over my head. I figured when Mother fell "in a state," it was harder on him than it was on me because he grew up without having to live with someone like Mother, whereas I was born into this situation. Papa was a nice man, which was not necessarily a good thing. Being nice and wanting peace didn't always work in our world; I'd already learned that much. Even so, it was Papa who taught me almost all my out-of-school-learning—where to fish with a deep-water line, where to troll over shoals, how to shoot and hunt, how and where to swim, plus how to barter for goods to be sold from our store and how he kept his books recording his sales. When I broke a fishing line or missed the one shot we would have at a flighty deer, or if I disobeyed his rules and swam where the currents were too strong, he always reacted with patience and explanations instead of anger, which made his earlier furor quite frightening.

"I'll take you across the river tonight. I know someone at the Detroit fort who'll take care of you while I'm with Hull's army."

With one ear I heard my father's words; the other could not avoid the questions swirling inside my head. *What will happen to Mother if we both leave? Will Joseph stay with me? Will Papa be killed? What will happen to me?*

"I may be rusty in the joints, but a little exercise will scrape it off and show there's still some steel underneath." Papa was talking out loud to himself. I thought he was trying to convince himself that he was ready for war. In truth, his belly was too big. His hair was beginning to move back from his forehead and what was left was beginning to go grey.

"Papa, are you going to have to fight against Joseph and Lieutenant Colonel Baby and all the people who shop at your store?"

"Guess I'll have to."

"Could you kill them?"

"I'm sure it won't come to that."

"But it might." Was Mr. Wickam right? Did Papa think that to be brave and noble and maybe die for his country was more important than to live out his life with his wife and son—especially his son who loved him so much? I was not really sure what Mother felt. The idea of my good father being willing to kill people I knew, people who were his friends, was so big and so horrible I decided to put it away and think about it later. My hound, Prophet, was looking up at me from the bottom of the stairs. "C'mon boy."

He crept up the stairs with his tail wagging. I put my arms out to enfold the dog in a drooling hug.

Papa ruffled the dog's ears. "Damnedest thing, naming the animal after that crazy Indian."

I put my head in Prophet's neck and remembered the stories Joseph told me about the Indian named "the Prophet."

Whenever Mother's explosions became scary, Joseph and I would go to our special place on the edge of the river with our fishing rods. I loved the way the reflections in the water jiggled. It looked like time was laughing. Joseph always took a bottle of rum and after a while he started mumbling in fractured English. He even forgot that I was there. I always just dipped my rod up and down, stared at the river and listened to his mumbling.

"The Prophet, he crazy crippled man with one eye but that eye, it see everything. He tell us not to sell our land to Mr. William Henry Harrison. He say the Indian lands belong to everyone. He tell his brother Tecumseh it be safer if Indians live together in big village at Tippecanoe."

Sometimes when he was very drunk he talked about the most horrible day of his life.

"My son, my wife and me, Deep River, sleep in our teepee. I hear shuffle sound. In moonlight under the teepee I see one shadow then two then three. I touch wife, touch son, touch lips, keep still. Ten shadows. Shadows shoot through teepee, through head of wife. I try to escape with son in arms but he shot too. Deep River not stay to help, Deep River run and run. I, Deep River, am big coward."

As the liquid in the bottle got lower, so did his voice.

"Tecumseh come home. Find town burned, food burned, crops burned; many dead. Tecumseh say, 'Long Knife Harrison!' Tecumseh say, 'No peace now!'"

Joseph would start to flick his ear with his hand and shake his head. I figured it was to try to rid his mind of the bad memories.

"I not save family, not help tribe, not fight for Indians. Black cloud blanket cover me. I not talk, not cry, not eat, not want to live. Tecumseh come. Say Deep

River must help Indians now. Must go north, take new name, watch English soldiers, send message to Tecumseh. I become Joseph. I work at store, watch boy, good boy, like son. Joseph watch soldiers, watch river, hear talk, send messages. Me Tecumseh's long-haired spy."

I looked up at my father. "Joseph says Mr. William Henry Harrison is a bad man."

Papa reached into his pocket for his tobacco pouch and started stuffing his pipe. "It's not that simple."

"Why?"

"Why? Because the Indians are grown people with children's minds. They think they can hunt and ride and fish without any responsibilities in life. They are going to have to learn that their lives and their land need fences."

The dog wiggled in my arms. "Are Americans better than Canadians?"

"I suppose not, just different, that's all."

"Why do you have to go, Papa?"

"That's not an easy question, Daniel, at least not one you would understand. It's about roots: mine are American. War makes you realize how damned strong they are. Roots have a memory, you see. They suck up beliefs and prejudices and emotions that are with you for life."

I thought I understood the roots part, but not the rest.

"Am I American?"

"Only half."

"So what kind of roots do I have?"

Papa gave me a big hug. "Your roots are still like the roots of a young sapling. They won't get a grip on you for a while yet."

"I think I'd better stay and look after Mother."

"She can look after herself. She doesn't want you along."

"I know, but I think I'll go with her anyway."

"Suit yourself. This won't take long in any case. I'll fetch you at Amherstburg as soon as the British surrender the fort."

The wagon was piled high with trunks and boxes, so many I thought that maybe she wasn't planning to return. She was wearing her red skirt and was talking too fast, both bad signs. She pointed up at Prophet who was sitting on the wagon between Joseph and me. "The dog cannot come, Daniel!"

A closed coach pulled to a stop next to the wagon, and Mother went over to join her friend Mrs. Baby for a more comfortable trip to Amherstburg. As she opened the door of the coach and mounted the step, she called over her shoulder, "Get rid of it, Daniel!"

"He won't do any harm. Joseph will keep him." I looked over at Joseph and whispered, "You will, won't you?"

"You heard me, Daniel! You may not take that animal to Amherstburg."

I hugged my dog and stuffed my face into his neck to hide my tears. "We'd better take him to the Wickams'."

"They not come?" Joseph asked.

"Nope." When I'd gone to warn the Wickams about Lieutenant Colonel Baby's evacuation order, Mr. Wickam said, "Well now, I don't think Clementine and me will be goin'."

Joseph pulled the wagon to a stop in front of their house and I climbed down. "C'mon, Prophet." The dog didn't move. He wasn't dumb; he knew something bad was going to happen. Joseph gave him a push and he jumped down, but his ears were back and his tail was pasted low between his legs. I pulled him by the collar, but he put his bum on the ground, forcing me to drag him. I turned back to Joseph. "Can't we take him?"

Mr. and Mrs. Wickam come out on the porch when they heard the wagon. I wiped the stupid tears from my eyes with the back of my sleeve. "Can you keep Prophet for me?" I tried to keep the strip of blue out of my voice. "Mother says he can't come."

Mr. Wickam came down the stairs and crouched down to my level. "'Course we will." He ruffled my hair. "It's probably better for Prophet to stay here anyway."

"I guess so." I knelt down and hugged Prophet.

Mr. Wickam held the dog gently by the scruff of the neck. "You'd best get on, young man."

As soon as I climbed back in the wagon, Joseph clucked at the horses and I waved goodbye to the Wickams, who were standing on the porch with Prophet sitting between them. The old couple looked like trees growing out of the wooden floor, and I knelt on the wagon bench waving at them until they were out of sight. The smell of Mrs. Wickam's bread, the sawdust in Mr. Wickam's workshop and my best friend, Prophet: I was leaving it all. I plunked myself back in my seat, reached in my pocket for my mirror and spoke severely to the reflection. "Dumb kid, you chose to go with your mother. Anyway, you'll be back soon." That felt better.

Because the Americans might shoot at us from the far side of the river, we could not go to Amherstburg by boat, which Joseph said would be a lot easier.

We went very slowly. There was a long line of wagons, and they made the mud in the corduroy road ooze up between the side-by-side logs and squish around the wheels. Some boys were playing tag and stomping the liquid out of the mud, but I sat close to Joseph and looked up, away from the confusion.

The sky didn't seem to understand what was going on below it. It was a happy blue with clouds that were sailing through the air like kites in a perfect wind. How could it be so wonderful up there when down below people were cross with each other and the horses' feet slipped and the wagons' wheels thumped over the logs and then sank in the runny black mud? How could it be?

When would Papa come back? How would he know where to find me? I stroked the cool mirror inside my pocket and then took it out.

"What you see?"

"A boy who isn't scared."

Joseph took the mirror, looked in it and nodded.

"What do you see?"

"See Indian."

"That's all?"

"No. Joseph see a shadow, a black shadow, big trouble."

Sometimes we passed through forest trails that were so narrow the branches of the trees grabbed at things in the wagon and I had to climb back to rescue them. In clearings, there were farms and wheat fields with the wheat standing only half tall. Joseph said a lot of the farmers were in the militia and had to go ahead to Amherstburg and that's why their families were joining our wagon train as we passed. It made the trip very long. Sometimes I fell asleep against Joseph's shoulder only to wake a few minutes later with a start.

Three miles from Amherstburg, we came to the River aux Canards, which was a muddy stream that was more like a giant marsh. There was only one bridge, so traffic was backed up. Some people climbed down from their wagons and went forward to see what was happening. Each man seemed to think he knew how to get the long line moving, and each screamed his advice to the people in front. If I had been in the front, I would have suggested to those noisy men that since they were such experts, they trade places and then the men from the front could bellow while the screamers tried to make things move faster.

While the men yelled, the women complained to each other in voices that peaked in a whine—kind of like the sound knives made on the whetting wheel. The words and the noise made me feel sick.

The fort at Amherstburg was called Fort Malden. At the gate of the fort, a soldier wrote down the names of the people in each wagon and directed them to continue along the road to different fields where they could set up camp. When it was our turn, he asked, "Be ye Joseph and Daniel?" We nodded and he said, "Yer mother said to follow her to the home of Mr. Matthew Elliott. She said Joseph would know the way, is that right?"

Joseph grunted and clicked at the horses. We were able to move a little faster once we passed the fort.

"Who is Mr. Elliott?"

"Friend Shawnee. He speak for Indians to redcoats. He important man—he got Shawnee children."

We turned at low stone columns that marked the entrance and drove for a long time through a lane lined with trees I'd never seen before. They had flat leaves that tossed the sun around and danced on branches that hung over the lane. Behind the trees were long fences that marked fields of hay and corn and oats.

The lane was smoother than the public road. It ended in a barnyard with three barns inside a white fence, but we turned off before we got there, wound around a lane and came to a huge house that looked down at the river. There was a big garden in front of the house and the drive curved around it. There was a cut lawn that ran all the way down to the river. I figured this Mr. Elliott must be very rich.

Joseph drove the cart around to the back entrance, which was good. We certainly weren't front-door people, what with me covered in mud and Joseph smelly as usual.

We walked through a kitchen where there was a black woman stirring a pot over the fire, another washing dishes and a third putting little pieces of food on a large serving plate. The whole room smelled of fried onions and baked bread. An old black man held one large plate that was already filled with little round toasts with cheese and bacon and appeared to be waiting for a second.

I'd have liked to stop to talk to these people and maybe get some of those toasts to eat, but Joseph pushed me ahead into a room off the kitchen.

An older man was sitting at a large table, tilted back in his chair. His sleeves were rolled up, his vest was only half buttoned and his coat was flung over an empty chair. His face was yellow and the skin had wrinkles everywhere, but most were around the eyes and mouth where there were deep smile crevasses. Papa described parchment faces like his as having hung over too many campfires.

Opposite him was a younger man who had the same eyes and the same smile as the old man, but he was dressed in English clothes. I didn't have to ask to know they were father and son. Between them, on the table, were sticks grouped into different piles.

The old man stood up and smiled when he saw Joseph. I went over to the table and stared at the sticks. The younger man who had remained in his chair was counting the piles, each of which contained sticks of different lengths, and was writing down the results. "What are the sticks for?"

"They're for the annual distribution of presents to the Indians." He looked up from his paper. "Can you count?"

"Of course, sir."

"Well, then you can sit down here and help me." He pushed a pile of sticks toward me. "Can you read what the paper on the top of the pile says?"

"Wyandot."

"Good boy, you can read too."

"Of course I can read!"

"Don't be insulted, young man, there are many around here who can't. Now, tell me how many sticks there are in the Wyandot pile."

I sifted through the sticks. "There are 50 longs, 30 medium and 75 short ones."

He wrote down the numbers beside the word *Wyandot*. "Good boy, now go to the next pile."

I pulled another pile toward me. "What are they for?"

"Each tribe brings a bundle of sticks representing the number of people in their group. The long sticks are for men, the medium sticks are for women and the short ones are for children. Now, what does the paper on the next pile say?"

The old man interrupted us. "You must be Daniel."

I stood up. "You're not Mr. Elliott, are you?"

"And why would I not be?"

"You don't look like a rich man, that's all."

"What's a rich man supposed to look like?"

"Rich men look like they've never worked and they are clean and they have long noses that look down at you." I'd never known a rich man, but I'd read about them in books.

The man laughed and shook his head. "Sorry ta disappoint you, young man, but I am Mr. Elliott and that man at the table is my son Alexander."

"I could tell he was your son. You have the same nose." I didn't say large nose, which I might have.

Mr. Alexander Elliott put his pen down and shook my hand like I was a big person. I liked him for it. "It's nice to meet you, Daniel. I hope you'll be around to help me with more counting. I can see you're very good at it."

"Yes, sir, I'm precocious."

Mr. Alexander guffawed. "You are, are you? And what does that mean?"

"I'm not entirely sure, sir. I think it means that I can count and read better than most of my friends."

He smiled and pulled me toward him. "Does being precocious get you into trouble?"

"Sometimes I get impatient with my teacher, and I guess I'm pretty creative at being bad."

"Well, if you are going to be bad, you might as well do it with flair!"

I liked Mr. Alexander Elliott, but I turned back to Mr. Matthew Elliott. "Excuse me, sir, but I've come looking for my mother, Margaret Brownell. Is she here?"

"She's in the front partyin' with the military who've come out to watch me distribute the food to the Indians."

The way Alexander looked away from his father's face and shook his head when Mr. Elliott mentioned the military, I figured there was more going on than I understood, but that was not important to me. "Is my mother all right?"

"Why wouldn't she be?" Alexander asked. Then it was I who looked away and shook my head.

CHAPTER 3
JULY 1812

▼

Matthew Elliott

The boy was of average height, with a head of light brown hair that had cowlicks standing up front and back. There was something that drew him to me, and it wasn't his limp. 'Twas probably his bright eyes that were looking everywhere and the tilt in his head that showed he was taking in every word and holdin' it there so's he could chew on it later. He could surely see my preoccupations, what with the way I'd been pacing back and forth.

I took a deep breath and brought myself back to the business at hand. Joseph was waiting patiently. I spoke to him in Shawnee. "Tecumseh is in Amherstburg with his men. He moves back and forth across the Detroit, leaving his warriors on the west bank to shadow the advance of General Hull's supply lines. Hull could cross with his army any day and once in Sandwich, they'll march to Amherstburg by land. That damned fool Procter wants ta 'wait 'n see,' believin' there'll be some peace agreement before the Americans invade."

"Will General Brock come?" Joseph asked.

"He's on his way, but 'til then we'll have ta rely on Tecumseh. Go to him and find out what he needs. I'll see what I can do with these redcoats to get a little backbone into their staff."

From the table, the boy said in Shawnee, "You sound richer when you're talking Shawnee. It's like the language dresses you in important clothes!"

Alexander burst out laughing. "The honesty of innocence, Da!"

"You speak Shawnee, boy?"

He nodded and smiled. "Joseph taught me!"

"And you're precocious!" added Alexander, a smile twitching on his lips.

The boy blushed and looked down at the bundles of sticks he was countin'. Alexander reached across the table to ruffle his hair.

Before I could return to my conversation with Joseph, Sarah came through the kitchen door with the babe in her arms and Boy, as usual, attentive at her side.

"Matthew," she said to me, "I want to attend to the baby. You've left me alone with the party inside much too long." She switched the baby to her other hip. "Why are we entertaining soldiers anyway? Shouldn't they be in Amherstburg preparing for an attack?"

I put my arm around my Sarah's shoulders, kissed the head of the babe and whispered, "Some of the officers have been sent here to watch the allotments to the Indians, and I invited the others to get their incompetent asses away from Amherstburg. Could you not keep them busy just a little while longer, my dear, while I try to get a little planning into this mess?"

She shook her head and touched my cheek. "If that's what you want, but remember your wife and two babes in your grand plan."

"'Tis already done. I'd not be able to think if you weren't safe. There are wagons ready to be loaded, and I have drivers prepared to take you east the minute Hull crosses."

"Is she your wife?" I heard Daniel whisper to Alexander.

"No, she's my stepmother," Alexander answered in a brusque voice. "And that baby is my half-brother."

"But I don't understand."

"Yah think I'm too old to be his da, do yah?" I put my arm around Sarah's shoulders. "This here's Daniel Brownell. He thinks he's extra smart, but I guess there's still some things he doesn't understand."

Sarah handed the baby to Boy and crouched down in front of the boy, whose puzzled expression pleasured me more than it should have.

"Daniel Brownell," Sarah said. "I've heard about you from my father."

Daniel eyed her suspiciously. "Who's your father?"

"Mr. Donovan."

"Mr. Donovan was your father? I learned more from him in two years than I did from Mr. Flaherty in the next three when he took over when Mr. Donovan died. I think your father was a great teacher."

"I'm sure of that." She straightened up. "Have you come to find your mother?"

"Yes, ma'am"

Sarah signalled a slave who was carrying an empty tray of food to the kitchen. "Joshua, find Mrs. Brownell. Tell her that her son is here."

I turned away from the domestic problems to Joseph and said, "Procter has only 300 regulars at the fort. He's working hard to gather up the militia. Tecumseh has the 400 Indians—"

The door to the party room opened and the boy's mother was blown through on a wave of noise and laughter that rang false—sittin', as it was, on top of shadows of worry. Every time I saw that woman, my nerves jangled; 'twas as though her tension was contagious. She had ivory skin and a straight nose and the bones in her face and her wrists and her ankles were so delicate she seemed like a beautiful bird with a broken wing. I could see that many a fool would want to pick her up and repair her, but my gut told me this creature could not be repaired, and I'd bet my arse that anyone who fell into the orbit of those large black eyes would probably be the one ta need fixin'. The major on whose arm she was hanging and who looked down at her with cow eyes was an obvious victim.

The woman's mouth jumped in and out of a smile, and one hand beat a rhythm on her dress while the other pulled at strands of hair that were loose around her ears. She twirled in a circle as though she couldn't decide whether to come forward or return to the party in the front room. I suspected she was a little off her head, but lookin' around I figured I was the only one who nursed such suspicions—except for the boy whose expression was frozen in dread. He knew.

The tall officer who'd followed her into the kitchen was very thin and fair and meticulously dressed in his military red with white pants tucked into shinin' black boots. I'd seen the man before, and I knew he was the postmaster of the regiment.

"Daniel, this is Lieutenant Mackenzie. You will stay with him at the fort. Mr. Elliott doesn't have any room for you here."

There was room here, but I bit my tongue. An idea was percolating in my head.

A lock of the soldier's hair fell across his forehead, and he brushed it back with long thin fingers.

In Shawnee, Joseph mumbled, "*Berdache.*" I had to agree. This Lieutenant Mackenzie sure as hell had to be from an important background to have the army accept him in spite of his sexuality.

Daniel's mother waved her beautiful arms as her words mounted in a crescendo. "You're too big to hide under my wing all the time, and you'd best start learning to live by your own wits."

"Me keep Daniel," Joseph said.

The soldier put his hand on the boy's head. "I can take care of the child. There's a cot in my quarters."

The mother tapped the top of her son's head with her fan, gave him an absent smile and taking her major's arm, returned to the tearoom. I felt everyone exhale.

Crouching down to meet him at eye level, the soldier said, "Find Drummer Jakes at the fort. He'll show you around. I'll meet you at my quarters at six o'clock." He offered his hand to shake. "I'm sure we'll get along very well, Daniel."

Daniel accepted the proffered hand and attempted a confident smile, which the *berdache* returned before he straightened up and followed the mother back through the double doors.

Daniel turned to all of us left in the room. "He seems nice," he said, but there was a question in his voice.

Nice he may be, but Joseph would have to warn the boy. I put my coat on and turned to Alexander. "Take your numbers to the clerks. The tribes will start arriving soon."

Officers looked down from my porch watching the allotment with suspicion, worried that I was skimmin' off the top at a time when it was their poor organization that had left them low on supplies. Had it not been that the army needed the tribes to fight with them, I was damned sure there would have been a harsh cutback on the amount of supplies the Indians received. And I was not skimmin'!

When Indians were involved, Boy was always there, especially if we were giving things away to them. He could find no fault with the Indians. He had said to me earlier, "It's our fault they're hungry, Da. We've insisted they come in huge groups and camp near so they'll be ready to fight when we want them. There's not enough food in the area for them to hunt, fish and farm to feed all of those who've gathered here."

I didn't disagree with him, but it didn't have to mean that everything the white man did was wrong. 'Twas the strangest thing, that two issues from the same parents could be so different. Boy was large and lithe on the outside but as rough as me on the inside, whereas Alexander was smooth and smart—a white, educated version of his mother.

"I'll get things started, Da. You'll speak at the end?" Boy interrupted my thoughts. I watched him go to the middle of the lawn to direct the clerks. We were vinegar and water, this son and I. Some would say he had the outward signs of an attractive man, but I sensed a snake lurking under his skin and had yet to figure it all out. I loved him, but my love was tinged with a little fear.

Daniel appeared at my side. "I've never seen so many Indians in one place!"

"I thought you'd gone to Amherstburg."

"I'm going, I just wanted to see the distribution Mr. Alexander was talking about. Is this because of the war?"

"No, we've bin doing this for many years now."

"What are the big stakes your men are planting all over the lawn for, and what are the signs they're attaching to the stakes?"

I'd forgotten about all the whys, whats, wheres and whens that emanated from curious 11-year-old heads. "There's a stake for each tribe. The signs are for the clerks; they say the name of the tribe and how many members there are. We know that number by them sticks you helped to count." The boy's chest expanded with pride.

We watched the clerks bring the supplies from my storehouses situated behind the house.

Boy directed the distribution of blankets, cloth, tobacco, scissors, needles, combs, hatchets, iron pots, kettles, guns, flints, powder, balls and shot. The assistants arranged the presents at the various stakes, and Boy gestured to the warriors to come forward and form a large circle.

"'Tis my turn now." I walked into the centre of the circle and addressed the Indians in their language. "Each year we give you presents. Now we are at war, and we ask you to fight for the father who has fed and clothed you for many moons."

The Wyandot chief stepped forward. "You must give us land and guns."

"When we defeat the Long Knives, you will be able to return to your land, grow your own food and use your guns to hunt food instead of men! I and my sons will fight with you and Tecumseh, who is waiting for you to join him!"

The Indians mumbled amongst themselves. "We will meet with Tecumseh and decide."

'Twas the best I could do. The rest would be up to Tecumseh. "I thank you in the name of the Great White Father," I said, backing away and gesturing to the young Indians responsible for gathering the goods.

"They sure are fast, those Indians! I bet they cleared the grass in three minutes!" Daniel exclaimed.

I watched the loaded canoes paddle across to the island of Bois Blanc where the Indians were camped. "Yep, now we have to see if it's been worth it—if they will fight for us."

Daniel and I walked up the lawn toward the house. "Do you know Tecumseh and the Prophet, Mr. Elliott?"

I grunted in the affirmative and smiled.

"What are they like?"

"He's a handsome son-of-a-bitch, Tecumseh is. He has piercing eyes and a tongue that can wind words around the minds of even his biggest opponents. The Prophet, his brother, is a one-eyed madman."

"But why are they willing to fight with the British?"

"It's like this: They were furious that the tribes were selling land to the Americans. 'Twasn't the measly sum they received for the land that bothered them but that they were sellin' the Indian way of life. Even now Tecumseh travels from village to village tellin' all who'll listen that, just as the sky, the clouds and the rivers belong to everyone, so too does the land and therefore it can't be sold. The young warriors agree with him and they're itchin' to do battle against the Americans, but the old chiefs are harder nuts to crack. When Tecumseh's words fail to rally the warriors, the Prophet gets into the act. Don't know what he takes to make him seize and jiggle and have his one eye roll out of his head, but whatever it is, it scares the bejesus out of the Indians!"

"How can the Indians believe in a madman?"

"I'm guessin' that when a nation gets hints of approachin' obliteration, it'll more easily fall in with a mystic who tells the people that if they rid themselves of everything associated with the arrival of the white man—alcohol, guns, foreign food, clothes, missionary schools—then life will return to the way it was."

"But it won't, will it?"

"Nope. No matter how smart the brothers are, they don't have a hope in hell of preserving their land unless they fight for it. Tecumseh knows it and needs me close to him so I kin persuade the British military not to back off when the time is ripe."

"That's a big responsibility."

"'Tis that, but I'll do my best."

The boy saw Joseph and waved. "I've got to go now, Joseph is waiting. Thanks, Mr. Elliott." And he ran off.

I shook my head and wondered how much of our conversation he'd absorbed.

Alexander came up by my side and we watched the boy run ahead. Still following the boy, I said to Alexander, "The soldier Daniel is to stay with is the postmaster at the fort."

Alexander turned his head to me, stared for a minute and then whispered, "And Procter's damning note is probably in his hands."

"The boy could solve that problem."

CHAPTER 4
JULY 1812

▼

Daniel

Joseph and I walked the mile back to Amherstburg. Joseph said there would be no place for the horses and wagon, and he was right. The town was like an anthill, with too many people moving too fast and not sure where they were going. There were soldiers directing long lines of wagons, traffic jams where carts were trying to turn around and drive in the other direction, people asking where to go, others pointing, shoppers running in and out of stores and screaming kids with barking dogs. The noise made by the kids seemed to make the grownups mad, which I didn't think was very fair. It was the big people making the music, the kids were just moving to the tune.

The fort was on the water at the south edge of town. People from Sandwich and the surrounding farms were camped in the shadow of two sides of the tall wooden palisades; Indians were camped on the third, and the fourth side was open to the river.

The gate of the fort was lopsided, and there were carpenters with leather belts trying to fix it while others were repairing fallen pickets, which had left holes that made the fort look like it had missing teeth.

The guard at the gate dropped his musket across his body to prevent Joseph and me from entering. Joseph presented the pass Mr. Elliott had given him, and we were allowed to walk in.

Inside, on the parade ground, militia who didn't have uniforms were marching to the screamed command of a scary-looking sergeant with a big moustache. They looked quite ragged, especially because on the other side of the parade ground the real soldiers marched like each man was a bit of one large piece, creating a completed puzzle. The noise was different inside the fort. It was the screams of command and the hush, hush, hush of marching feet, but it was an unsettling noise, one that was waiting for bad things to happen.

Joseph had hold of my hand and dragged me away from the parade ground past long, low buildings that had fires burning outside, ratty-looking women tending them and soldiers leaning against the doors. They sure didn't look like my neat and clean toy soldiers. Most of them looked smarmy, like people I shouldn't talk to.

We stuck to the dusty paths.

Two militia officers almost knocked us over. One was saying to the other, "I can't stay here forever, there's no one to take in the crops." They didn't even notice us. We passed an important-looking building where officers removed their tall stovepipe hats and ducked through the door going in and coming out. Behind the building was a fenced-in patch of grass where a lady with an umbrella was walking back and forth.

There were even some Indians inside the fort. They had shaved their hair everywhere except for a strip running from front to back in the middle of their heads, which they had greased so well it stood up tall. People stopped talking when they passed. I asked Joseph why they had their hair like that, and he said that when they put war paint on and started screaming at the enemy, it made them very frightening. I was sure it was so. They were really scary even without the paint.

I remembered Joseph sitting on the edge of the river moaning that he was just a long-haired Indian. Now I understood what he meant: He was no longer a Shawnee warrior. It was funny how old sentences fit into new slots.

We passed a boy who was wearing an army coat that was too big for him and a bag tied around his waist. He was a lot smaller than me, but the shadow on his upper lip made me think he was a little older, maybe 13. He was walking toward us with a stick in his hand, and an excited dog was nipping at it. He stopped to watch us go by. I turned to stare at him. Under his messy mop of hair, he had a quiet face and a mouth that was sending me a half-smile. Why was it that I liked him before even talking to him?

Tecumseh was near the water, crouched in a circle that had a number of important-looking chiefs. I could tell they were important because they had beaded moccasins and belts, silver hanging from their ears and noses and medallions hanging around their necks. Two of them even had an eagle feather hanging down the side of their heads. Tecumseh had his head shaved like the others and wore buckskin pants and was naked on top. Even though he had no jewellery and no feather, I knew who he was 'cause of the space that was left between him and the others. When he saw Joseph, he stood up and came over to us. He hugged Joseph. "I have missed you."

"And me you," Joseph answered.

"You are well?" Tecumseh was looking deep into Joseph's eyes.

Joseph couldn't look at him. I think it was because of his drinking and memories that still brought tears to his eyes. I took his hand.

Tecumseh saw everything; I guessed that was why he was the top Indian. "Your messages have helped." He put an arm on Joseph's shoulder. "Through them and others, I have been able to judge the British intentions. Finally, they are forced to go against the Long Knives."

"That's only 'cause they have to, what with General Hull about to attack, otherwise they wouldn't; I'm quite sure!" I spoke in Shawnee with an adult voice to make sure he'd know I was precocious.

The way Tecumseh looked at me, I thought perhaps it would have been better not to speak. I just wanted to be part of the simmering I felt in the air. I looked at the ground, ashamed of my outburst.

"You speak Shawnee." Tecumseh's cold voice said without saying that children who interrupt get scalped.

"Joseph taught me—sir." I kept my head down but raised my eyes to see whether I would be alive to see the sun rise again. I couldn't tell, because Tecumseh was rubbing his finger up and down his nose and his hand covered the talk on his face.

Joseph said in Shawnee, "This is Daniel. He is like a son and he learns well." His voice was serious, and Tecumseh nodded his head. For the moment, I was saved. They continued to talk, but it was all about the war and people I didn't know, so I let the words float around my head and looked at the goings-on down by the water.

At the wooden dock that was shaped like the letter T, there was a ship with three masts that had the sails pulled up, making them look like draped skirts. Navy officers wearing blue three-cornered hats were yelling at sailors in blue trousers and tops who were unloading supplies from the ship, and army officers in their red coats and stovepipe hats with feathers in them were busy bright dots in the sea of blue.

The boy who followed us was leaning against a cannon that was aimed out over the river. He had the dog with him and was throwing a stick for it, but I suspected he was really watching us. I walked toward him; he pretended he didn't see me and continued to throw the dog his stick. I watched for a while without saying anything and then leaned down to pat the dog when he delivered the stick. "What's his name?"

The boy squatted down and patted the dog too. "Bruno. He's jist a stray, but he seems mighty 'ttached to me."

"How come they let a kid like you sign on?"

He threw the stick again. "I'm small and I have all my teeth . . . and I didn't exactly sign on."

"Are you Drummer Jakes?"

"That's me."

"I'm supposed to get you to show me around and then take me to Lieutenant Mackenzie's rooms at six o'clock."

"You going to stay in his room?"

"I guess so."

"Better not turn yer back to him."

"Why?"

"You see them two dogs over there?"

I looked to where he was pointing. One dog was mounted on the back of another dog. I knew all about that.

"That's what Lieutenant Mackenzie likes to do to boys."

Surely that couldn't be true. I searched Drummer's face for a hint that it was a joke, but he looked serious. "I'm certainly not going to stay in that man's room!" *I don't care what Mother says! She probably won't even know where I'm staying, or care.*

Drummer Jakes stuck a piece of straw between his teeth, which made me think of something he said before. "What difference does it make if you don't have all your teeth?"

"Oh, they don't care if you don't have 'em all, but you got to have at least one on the top and one on the bottom that can touch and since I've got so many, even if I lose some I'll still be okay."

"Why do you have to?"

"'Cause if you don't, you can't open cartridges."

I took the stick from Bruno and threw it. It must hurt to open cartridges with your teeth. I bet it would cause more and more lost teeth. We watched

Bruno retrieve the stick and come rushing back. "What does the drummer have to do?"

"Lots of things, but the most important is to learn to drum or bugle to communicate manoeuvres so other regiments can hear but the enemy doesn't understand. The worst is when I have to take the cat out of the bag."

I looked at the bag hanging around his waist. "What does that mean?"

"I don't want to talk about it, you'll see soon enough." He looked over at Tecumseh and Joseph. "You know that Tecumseh?"

"I just met him. Joseph, the other one, is my friend."

He pulled his oversized red coat down, straightened his crossed belts and asked, "Want to see the rest of the fort?"

"Sure."

"Don't you have to tell that Joseph guy where you're going?"

"Nope, he never asks."

Drummer Jakes's steps were shorter than mine but he moved faster, so he had to turn around and skip backward to talk to me.

"What do you mean you didn't sign up?" I asked

"I didn't. I was snatched down on the London docks. They bonked me on the head and threw me in the army."

He didn't sound too upset about it, but his words made me stop so I could absorb the whole story, which sounded horrible to me. "But the army doesn't take kids like you, and it doesn't bonk people on the head! Does it?"

"Sure, they do it all the time."

"Why would they want a kid like you?"

He took the straw from his mouth. "To be a drummer. They like 'em small so the enemy can't see 'em and they don't get kilt so easy."

"Was it horrible? Don't you miss your Ma and Pa?"

"Don't have a Pa and me Ma was probably glad to git rid of an extra mouth to feed. Anyway, once they got me out in the country and took the leg irons off, 'tweren't so bad. The place was more like a school than the army. It was full of other kids who'd been bonked, and we were all trained to be drummers and buglers." He threw the stick for the dog as he talked. "The drum major was damned mean, but I learned real quick so I didn't have too many problems."

"What did you have to learn?"

"Different drumbeats, which mean different things."

"Like what?"

"Like one for attack and one for retreat and lots of others."

"Have you been in battles?"

"Till now, I've only had to drum troops to attention and drum the beat for marching and things like that, but I s'pose now that there's war, 'twill be different."

We stayed crouched facing each other, patting the dog and not talking. Finally, I stood and looked around. The fort was so big that down at the water, you didn't think about the palisade walls.

We went back up the path and cut across in front of the officer's building and made our way to the soldiers' barracks. They were the low buildings I'd noticed earlier, lined in a neat row and looking like the blocks I played with when I was little.

Drummer Jakes pointed to a middle building. "That's where I bunk." We sauntered toward it.

Bruno followed us inside and a big soldier with bright red hair and a dirty red beard kicked him viciously, making the poor dog scream in pain and scuttle out whining. We skirted around the table where the mean soldier was playing cards, and Drummer Jakes directed me to his bunk. We passed a soldier who was peeing into a wooden tub that was almost overflowing. It made the place smell so bad that I had to breathe through my mouth. Next to that tub was another tub where a soldier was washing his hands and his face. I sure hoped none of them confused the tubs when they woke up in the night. I sat on Drummer's bunk and looked around. There were 16 bunks: the one in the corner had blankets hanging over it. Drummer saw me staring. "That's cause he brought his wife."

"Do you like it, being in the army?"

"At the beginning it's tough 'cause they take away yer clothes and make you dress like everyone else, then they yell and scream at you until it's easier to do what yer told than to fight it. When that happens and ya accept that yer goin' to sleep, eat and even shit without no privacy, ya become a real army man, which is what they want."

"Does that mean you're not supposed to think for yourself?"

"Yup!"

"Why?"

"I guess it's 'cause if we thought for ourselves in the middle of a battle, half of us would turn tail and run."

I took my mirror out of my pocket and rubbed it with my hand.

"Whatch'a doing with that?"

"It's my mirror. I always look in it when I have things to think about."

"What're ya thinkin' about?"

"About you being sucked into this giant army and not being allowed to think for yourself."

He took the mirror from me and stared at his reflection. "There's lots of thoughts behind them eyes, but I guess they'd better stay where they are."

Outside, Drummer called, "Bruno, Bruno!" and said, "Dogs aren't allowed in the barracks. I don't see why, 'cause Bruno is cleaner and more polite than any of them." When we caught up with Bruno, Drummer crouched down to give him a hug, which seemed to satisfy the dog because he ran off again.

"What's that place over there?" I pointed to a long fenced-in area that ran the whole length of the fort.

"That's the rope walk where they make rope from hemp fibres and then braid and tar 'em." We went and leaned on the fence, but there was no work going on at the moment. There were long, long ropes lying on the ground, some so fat they could hold a ship down in the toughest storm and some so thin that a man could wind them up and carry them on his shoulder.

Leaning on the fence, we rested our chins on our crossed arms and stared at the different ropes. My mind started wandering and I guessed his had too because we were very quiet.

"Why do you gotta stay in that soldier's house?"

"My mother is staying at Mr. Elliott's and she says there's no room."

"I bin over there. There's enough room for an army."

"Guess she just didn't want me there."

Drummer took the straw out of his mouth like he was going to ask more, but after he looked over at me he put it back in his mouth and chewed at it. I wondered whether I should say more when a bugle call interrupted.

Drummer threw his well-chewed straw into the rope-walk. "That means we all have to go to the parade ground."

Soldiers poured out of all the barracks and a sergeant yelled, "Get the cat out of the bag, Drummer!" as he went by.

Drummer was dragging his feet. I figured he didn't really want to go. "What's the cat?"

"This." He pulled a whip with nine different strands out of the bag hanging from his waist. "They must have caught a deserter."

I followed him to the parade ground, but once there Drummer stopped and turned to me. "You can't go no further." So I went over to the barrack wall and slid along it until I could see what was happening.

Drummer disappeared through the door of a building that looked like a jail. The three platoons were formed up in the shape of a U, each side five rows deep. The silence felt like it was at attention too. I was sure I was not going to like what came next.

I heard the drum thump a beat that sounded like a dirge before I saw Drummer leading a procession made up of three slow-marching officers followed by two prisoners, each with hands tied behind his back and escorted by big soldiers at each shoulder.

Drummer marked time beside a cross of wood cemented into the ground at the open end of the U and then, without warning, stopped drumming, leaving a tense silence hanging in the air. The escorts tied one of the prisoners to the cross, tummy first, while the second man was stopped next to the cross and a hood was put over his head. The leading officer—I figured he must be the Lieutenant Colonel Procter who Mr. Elliott said was in charge—stepped in front of the prisoners and bellowed at the soldiers, all of whom were standing at such muscle-straining attention I didn't know how they could even breathe.

"These men were caught trying to cross the Detroit. They knew the penalty for desertion." He turned and spoke to the man tied to the cross. "Joseph Adams, 25 lashes and a branding!" Then turned to the hooded prisoner. "Bruce Haverford, you not only deserted, you stole rifles and ammunition to deliver to the enemy. You are therefore sentenced to stand barefoot on the spikes for 24 hours!" The soldiers in the U didn't make any noise, but it was like they all inhaled at the same time.

Lieutenant Colonel Procter nodded his head to Drummer Jakes and my new friend handed the whip to a big, mean-looking soldier who, with the handle of the whip in his right hand and the nine tails in his left, stood to the side of the prisoner on the cross and, using his whole body, slashed the cat across the man's bared back. The prisoner moaned in pain.

I watched five of the 25 strokes. The prisoner was screaming and I felt vomit in my nose. Could they do that to Papa if they caught him? I put my hands over my ears and backed away. I squeezed into the middle of the crowd gathered at the rear of the parade ground. A forest of legs surrounded me, some even standing on tiptoe to get a better view. The man's moans were getting faint; 23, 24, 25. Heels around me returned to the ground but didn't move. What was happening? Was the soldier dead? I wanted to see, but I didn't want to see. I peeked through between shoulders and hated myself for looking. A branding iron was taken from a fire burning near the jail wall and pressed into the whipped man's skin just below the armpit. The stink of burned skin mixed with the man's screams. The brander pulled the lid off a cartridge with his teeth and poured gunpowder into the wound. It was too much. I hurried back to Joseph and the Indians.

Joseph and Tecumseh and many chiefs were standing by the water when I approached. I figured it wouldn't be wise to interrupt, so I just stood there and held my ground until they realized I had something important to say and they came over to me, leaving the other Indians behind.

I would have been happier to speak to Joseph alone, but that did not seem possible, so I held my breath and spouted my worries. "Drummer Jakes says that lieutenant, where I'm supposed to sleep, likes to mount boys like a male dog mounts a bitch."

Joseph grunted, which I thought meant yes.

"I don't want to stay in his room!" I tried to keep the tears out of my voice.

Joseph hugged me. "You stay with me."

"Thank you!" I felt better and started off to find Drummer.

"Boy!" Tecumseh called, bringing me to a very fast stop. I wondered what I'd done.

"You limp!"

"Just a little." I frowned at him. It made me cross when someone brought it to my attention, because otherwise I never noticed.

"How did it happen?"

"Don't know. I was a baby." I had a shadowy memory of my parents screaming at each other and pulling me from one set of arms to another, but maybe that was a dream. "Anyway, it is not important, and there is no need to talk about it!" It was silly to talk to Tecumseh like that, but I was mad! "Sir," I added. Maybe that would help.

Tecumseh started toward me with a serious look on his face, which frightened me, 'cause I didn't know what I'd done or what he was going to do . . . and then, in a flash, I knew! Tecumseh limped too! Smiles hit our faces at the same time. His smile was around his eyes. I'm sure my grin covered my whole face!

As I turned to go to find Drummer, Tecumseh and Joseph returned to the chiefs and I heard Tecumseh say, "Procter is a turtle who is too slow to attack. If we don't fight now, I will lose the tribes that have gathered. Elliott must convince the military. He is our only hope. We attack or we die!"

CHAPTER 5
AUGUST 1812

▼

Daniel

It was getting harder to watch over Mother and keep an eye on Joseph, who was drinking again. It was like they sat on opposite ends of a teeter-totter and when one was up the other was down. My job was to stand in the middle and use my weight to keep the thing balanced until the war was over, but I wasn't that heavy and I was beginning to think it was impossible.

Everybody was hysterical and that included me. That was because General Hull had crossed the Detroit and invaded my town, Sandwich, on July 12, and we'd been expecting him to march against Amherstburg ever since. It was already August 9 and he still hadn't attacked. I was beginning to think waiting was worse, 'cause living with scenes made in the imagination was making everyone very ratty. Drummer Jakes had to take the cat out of the bag many times so the big brute sergeant could whip nervous soldiers who had tried to desert.

Tecumseh and his men had crossed the river 'cause they wanted to attack the supply line that was travelling up to Fort Detroit. I was not quite sure what a supply line was. Did they pull all the supplies on a rope?

I found Joseph at the edge of the river with an empty bottle of rum lying on its side between his straddled legs. He had cut off his hair, leaving the centre untouched just like the other Indians, and he was soaping and scraping the stubble on either side of the crest. I took my mirror from my pocket and held it up for him. Mr. Wickam's razor worked better than the knife Joseph was using, which made him bleed a whole lot.

There were two pots beside him. He used the first to grease the middle hair and then dug his hand into the other pot containing black guck, which he pasted all over his face. His hand was not very steady and he missed lots of places with the paint. I put the mirror in my pocket so he wouldn't see the mess he'd made of himself. He stood up and staggered down the bank to his canoe, falling a couple of times, which made me realize he was not going to manage on his own. I ran ahead of him and jumped in the canoe. He didn't seem to notice or understand that I was going with him.

Paddling across the Detroit seemed to take a lot longer than usual, and I was tired and quite frightened because I didn't know what was going to happen next. I took my mirror out of my pocket and told my reflection to be calm.

We pulled in amongst reeds in Brownstown Creek and didn't get out of the canoe. Joseph seemed unsure of what to do, and I was thinking that this escapade had not been a good idea at all and that we should probably just turn the canoe around and paddle back to where we came from.

I heard gunshots in the distance and the rustle of Indians moving through the bushes. An Indian with his face painted white appeared on the bank, motioning with his hands to tell us to get out of the canoe and pull it into shore and be quiet about it. He had not said a word, but I knew what he meant. We sneaked along the riverbank to a very narrow part of the creek where, hidden in the bushes, I saw Indians with their faces painted either all black or all white and with their hair oiled to stand straight up, which made them look very scary.

The Indian we followed signalled Joseph to hide in the bushes but took me by the hand across the creek into a cornfield where he signalled me to lie down and lay beside me. I could feel my heartbeat all the way up to my ears. It was hard to stay still. Every time I moved, the Indian put his arm across my back. There was a noise coming from the north; it was horses snuffing, and then I heard leather squeaking and weapons clanking. American soldiers on foot came through the woods and marched toward the creek. I could see their legs. They crossed in a double file, with officers on horses marching up and down on either side of the line.

Dressed only in loincloths, with bodies painted half black and half white, the Indians shot out of their hideaways, firing guns and bows and arrows, waving tomahawks and war clubs and screeching war cries that hurt my ears. I stood and pulled aside the tall corn to see if I could see Joseph. He staggered into the middle of the battle, stabbing his knife in all directions and screaming with all the rest of them. Bodies appeared and disappeared in the smoke caused by the muskets and dust raised by the horses.

Through the haze, I saw one man shot in the face, blood spurting out from his eyes, and another running in circles and screeching in agony trying to stuff his intestines back into the huge hole in his stomach. There was a stink of burning from the muskets mixed with the smell of wet mud and sweat and poop and a horse was shot and fell over almost on top of me, its eyes popping out in pain. The officer from the horse was thrown to the ground and his musket flew from his hands, and the Americans were bumping into each other trying to get away. The officer tried to stop them with words, but they paid no attention and ran into the woods, stomping on dead bodies as they fled.

Two American soldiers ran right into me and we all froze for a minute, and then one of them put his hand over my mouth and pushed me into the ground. He yanked me backward out of the cornfield and down the bank of the creek, where both men lay flat and one held me down. My face was scratched and my hands were bleeding from being dragged over the sharp cornhusks.

"My God," one of them whispered. "What'll we do now? Where can we go?"

"Quiet!" The one with his hand over my mouth hissed. He took his scarf off and tied it around my mouth and then he unbuckled his belt and, with his free hand, released it from his waist and used it to tie my hands behind my back. "We wait and pray."

The other one got to his knees. "No! I'm going now," and he took off splashing down the middle of the creek.

My captor shoved my face into the mud and banged me on the head. I don't know if I lost consciousness or not, but when I heard British soldiers marching toward the battle I got up on my knees and staggered forward, at the same time struggling to release my hands.

British soldiers, militia and even Mr. Elliott were climbing the bank and marching to the narrow crossing at Brownstown Creek.

Mr. Elliott broke away from the marchers, pulled the gag off my mouth and untied my hands. "What happened?"

"Two American soldiers caught me." I pointed down the creek. "They went that way."

"Stay here," he ordered and turned back to join the soldiers.

I was too frightened to stay alone where another escaped American might appear and this time kill me, so I followed the marching soldiers at a distance and stopped behind a tree at the edge of the battlefield.

The place was strewn with dead horses and scalped bodies that had been stripped and forced onto sharp stakes that held them upright by piercing them through the bums and travelling up into the stomach.

The Indians were tying an American prisoner to a stake.

The British soldier in charge marched over to them and said, "Let me speak to Tecumseh."

"Gone," an Indian answered. "He take American soldier papers to General Brock."

"Turn this prisoner over to me. We need to question him."

The Indians stared at the Major.

"I have a barrel of rum I can leave you." He signalled a soldier to get the rum from the boat.

The Indians waited, mumbling amongst themselves. Some wanted the rum; others wanted to kill the prisoner.

Mr. Elliott spoke to them in Shawnee. "Tecumseh would not allow you to kill a man once he becomes your prisoner."

"Tecumseh not allow plunder, not allow rum, he not say don't kill," an Indian argued.

Just as the soldier appeared with the rum, screams came from the woods. A group of Indians broke through carrying the body of one of the chiefs; I could tell he was a chief because he had an eagle feather in his hair. They carried his body to the centre of the gathering and dropped it in front of the prisoner. All the Indians began to cry and yell and whoop and wave their tomahawks around the face of the prisoner.

The American peed his pants and his face drained of blood. "Major, please don't let these savages kill me!" His words were almost drowned out by the screams and cries of the Indians.

The Major turned to Mr. Elliott. "Can't you do something?"

Mr. Elliott pulled aside the Wyandot chief and pleaded with him, "Don't do it! I speak for Tecumseh."

But the chief, looking as wild as the rest of the Indian mob, lifted his tomahawk and slashed the air in front of Mr. Elliott, forcing him to back away from the threat, and then the chief turned away to join the screams of the Indian mob.

Mr. Elliott went back to the Major. "We'd best back off, Major. The Indians are out of control, and they'll avenge their chief no matter what we do. You can see that if we try to stop them, they'll turn on us." He sounded sad and tired, and he walked away from the crowd.

I put my face into the tree, inhaled huge sobs and shook my head back and forth, not wanting to believe what was happening.

The Major hesitated and then backed off, not looking at the prisoner.

An old Indian chief gave a signal and a group of Indian women melted out from the woods. The first female to arrive in front of the American pierced his ear with a knife, the next stabbed him in the side, another dug out his eye with a knife and the oldest of the Indian women attacked his neck with a tomahawk. They kept at him and at him well past the time his screams stopped, and they were still tearing at strands of skin when I ran back along the bank to the Detroit.

Joseph was there, screaming with the rest of them, letting it happen. Tears mucked up my vision and snot ran from my nose.

Not wanting to have anything to do with Joseph, I left our canoe where it was and went back to Amherstburg in a British boat. There were people waiting at the shore to find out what had happened at Brownstown Creek, but I jumped out of the boat and ran past their questions to the teepee I shared with Joseph. I threw myself, stomach down, on my pallet and shut my eyes and put my hands over my ears because I didn't want to see or hear or think of what had happened on the other side of the river. It didn't work.

I got up on my knees and elbows and tried to rock away the visions. I couldn't stop crying. If I hadn't followed those soldiers, if I hadn't gone with Joseph, I might still be a kid who could sleep without nightmares. But I'd wanted to look after him and now I was saddled with a black memory that I knew would never be wiped away.

Joseph came into the teepee and wakened me. I turned on my back and stared up at him.

He crouched down and put his hand on my head. "You are angry," he said in Shawnee.

I answered in the same language. "I don't like you with your hair like that. There was saliva dripping out of your mouth when you were killing soldiers. You were not my Joseph over there."

"That man is gone. I am Deep River again."

I turned away from him. "I don't like Deep River. I want Joseph back."

"Understand, little one. I must fight with Tecumseh. The Long Knives have taken our Indian land."

I sat up and looked at him. Perhaps I could change his mind. "You fought the Long Knives at Tippecanoe. Don't you remember what happened to you then?"

"You know that?"

"You talked about it when you had too much rum."

Joseph stood up and wiped his hand on his crest of hair. "Memory must be swallowed. The Long Knives killed Indians and Indians must kill Long Knives."

"You will become like Mr. William Henry Harrison then?"

"Uunh."

I stood up and threw my arms around his waist. "I want Joseph back!"

He crouched down and looked me in the eye. "Your pain and my pain are dust grains in the storm over Indian nations. Deep River must fight. I must say goodbye. Be brave like Joseph taught you." He stood away from me and stared into my eyes. I looked back at him and tried to be brave, but gulps snuck out of my mouth. "Remember, we are friends forever."

He was gone. I turned around in circles. What could I do? Where should I go? I'd lost my only friend. I had to be brave. I didn't want to be.

CHAPTER 6
AUGUST 1812

▼

Matthew Elliott

Sarah had me wash and change my clothes to receive the guests, but 'twas impossible for me to scrub off the filth of battle, so I sat there, weighted down by my inability to stop the savagery of the Indians and glared if anyone attempted to approach.

'Twas a bit like a dream watchin' my servants pass trays of food to soldiers in dress uniforms, sipping drinks as they leaned over the ladies, twittering birds dressed in bright tea gowns and all of them ignoring the noise of shootin' and drummin' that floated across the river from Bois Blanc as the Indians celebrated today's victory. I knew 'twas at my insistence that these people were invited, but that was before Brownstown.

The handsome major sportin' a lush moustache and slicked-back hair was leaning his sleek body over the boy Daniel's mother—salivatin', no doubt. No question, Margaret Brownell was beautiful and lively and more vibrant than the flowers behind her, but I sensed that the streak that brightened her was as dangerous as a bolt of lightning.

I watched a canoe pull in down by the dock. Daniel climbed out and came slowly up the grass. He stood on the edge of the crowd and stared—unable, I guessed, ta connect what he saw today with what he was seein' now. Couldn't blame him. He stared at his mother till he got her attention. I eavesdropped.

"Daniel, where have you been? Lieutenant Mackenzie said you didn't go to his room!"

"I stayed with Joseph and we were at Brownstown and—"

"You're filthy! You can't stay here! Go to the river and clean yourself up." She called a servant. "There are clothes in the trunk in my room. See to it that he's made respectable. Give him some soap to take to the river." She looked cross. "When you come back, I want you to apologize to Lieutenant Mackenzie"

The boy followed the servant and reappeared with soap and a pile of clothes, which he took down to the river, out of sight of the festivities.

My eyes must have drooped for a few minutes, because I jerked awake to find Daniel standing in front of me, washed and in clean clothes and with his arms crossed tight in an effort to stop the shiverin' that had taken over his whole body.

"Mother was right. I was dirty and I went to the river with my clean clothes and tried to scrub away the memories, but I couldn't get the stink out of my nostrils or the screams out of my ears or the vomit taste from my tongue."

The boy was babblin', which I understood. If I, an old man, couldn't shake the memory of the Yankee soldier, the things he saw must have smashed this child's world.

Still shivering, he stared over at his mother, who had returned to her flirtation with the Major. "I understand that Mother's too frail to think about me as anything but a burden, and that doesn't matter. I have to be strong to look out for her." His face contorted and he burst into tears. "But now, I'm not." His sobs screeched. "I hate the men who made this war."

In a minute he would be yelling, so I stood up and put my hand over his mouth to stop the prattle and, though it's not a gesture I'm accustomed to, took him into my arms and lay my cheek on his head, which, of course, brought on more blubber. He sucked in huge gulps of air tryin' hard to get himself together, but it took a while before he pulled himself away and looked up at me, smilin' a half-smile through his tears, and said, "Thank you."

For the first time, he seemed aware of the gathering and said in Shawnee, "How can you have a party after what we saw today and knowing General Hull could attack any minute?"

I answered him as I would an adult speaking in Shawnee so no one close might overhear. "These people are of no consequence, Daniel, it's better that they're kept out of the way. When they become involved, confusion destroys what little organization there is." I was about to go on when Boy appeared at my elbow.

"Lieutenant Colonel Procter's in the parlour wanting to talk to you."

"Damn!" I took Daniel's hand and we went up to the house. As we passed my office, I opened the door and pushed the child inside. "Wait for me here. I have to see to this." I followed my son to the parlour where the world's most important man was standing feet spread, seemingly glued in place and holding his tall stovepipe hat in one arm.

I didn't offer a seat or a handshake or a greeting, all of which would have been received with a negative response. Instead, I just started right in. "I suspect yer havin' a bit of a task seein' the fort right since the soldiers have taken to drink to celebrate the Indian's victory today." I knew I shouldn't spout such digs, but I couldn't resist scratchin' at the nerves of the pompous son-of-a-bitch.

"You needn't worry about the soldiers, sir, they are my business and I'll have them in shape in no time. I'm here to find out how many Indians you can rally to fight against Hull."

"That's difficult to say. It could be anywhere from 400 to 800. It depends on a lot of things."

"What things?"

"Well, how many Tecumseh can convince to fight, how many have lost their land to the Americans, how many are hungry and how many are angry. There's about 300 we can be sure of, but my guess is that after today a lot more will cross over. Could be we'll have 600 warriors in a few days."

"I'm surprised you can't be more accurate than that." He began to wander around the room, fingerin' the furniture and lookin' everywhere but at me. "You store and distribute the supplies to the Indians."

It was not a question, but I answered anyway. "I do."

"I'm afraid we'll have to change that." His tone was that of an overlord talking to his serf, which should have stuck in my craw, but I knew he was attackin' from weakness.

"What do you propose, sir?"

"The supplies must be kept in the fort and brought to you only when it is necessary to deliver them."

"I see." I rubbed my nose to contain a smile. 'Twas a battle we were to have. "I would be more than happy to accommodate ya. You do know that the wheat and corn come from my farm, so I'm afraid I'll have to charge you for the transportation and ya will, of course, have to construct warehouses to store it."

He looked down his barrel chest over his protruding stomach, pulled his chin back and flared his nostrils as though he was inhaling a bad smell. "There are facilities to store supplies at the fort, and we will not pay transportation! You will organize the transportation immediately, do you understand?"

I smiled up at him, knowing the task was next to impossible. "Well now, I believe you'll have to be more specific, as my warehouses are four times the size of any facilities at the fort. I'll have to think about that, sir, 'tis a huge undertaking you're suggesting."

"It's just the foodstuffs and guns I want. The rest—blankets, tents, cooking equipment and such—can stay here."

"I'm afraid with all these Indians arriving, there will be a need for more foodstuffs than I have in all my warehouses." I stroked my chin. "Which would mean the price of my oats and corn could rise fast, 'specially if I had to absorb the cost of transportation." Proud I was that my tone of voice remained practical, as though there was no tension existing between me and the twit.

He gritted his teeth and snarled, "The army doesn't want you, Elliott. The letter is with the postmaster and will leave on the next ship."

With that he stomped out.

The boy was sitting at my desk staring out of the window. I hesitated to burden him any more, but war was war and I needed his help.

"Daniel, there's somethin' I want you to do for me." I leaned on the desk as I talked.

The boy snapped his eyes to shutter whatever was swirling in his head and stared at me.

"Lieutenant Mackenzie is in charge of the post, and there is a letter I want that is probably on the desk in his room. It would be addressed to the Superintendent General of Indian Affairs in Quebec." I stopped with a sudden thought. "You can read, can't you?"

"Yes, sir."

"I need you to find the letter with that address. Do you think you can do that?"

"I don't know. Drummer Jakes told me Lieutenant Mackenzie liked to mount young boys."

"Mackenzie is here now. I'll make sure he stays. You go to the officers' barracks and tell them that Mackenzie is expecting you, which is not a lie."

"I guess I could try."

"That's a good soldier."

"Then do I come back here? Can I sleep here?"

"'Course you can. Where've you bin sleeping?"

"With Joseph."

"And where's Joseph?"

Tears brimmed on the boy's eyes. "Gone with Tecumseh. He's Deep River again."

"You come back here, Daniel, and we'll take care of you."

I handed the boy off to an Indian with orders to take him to Fort Malden in a canoe and wait to bring him back, after which I spent an hour with Boy discussing how we should deal with Procter and his rigid ideas. Unlike Alexander, this son was against compromise of any kind.

"You can't listen to him, Da. We're at war and we must go at it Indian-style, attacking and retreating, attacking and retreating. Going by the book and fighting beside bright red coats will end in disaster."

"You're more Indian than white, my Boy."

"Why wouldn't I be? I've spent most of my life with them. I have Indian skin and I didn't go east for an education."

He spoke in a practical voice, but I heard the undercurrents.

I returned to the party and sought out Lieutenant Mackenzie. He turned away from the group of officers with whom he was talking when I tapped him on the shoulder. "The boy had wanted to spend a final night with his Indian friend but will stay with you starting tonight." I beckoned a servant to refill the Lieutenant's glass. "You interest me, Lieutenant Mackenzie. Tell me about yourself, where are you from? How long have you been here? What do you think of this part of the world?"

He looked at me with curiosity but swiped his falling hair from his forehead and answered my questions with grace. Rather than listen to his responses, I tried to conjure up more questions so as to keep him occupied and away from the fort, but my scheming was interrupted by an announced order for all soldiers to return to the base.

I sure as hell hoped the boy would not get caught.

Sarah's Diary

Matthew has been very quiet since he returned from Brownstown. In bed last night, I tried to get him to talk about it. He took me in his arms and rubbed his chin on my head, but all he could say was, "I've known about savage battles for a long time, as have most adult men in this part of the world, including Alexander and Boy, but today I saw Daniel Brownell lose his innocence, and it made me sad for us all."

He kissed the top of my head and turned his back to me, leaving me wide awake wondering what I should or could have done to console him. He is my husband. I must keep telling myself that: I am the wife of Matthew Elliott Sr.!

CHAPTER 7
AUGUST 1812

▼

Daniel

One of Mr. Elliott's Indians paddled me back to the fort and said he'd wait. I got out of the canoe slowly. I was not looking forward to my job.

Drummer came over the hill with his drum still hanging down his front, held there by two thick white straps that crossed on his chest. I figured he'd come straight from being dismissed on the parade ground. "Did ya find a place to stay?" he called.

I trudged up to meet him. "Mr. Elliott says I can stay there, but first I have to do something for him."

I looked around to see if anyone was listening and whispered, "I'm supposed to steal a letter from Lieutenant Mackenzie's room."

"Who for?"

"For him, for Mr. Elliott."

"How're ya goin' to get into his room?"

"Mackenzie is at Mr. Elliott's so I guess I can just go in and tell anyone who asks that I'm supposed to meet Mackenzie and then I could get the letter and skedaddle out of there."

"I already warned you about him. If he catches you, you'd better not turn your back to him!"

"I know!" I thought about the two dogs and chewed my lips. "Maybe you could stand guard for me."

"Guess I could, but I'll get the cat if anyone finds out." Drummer picked up a stick. "I'll stand by that building across the way and watch, and if I see him comin' I'll throw the stick for Bruno and tell him in a real loud voice to go fetch it."

"Maybe I'll go with you so we can discuss it a little more." We situated ourselves in a place with a good view of the barrack door and discussed our tactics. "What'll I say to the officers inside if they tell me I should wait for Lieutenant Mackenzie before going into his room?"

"Say yer s'posed ta clean his boots."

"What if he has only one pair and he's wearing them?"

"Officers gotta have more'n one pair, I'd guess."

I didn't find the idea very appealing. While we talked, I took Drummer's stick from his hand and traced the letters S-U-P-E-R-T-I-N-T-E-N-D-E-N-T in the dirt. "Does that look like the way you write *superintendent*?"

Drummer looked down at my writing, took the stick back and traced the letters. "Could be."

I looked at Drummer and he looked away. I didn't mean to embarrass him. Stupid me! Of course he couldn't read! "Well, I guess I'd better do it." I took a deep breath and pushed myself away from the wall. "Here goes!"

I pushed the door open and peeked around it into what looked like a sitting room with chairs gathered round a fireplace. There was only a man with a broom cleaning the place, so I walked in and said, "I'm supposed to get something from Lieutenant Mackenzie's room." I lowered my voice to make it sound like I knew what I was doing but it wobbled, giving me away.

The man didn't seem to notice, just nodded his head and said, "Third door on the right."

With my head down I hurried past him, through the sitting room and down the hall to the door he had indicated. I had never been in an officer's bedroom before. It was small and stuffed with so many things that I had to turn in circles to take it all in. Hanging on the walls were snowshoes and a pistol and a musket and clothes and hats on hooks, while leaning against the walls were a washstand, a commode and four trunks of different sizes all standing on end. I didn't know where to look for letters.

Each of the trunks was opened a crack, so I figured I'd better see if any of them held papers. The first had drawers; maybe they were in there. I opened the trunk a little wider and sneaked my hand into a drawer, but it just had clothes. I heard footsteps and a cough outside the door and almost peed my pants, but they went past. I had to hurry. Where could the letters be?

The second trunk opened up into a bookcase—no luck there. Uniforms hung in the third. The fourth was my last chance. I opened it and a folding desk clunked down with a noise that sounded like a bomb. I froze. Nobody came. I let out my breath and pulled a postal sack out of a rack in the wall of the trunk.

It was full of letters. I dumped them on the desk and sorted through them until I found the one Mr. Elliott wanted and quickly returned the others to the sack and the sack to the place I had found it. I was stuffing the letter in my pants when I heard Drummer screech, "Fetch, Bruno!"

I tried to push the desk back into place but it kept falling, with the legs almost hitting the floor. Finally I got it in place, pushed the trunk so that it was almost shut and headed for the door.

Too late! The handle was turning.

The Lieutenant opened the door to find me sitting on the floor. I had to do that to save my bottom!

"Ah, Daniel. I'm glad you've come, but what are you doing on the floor?"

I pushed my back against the trunk holding the books, and some of the books fell out. I couldn't turn my back to him to pick them up, but I couldn't leave them there. The only solution was to fish around with my hand to try to find the books and replace them in the trunk. He stood at the door and watched me with a puzzled look on his face.

"Are you feeling all right?"

"Oh! I'm okay for the moment, sir." I found a slot for one of the books and got to work on a second, never looking away from him.

He closed the door, which was very worrisome.

"Just for the moment?"

"I've felt pretty bad ever since the battle at Brownstown." I wanted to bite back the words—why would I bring Brownstown up at a time like this? "Would you like me to clean your boots, sir?"

He patted the bed, motioning me to sit down. "Were you there? At Brownstown?"

I stood up and slid toward the bed, never turning my back to him. When I sat down on the mattress, the letter hidden in my pants crinkled. "Yes, sir, and it was horrible. Everyone was horrible, the Indians, the British and the Americans. It was like they all caught the same disease—they were drooling like my dog, their eyes were wild and they were all screaming. They were cutting and shooting and stabbing, and it was like they had fire in them and it was making them crazy." I knew I was babbling, but I was too nervous to stop.

"How did you get there?" He sounded angry, and not at me.

"Joseph, the Indian who looked after me, was drunk, and he decided he wanted to cut his hair and become a warrior. I jumped in his canoe to look after him."

"You're too young to have been there; too young to see how men mangle the rules of war." He put his arm around my shoulder, and I froze like a deer caught in a light and started to vomit more words.

"Joseph is going to fight with Tecumseh now. He's changed his name to Deep River. He's not going to look after me anymore."

We sat like that and he rubbed my shoulder. I tried to figure out how I'd escape. "I'm sorry, Daniel, but you'll not be able to stay here. I'm going away."

"That's too bad, sir," I lied.

"Will you be able to find a place to stay?"

"I think so, sir. I think maybe Mr. Elliott has room for me now 'cause some of the visitors have left his house."

"You could stay in your mother's room with her."

"If she'd have me, I guess I could, but I'm not sure she's much interested in having me with her. I'm an extra burden, you know."

He ruffled my hair. If people kept doing that, I'd soon be bald. "An extra burden?"

"She thinks she would be better off without me." I moved a little bit to the side of the bed so our bottoms weren't touching. "But she really does need me, so I try to ignore her."

"I think you are a good son, and I wouldn't—"

A stone came crashing through the window. I swore to myself. I'd forgotten about Drummer!

"What on earth?" Lieutenant Mackenzie went to the window and then headed for the door. He dashed out after Drummer, forgetting about me.

I ran out after him, through the main room and around to the back of the barracks to where I heard Bruno barking.

Lieutenant Mackenzie had Drummer by the scruff of the neck and was shaking him. "You devil, I'll have you whipped for this!" Before I knew it, my friend was being dragged toward the prison. I had to do something.

"No, please, Lieutenant, it's my fault!"

Lieutenant Mackenzie stopped but didn't let go of Drummer.

"He did it for me—in case—because—" I didn't know what to tell him, but I had to save Drummer.

The Lieutenant stared down at me. "Because what?"

If I didn't tell the truth, Drummer could get the cat. Maybe I could lie and say I had dared Drummer Jakes to do it, but maybe it wouldn't help my friend anyway. It wasn't nice to have to tell the truth, but I guessed it was my only option. "Uh-m-m, because I was told you might want to mount me," I was talking fast. "And I was scared and I asked Drummer to wait for me and I guess I was in your room so long he got worried and threw the stone in your window to distract you. It's my fault, sir, please don't do anything to Drummer."

"Mount you?"

"Yes, like a dog—that's what they said you would do."

The Lieutenant let go of Drummer, turned his face up to the sky and let out a deep sigh. "You needn't be frightened of me, Daniel. I'm not going to 'mount' you. When people don't understand something, they make up ridiculous stories."

Maybe he was telling the truth. He had certainly been nice to me.

"It's a very hard thing to live with," he added.

"What's hard to live with?"

"It's not something you would understand."

"That he likes little boys," Drummer explained with the same tone of voice he used when he told me about drumming or shooting or cards—a teaching, practical voice.

"That's not true, young man. Never in my life have I accosted a child."

"If it ain't kids, it's men," Drummer insisted.

"And for suspicion of that, nothing more than suspicion—as I've done nothing—Procter is kicking me out of the army." He looked down at me. "That's why I'm leaving."

"How can they kick you out for suspicion?"

"They can't, really, but they can make life very miserable if they wish you to leave and you refuse." He leaned against the wall. "I'm not up to that kind of harassment."

"Where are you going?"

"Back to England, I suppose. I don't know yet."

He looked slumped and sad. It had to be hard to be different. "I don't care what they say, you're a nice man and I like you."

He squatted down and gave me a hug. "Thank you, young Daniel—it is very special to be liked by you, so much so that I will forgive your friend." He stood up and put his hands on his hips and glared at Drummer.

I felt really bad about the letter that was crinkling in my waistband.

Drummer and I and Bruno walked down to the river to find the boat that would take me back to Mr. Elliott's.

"That was close," Drummer said.

"Yah! If we'd known what Lieutenant Mackenzie was really like, you wouldn't have had to throw the stone."

"Maybe not, but he was sure to discover the letter in your pants if you stuck around too long."

I wondered what was so important about the letter and if I had done the right thing, stealing it for Mr. Elliott. It was too late to worry about it, though. "You're right! Thanks!" I stopped and gave Bruno a pat. "I forgot about the letter 'cause of our conversation with Lieutenant Mackenzie. What do you think about him?"

"Guess he's okay. Still, it ain't normal to like men like that."

"I guess there are lots of things that aren't normal, but who says they're wrong? Is there a list somewhere that says this is normal and that is not?"

"I'd bet there is in the Bible."

"Even if there is."

Whew! Another thought I'd have to put aside and think about later!

At the dock, the Indian who brought me upriver was waiting. Drummer grabbed my arm and stopped me before we got to the end of the dock.

"Daniel, we're crossing the river tomorrow."

I could feel the fist in my chest closing. "How do you know?"

"I had to drum up and down the streets of Amherstburg to get the militia to report to the fort." He took Bruno's collar. "Do you think you could keep him till I get back?"

"'Course I could."

I was slow getting Bruno into the canoe, as I was worrying about what Drummer would see tomorrow, worrying that he might be injured or killed, worrying that he might be captured and tortured and scalped. Of course, it would be dumb to let him know what I was thinking. "Good luck tomorrow," I called from the river. "I'll be waiting for you when you get back."

I watched Drummer wave and turn and slump off to the barracks.

CHAPTER 8
AUGUST 1812

▼

Matthew Elliott

"Where's my brother?"

Not knowin' when we'd have another feed, Alexander and I were pilin' into a meal so large 'twas impossible for me to finish, but not so my son, who was doin' justice to a piece of beef that was so large it hung over his plate and had been reduced to strips of fat relieved of even the slightest edge of meat. I wondered if courage sat easier on a full stomach. I replied, "He's going to stay behind and watch over Sarah and the babes."

"They'll be fine here without him. He should come with us." Alexander pushed away his empty plate.

"I want him to stay behind, to keep an eye on Sarah and the babes."

"I think he should come with us, Da. This is his fight too. It's like you're leaving him the position of the man of the house, and I don't think that's a grand idea."

"Don't you worry, I'm still the man of the house, but it makes me feel better to leave him here watching over Sarah and the babes." I could have added that I didn't want Boy with us, fearin' he'd find fault with whatever we did.

Alexander mumbled into his damned napkin, preventin' me from hearin' his words clearly.

Before I got a chance to question him, he threw his napkin on the table and said, "We'll have to cross tonight, Da. Hull has sent a huge force down from Detroit to make sure his supply train gets through. Tecumseh's scouts are shadowing them and sent a message saying the Long Knives are 'mosquitoes in a swamp in number'!"

"Who're they sending from the fort?" I sure as hell hoped Procter didn't try to lead them.

"Major Muir."

"He's a good man. Worked his way up through the ranks. His accent is wrong and his words rough: a man I can understand."

"He wants to meet with you and Tecumseh when he crosses, which will be before light, so we'd best be off within the next hour."

A servant cleared my plate and I was leaning my achin' body back in my chair so's to be able to rest my feet on the table when the back door opened and young Daniel appeared.

"Here's the letter, Mr. Elliott." He lifted his shirt, pulled the letter out of his pants and, with pride on his face, presented me with a very wrinkled missive.

"Good boy." It was good to get that small problem taken care of before we headed out. I handed the letter to Alexander, who opened it and checked to make sure it was the correct one.

He nodded his head. "This is it, Da."

"Rip it up," I told him.

"Can't you read, Mr. Elliott?" the boy asked.

"Never had the time for it," I grumbled.

"I could teach you."

"'Tis a tad late for an old man, but thank you, Daniel." I should have been ashamed that an 11-year-old had offered to better me, but I could add, subtract, multiply and divide in my head, and I'd done well by it, so I guessed I had better not complain about not having received any schooling.

As he tore up the letter, Alexander got up from the table and went toward the back door. "We'd better leave in half an hour, Da."

"I'll be right there. I just want a word with the boy."

"It's Mother, isn't it? Is she bad?"

Is she bad, he asked, not *What's the matter* or *Has something happened* or *I don't understand*. He knew. What must he have suffered havin' that beautiful witch for a mom? "She's real bad, Daniel! Yesterday she announced she was goin' to York with the Major, and when Sarah said she didn't think it was a good idea, her bein' married and all, your mom started screamin' that she wasn't going to stay here and watch grown men 'wallow in war,' and she threw plates across the dining room, breaking pieces of Sarah's good china and making a fekin' mess. I'm sorry, boy, but this is not a good time to have to deal with her problems. If in the morning she is still raving, we'll have to send her away."

He drew an imaginary circle on the table and doodled his finger inside the circle; looked like he was tracin' a star. "Papa and I call it 'being in a state,' and I've been really worried 'cause there were lots of bad signs, like talking too fast, wearing bright colours, not listening to anyone and doing crazy things, all of which means she has 'gone away.' Up till now, she's snapped back and doesn't even remember what's happened, so maybe she'll wake tomorrow and be all right and change her mind about leaving with the Major."

"I hope so for your sake, 'cause I don't believe Sarah will tolerate much more of this, and I can't deal with it bein' as the war is on my doorstep."

"Is it true you're crossing over tonight?"

"I'm afraid it is, and soon. You'd best be off to bed, and we'll talk about your mom when I get back." *If I got back.*

"You said I could stay here, but where do I go to bed?"

"A servant made up a bed for you in the attic. Off you go now."

"I guess I can't see mother now."

"She's asleep, Daniel, best leave it till the morning. Just go to the top of the stairs, and you'll see an open door along the hall. You'll need a candle from the kitchen."

The river was a black tongue lapping at our flatboats, swallowing us into Hell. Dockin' again at Brownstown Creek, we couldn't avoid marchin' past the dregs of last week's battle. Mother-O-God, the stench was overwhelming!

Scalped and bloated bodies of blue-coated cavalry officers littered the field, and the impaled bodies of foot soldiers had bin gnawed and pecked by animals and birds. Ravens had carried the entrails of chewed bodies into the trees, where they drooped on dead branches. 'Twas a field full of the defecation of evil. Alexander held my elbow and I didn't shake him off.

Tecumseh and Muir were waiting just past Brownstown. Tecumseh was painted up for battle. I greeted my Indian friend with a deep-armed handshake. "You've travelled far since last we met," I said in Shawnee.

"The battle at Brownstown has made many tribes believe the English could win. I have travelled far to gather warriors."

"How many?"

"We have 500. I will find more." He pulled me aside and continued in his own language. "I do not like these British, Elliott. I do not trust them. Are they men of their word, Elliott, can I believe them?"

"I s'pose we have ta believe them. 'Tis the only road left."

Tecumseh frowned and stared at the shadows between the trees. What was this driven man thinkin'? I'm damned sure if he could have come up with any other options, he'd have been out of there like a flash.

"They have made many promises and kept very few."

"They need you, Tecumseh. Without you and your warriors, they can't win, and without them you haven't a hope. It's an unhappy marriage, I know, but I'm afraid you're forced to stay together."

He turned away from the shadows and his eyes wrinkled. "We will be difficult brides!"

Muir was crouched over a map, and a sergeant was holding a flame over it, shielding it with his hand so it wouldn't blow out.

"This man, is he a real soldier?" Tecumseh asked.

"I don't know him well, but they say he's a good man." We joined him at the map.

Muir pointed to the Brownstown field shown on the map. "The best place to wait is Brownstown Creek." He had a thick Scottish accent. "It worked last week, and there is no reason it won't work again." He drew his finger along the strip where he proposed to do battle.

"Not good." Tecumseh's tone was vehement. "This time there are many more soldiers marching against us. We must go to the Indian village Maguaga, here." He pointed to the place three miles north. "In that place, the army can wait in this ravine while I take half my warriors to the cornfields on the left with me and the others can go on the right with Elliott and his son."

Muir didn't argue. Seems the man was smart enough to realize who knew the area best. He closed the map saying, "We'd best get on with it."

With Alexander beside me, we slogged along the muddy path, our footsteps makin' slurping sounds that, in this situation, seemed to be louder than the crack of a rifle

The sky had swallowed the pitch-black night and become a dark dirty grey that made shadows of the lithe bodies of the Indians slippin' between trees, of the soldiers marchin' along paths with military precision and of the basswood protrudin' from the caps of the militia.

"Da, that tree up yonder has a solid V that'll hold your rifle for a better aim," Alexander whispered.

He knew that these days, my gun got heavy real fast. The tree was on a rise that gave a good view, so I didn't argue, 'specially as I'd be able to lean a little and relieve the damned pain in my back.

Before the sun rose, we were all in position. It had been agreed that we would wait for the first volley of musket balls before risin' to the attack.

They appeared through the woods and the shootin' started. Our centre was pounded by musket fire. Guns screamed; soldiers slashed with bayonets and got sliced by swords; bodies appeared and disappeared in the brown vapour; horses slipped in the mud, tossin' their mounts, turnin' them into victims of screamin' Indians and their tomahawks.

Tecumseh attacked from the left, tryin' to turn the American flank, and my Indians were attackin' from the right, but it was not goin' well on my side. "Drop back!" I ordered them in Shawnee and kept shooting to cover their retreat. Our own soldiers started shooting at us! Alexander tore out in front of the Indians and waved his arms and screamed at them "Stop!"

A musket went off, and my son collapsed on the ground.

I tore out from behind my tree. "We're on your side, you dumb sons-of-bitches!" I screamed and ran to Alexander.

An army sergeant screamed back, "How the hell were we supposed to know? Ya can't tell them damn Indians apart!"

I tried to help my son up. "It's all right, Da. Just a scratch." With his arm over my shoulder, he limped to the shelter of my tree.

Comin' up from the south I saw a new crop of soldiers bein' led by Procter and was damned relieved to see the British prick!

The centre was drivin' the Americans back, and Muir had the drummer drum the bayonet charge. Knowin' Procter's men were behind us, I screamed "Attack!" to my Indians, and they charged forward once more but fell under the barrage of American bullets. Where was Procter? I turned to check his progress, and all I saw was their damn backs as they marched away from the battle. Where the fekin' hell were they going?

The Americans had pulled up a six-pounder and were spraying grapeshot at our chargin' troops, killin' hundreds and injuring many so badly their screams of pain could be heard over the blasting guns. Those that still could retreated in a confused mass. Tecumseh was doin' his best to draw off some of the Americans, giving Muir and my surviving Indians time to escape to the boats. With Alexander leaning on the tree for support, we positioned ourselves to protect the retreat of our Indians, but the smoke was so damned thick we didn't dare shoot for fear we'd kill our own men who burst through, dragging their wounded over stinkin' mud and dead, bloodied bodies of fallen brothers and their horses.

I was seethin' in furor over Procter's actions as I joined the Indians in a mortifyin' retreat across the river. "Why did the fekin' idiot turn away from the battle? What in God's good name was he thinking?"

Sarah's Diary

They're back in one piece. Alexander was hit in the leg but it's not serious. I'm staying away from Matthew's office, where he is venting his anger at yet another problem with Procter. It must be very bad this time, because he can be heard throughout the whole house, and the words he's spouting would infect any Christian ear that was exposed to them.

Boy plans to go and join Tecumseh.

I must go to confession!

Chapter 9
August 1812

▼

Daniel

Even though Mr. Elliott said not to disturb her, I thought I should see Mother before finding my bed in the attic. Since all the men were gone, I creeped up the front stairs, knocked on her bedroom door and waited. Nothing happened, so I knocked again. "Mother, it's me." And waited again. Finally, she appeared at the door, clutching her dressing gown closed.

"What do you want, Daniel?"

"Can I come in?"

"No, you may not. I . . . I'm busy. Now off you go."

"I just want to talk to you for a minute."

"*Not now, Daniel!*"

She slammed the door. I stood with my nose practically smooshed by the door and couldn't decide whether she was back or not, and then I heard the voice of a man inside the room saying, "Come back to bed!" I knew that voice. It was the Major who was going to fight with Wellington. I should have known. I slumped along the hall dragging my hand on the wall. Just before I turned the corner of the corridor, I heard a door open and saw Mrs. Elliott tiptoeing out of Boy's room. I wondered what she was doing there.

The attic air smelled thick and dusty, and the candle made shadows dance, but there was a little window through which I could see the sky with millions of stars, and I tried to concentrate on them and ignore the ghost-shadows that were trying to climb under the covers with me.

One ghost tried to make me look at the battle at Brownstown, so I turned on my other side and consoled myself that Mother was not always horrible.

There was a day when Mother took me by the hand and, skipping backward, pulled me to a patch of wild raspberries she'd discovered, and we picked and laughed and then, with containers full, sat at the edge of the river to eat our cache, each staring quietly out at the calm water until, out of the corner of my eye, I could see some nonsense forming in her crooked smile. When she grabbed a fistful of berries, I knew immediately what was coming and tried to slide away while shaking my head and laughing, "Oh no you don't!" But she caught me and smushed some berries on my face, and I knew it was in fun so I took some of my own with the idea of returning the favour, and she tried to roll away from me but I caught her and smushed her face, and she put her arms around me in a giant hug, and we rolled around on the ground, laughing as hard as we could.

I woke to yelling in the kitchen, so with Bruno on my tail, I crept down the stairs and opened the door a crack, through which we saw Mr. Elliott appearing and disappearing as he stomped back and forth, kicking at every available piece of furniture. "What did the lily-livered son-of-a-bitch think he was doing? Jaysus, Mary and Joseph, I'm goin' to murder the feker!"

"He said the drummer drummed a retreat, not an attack," Alexander answered from a place I couldn't see through my crack.

"Jist like him to lay the blame on a boy. He'll probably try to court-martial him!"

Are they talking about Drummer?

"You'd best calm down, Da. If you roar around in a furor, it's not going to do anyone any good. We've got to keep Procter happy until Brock arrives, then we'll see."

Mr. Elliott kicked another chair. "Mother o' God, where do these officers come from? They must be the dregs of the British military!"

"Face it, Da, war is just a series of mistakes, so chalk this one up and forget it. We can't afford to dwell on it."

I pushed the door open and stepped into the kitchen.

Mr. Elliott was slumped in a chair, arms crossed, chin on his chest and a giant scowl on his face. Alexander was leaning toward his father with crossed arms pressed hard into the table.

Mr. Elliott saw me out of the corner of his eye. His chin stayed glued down and his eyes were crinkled in anger. "What are you doin' here?"

"The drummer, it wasn't Drummer Jakes, was it?"

"It could be. I'm not sure which drummer it was."

"Will whoever it was be court-martialled?"

"Not if Major Muir stands up for him, but right now I'm not believin' any of those red-coated peacocks!"

"He's a good man," Mr. Alexander said. "He'll do what's necessary."

I had to find out if Drummer Jakes was in trouble. "Can I take a canoe to Fort Malden? I need to see my friend."

Mr. Elliott waved me away with a nod.

Being lighter, I paddled in the front of the canoe while an Indian paddled in the back. At the Amherstburg dock, I jumped out and headed straight for the barracks, hoping to find Drummer Jakes.

The soldiers I passed talked in low voices and were not smiling; it was like the whole place was suffering from a giant wound. I found Drummer lying on his bed. He seemed to be in one piece—at least he wasn't bandaged or limping like some of the men I saw—but his eyes were flat, and his smile was pretty small.

"You okay?"

"I s'pose."

"It's horrible, isn't it?"

"That is for certain sure!"

Drummer looked up at the ceiling and I knew he was looking inside his head at what happened, and I knew he'd never get it out of his head.

"Tell me."

He continued to stare at the ceiling. His voice was flat. "Ya heard only one noise: left, right, left, right. There weren't even a whisper from the soldiers. Beside us and in front of us the Indians, naked 'cept for a loincloth and painted from head to toe, ran through the woods without making a sound. My stomach were down in my balls, I can tell yah!"

"You must have passed Brownstown," I said, not looking at my friend.

For a minute he didn't say anything. "We did. 'Tweren't easy to get past without vomiting."

He shook his head hard, shut his eyes and crossed his arms over his face. "Can't tell you about the battle 'cause a thousand things were happening at the same time. There was noise and blood and stink and war whoops and I didn't even know what I was doing. I just stuck to the line while the soldiers shot and moved back, shot and moved back."

"You don't have to tell me that part, I saw it myself—I know what it's like." I pushed his legs aside and sat down on the cot. "I guess the Americans won, then?"

"Ta tell the truth, I've no idea."

"Were you the one who drummed the bayonet charge?"

He rolled over, turning his back to me. "Yep."

"I heard that Lieutenant Colonel Procter said you drummed a retreat instead of charge."

"He said that. It's not true, but there's goin' to be a hearin'."

"Will Major Muir stand up for you?"

"He will, but he's only a major, what can he do against the word of a lieutenant colonel?"

I put my hand out thinking I might touch his shoulder to reassure him, then hesitated thinking the touch might bother him, then did it anyway. "Don't worry, I heard Mr. Elliott talking about it. He hates Procter, and I'm sure he won't let anything happen to you."

Drummer Jakes turned back toward me. "Is that the truth?"

"Yup!" *I hope I'm right.*

Two soldiers blocked the door, preventing me from leaving. They barged into the barracks and headed straight for Drummer Jakes and grabbed him under the armpits, lifting him right off the floor. "You're under arrest, boy," one of them said, and they pushed me aside as they dragged him toward the jail.

"I'm going to Mr. Elliott right now, Drummer." I ran to the canoe.

Mr. Elliott wasn't in his kitchen office. I ran through the house looking for him and found him in his real office in the front of the house. There were a group of men with him, but I didn't care. "Mr. Elliott," I cried. "They've put Drummer in jail!"

He looked up from the map he was studying and didn't seem to understand. "What's that your sayin', Daniel?"

"They've arrested Drummer Jakes!"

He slapped his hand on the table. "That pissin' Procter is tryin' to make the boy a scapegoat!"

"You have to do something, Mr. Elliott! He swears he didn't drum a retreat!"

"Don't worry, lad, we'll take care of it." He swivelled his head to include everyone in the room.

Only then did I realize who else was there. Alexander Elliott was sitting at the desk, and Boy was standing with Tecumseh against the far wall.

"Can you do it fast so he doesn't have to stay in that jail?"

"As fast as we can, Daniel." He looked around at all the men who, it seemed to me, were like a team planning some tricky play, and all their eyes were focused on me. "But there's somethin' we want you to do for us in return." He put his hands on my shoulders. "We've received a letter from General Brock, askin' us to have General Hull capture a letter that will deceive the American general into believin' we have more troops and more Indians than we really have."

"We've been trying to decide how we get this letter into Hull's hands." Boy added. "Tecumseh said you are the perfect young soldier to do the task."

"Me? How? Why?" That old fist in my tummy was doing its worst.

"Your father, he crossed the river, no?" Tecumseh asked.

Joseph told him, I was sure.

"Ya tell the General you want to cross to be with your father and that you stole the letter to help the Americans," Mr. Elliott added.

"No, I am not going to trick my father and his friends."

"They are the enemy." Tecumseh looked angry.

"They're not the enemy, sir! It's about roots and memory. He loves the place he was born in."

"You know that means he's a traitor?" Alexander said gently.

I thought that was the silliest thing I'd have ever heard. "No, he's a trader, not a traitor. He's always been an American, so how can he be a traitor?"

"He was living here and he crossed over, did he not?" Alexander the lawyer asked.

"He crossed the river, that's all."

"In our estimation, that makes him a traitor, and when they are captured, traitors are put to death."

They all grunted in agreement.

"You're wrong. I know you're wrong. He's my father, and he is a good man."

Mr. Elliott leaned down to my level. "Daniel, we've promised to get yer friend out of jail, so I figure you should be willing to do something in return. If ya do this for us, I'm sure we kin convince General Brock to promise not ta kill your father after he's captured."

All of a sudden, I didn't like anyone in the room.

"You can say ya stole the letter from the mailbag before it was sent, and you hoped it would help your father if ya delivered it to Hull. You have to choose between a whole country and your father, Daniel."

If these men had mirrors to see themselves, I bet they wouldn't force a boy my age to do their dirty work. "I guess I have no choice, but if I can avoid it, I'm not going to cross the river 'cause I need to be with my mother. I'll get the letter to General Hull, but after that, even if I have to cross to put on a show, I'm going to sneak back as quick as I can."

The four men looked at each other and nodded their heads.

"But you have to promise to get Drummer out of jail immediately."

"Agreed." Mr. Elliott shook my hand. "Now, wait outside till we finish in here." He unfolded some maps and gestured to Tecumseh to have a look. They bowed their heads and forgot about me.

Outside I slid my back down the wall until I was sitting with my legs bent. This was not a good thing. I would have to figure a way to work around it.

Chapter 10
August 1812

▼

Daniel

Mr. Elliott walked me down to the canoe. He had his arm around my shoulder.

"I can't say your arm is making me feel any better, sir."

"I know, Daniel. It's a hard thing we've asked, but we've made a deal. We'll get your friend out of jail if you do this for us."

I didn't feel much like talking to Mr. Elliott. I was still pretty mad at what they had all said about my father.

"I wouldn't have you do this, Daniel, if wasn't so very important."

I didn't answer him, and when we arrived at the edge of the woods where an Indian waited to take me some of the way on the back of his horse, Mr. Elliott stuck out his hand for me to shake, but I shook my head.

He chewed his lower lip.

I was glad he looked miserable. "If I don't come back, please take care of my mother."

The Indian dropped me off at the edge of the road about a mile short of the closest American outpost at the River aux Canards. The morning sun was just a hint creeping through the dark woods as I walked along the road out in the open and whistled so the guards wouldn't shoot at me. I was so scared, my whistle was just a squeak sitting on wind, and I could pee my pants any minute.

At the bridge, I stomped hard on the wooden planks. Where were the soldiers? I kept going, attempting my dry whistle, humming when it failed, and every few minutes I turned in a circle to make sure I hadn't missed anything. All of a sudden, out of the forest on both sides of the road, soldiers appeared, all aiming their muskets at me.

I threw my hands up in the air and some pee did dribble into my pants. The soldiers lowered their guns when they saw I was just a boy.

"What do you want, boy?"

"My name is Daniel. Daniel Brownell. I'm looking for my father. Ezra Brownell. He's in your army. He has a store in Sandwich. He crossed over. I have something for him. I haven't done anything. I was in Amherstburg with my mother, but I want to be with my father." I knew I was babbling, but I couldn't stop. "I stole some papers from the mailbag." I pulled them out from under my shirt and held them forward with two hands. "Maybe they'll help."

One of them took the papers and, holding them upside down, looked at them for a few minutes, and then he grabbed me under the arm and practically lifted me off the ground as he marched forward. "We'll see about all this."

They dragged me all the way to Sandwich, where there seemed to be a lot more militia than real soldiers—I could tell because they were dressed in homespun jackets and breeches and felt hats and had a real mix of weapons ranging from muskets to sporting rifles to army rifles. I tried to see what was happening at the store. Was Papa there? The soldier dragged me up the stairs of Lieutenant Colonel Baby's house just across from our store, knocked on Baby's door and told the man who answered it who I was, showing him the papers I'd brought with me. The officer looked at the letter and without letting go of it opened the door wide, gesturing for my captor to drag me in.

With the soldier still holding me tight, we waited in the hall. The officer went into another room, where I could hear voices mumbling, and then the door opened and the officer said to the soldier, "Bring him in."

In the room, my captor stood at attention and saluted the man standing behind the desk. "General," he said.

It must have been General Hull. He was an old man, fat, with puffy skin, but he had eyes that seemed really gentle, which was surprising 'cause I wasn't sure generals should have gentle eyes.

The letter lay open on his desk. "Tell me how you got this, young man."

I launched into my prepared story. "That's our store out there, General. My father left it to go and fight with you." I got a teary look on my face, which wasn't entirely false. "My mother wouldn't cross over with him and although I really, really wanted to go to Detroit, Papa thought I should stay with mother at Amherstburg."

The General sat in his chair and beckoned me to come around to his side of the desk.

"But my mother doesn't want me with her." I was crying real tears, even hiccupping a little. "She wants to go away with another man." I made a fist and dried the dumb tears from my eyes. I was a better actor than I would have imagined. "So I decided I wanted to come back and find Papa, but I figured I'd need something to help me get through."

The General lifted the corner of the letter. "How did you get hold of this?"

"Oh, that was easy, sir. The Major, he's the man who is going to take my mother away, is leaving in the morning for Niagara with General Brock's mail. We were all staying in the home of Mr. Matthew Elliott and when he and my mother went—" I looked out of the window and inhaled with a couple of stuttered breaths "—went to bed, he left the packet of letters in the room off the bedroom. I just snatched one from the mailbag and took off." Tecumseh and Mr. Elliott had told me to say I wanted to join my father, but my story just popped out when the actor in me took over.

"Did you read the letter?"

"No, sir. Does it help you, sir?"

"I'm not sure. Tell me, are there many soldiers in Amherstburg?"

"Yes, sir, there are so many, the Indians have had to move out to the island across from the fort. The town and the fort are overflowing, and some of the soldiers are sleeping in tents outside the walls." That was the biggest lie yet.

"And the Indians. Are there a lot of them?"

"Yes, they all came after Tecumseh arrived. They have been crossing the river to fight your soldiers, and they come back with scalps and do war dances on the island Bois Blanc. They are really scary!" At least that was the truth. "Mr. Elliott asked Tecumseh to tell them to stop shooting off their rifles, because they're wasting ammunition."

General Hull stroked his cheek with his hand as though he didn't want to think about what I was saying. "Thank you. You can go now."

"My father, sir? Is Papa here or at the fort? Is he all right?"

It was like I was pulling General Hull back from deep thoughts. "Your father? What is his name?"

"Ezra, sir. Ezra Brownell."

"I don't know him." He looked at the soldier who dragged me in and was still standing at attention. "Find out if Ezra Brownell is in our militia."

"Yes, sir. What do I do with this young man?"

The General flicked his lower lip with a finger and stared at me without saying anything. If I looked away from him, it would look like I was lying, but it was difficult to stand there frozen on the ground and hold his stare, so I pretended I had an itch on my head.

The General put his elbows on the table and wrung his hands together. "You'll have to put him under guard until we make sure he's telling the truth."

"Where, sir?"

"Where? Where what?"

"Where should he be put, sir?"

"Oh, with the other prisoners, I suppose." He looked at me. "It shouldn't be for long."

My captor led me out the door and once outside pushed me ahead of him so hard I had difficulty staying on my feet. There was no yesterday or tomorrow or an hour ago or an hour in the future, there was just me stumbling ahead too frightened to think.

The Sandwich jailhouse was one big room that had never seen many occupants before the war. Sometimes a drunk was thrown in to spend the night, and once when I was nine a trapper who had murdered his wife was kept there for a few days until the authorities came to take him away. I never imagined that I would be on the inside as a prisoner, especially not at my age.

My captor unlocked the door and pushed me so hard I fell onto my knees.

Someone helped me up. "Daniel!"

I knew the voice immediately. It was Mr. Wickam. "Mr. Wickam! What are you doing here?"

"Just a small misunderstanding. It will be fixed soon." He put his hand on my shoulder and steered me past the other men in the room to a place under the barred window. "Now, tell me what's happened. Why did you leave Amherstburg?"

I shook my head and whispered, "I can't, not here, not now." I was shivering.

He pulled me to him and said, "It'll be all right."

"Why are you in jail?"

"It's nothing serious. Soldiers moved into our house and they thought if they put me in jail, Clementine would be more willing to cook for them. She's promised to keep cookin' if they release me, so I should be out by tomorrow."

"And these men?" There were five of them, farmers who were in the militia—men I'd seen training here before the war.

"They snuck back from Amherstburg to save their crops but were caught."

There was a pail to pee in and otherwise just the hard floor. We all sat as far away from the pail as we could and leaned against a wall, not talking much. I took out my mirror and stared at the boy who had new memories in his head—unforgettable memories of good men who did bad things.

The door was unlocked, and I stood up expecting to be released, but it was Mr. Wickam who was called out. With difficulty he rose to his feet on creaking bones. "As soon as they release you, come home, Daniel. Come to the back."

"I'll probably be there soon." I had thought I would be released before night came, but I was not. Maybe they didn't even go looking for Papa. Maybe I'd be left and forgotten.

At night on the hard floor, with the stink of piss in my nostrils, the snores of the one man capable of sleep, the outside hoot of an owl and a sad song from a loon on the river, I was unable to sleep. Instead, I made up things I was going to say to Mr. Elliott if I ever got out of this situation.

In the morning, the door opened again. A soldier brought in bowls of gruel for the farmers and said to me, "They've found your father. You can go, but General Hull says you must stay in the area. I'm to find you a place."

"It's all right, sir. I know a place."

There were soldiers going in and out the front door of the Wickams' house. I thought they might not want me to stay with the Wickams, so I lurked at the edge of the property waiting for them to disappear—but then my dog, Prophet, appeared from around the corner in the back and, seeing me, came galumphing toward me with his big ears flapping. I crouched down prepared to hug him, and he knocked me onto my back and licked my face, he was so glad to see me. Laughing, I hugged him and twisted my head to the side to avoid his giant tongue, and I rolled around on the ground with him, not wanting to stop, not wanting to lose the feeling of happiness in my belly.

Out of breath, I crouched with my arms around my dog and watched the American soldiers walk by us. I'm not sure if they saw us, but if they did, we were of no interest to them. When they had all gone into the house, I stood up. "Let's go! Take me to Mr. Wickam, boy."

Obediently, he led me around to the side where there was a door to the back kitchen, the place where vegetables, preserves and everything that didn't fit in the real kitchen was stored. I went in and found it all changed. The extra chairs and pots and lamps and basins were piled high beside the shelves that held preserves, making room for a bed that had been made up, with enough space beside it for a table to hold an oil lamp.

I crossed the splintered, weathered, unpainted floor and opened the door to the real kitchen. Clementine Wickam was just where I had left her, tending her cooking pot in the fireplace, but I could see she was not the same, 'cause there was a new frown line that ran up and down between her eyes, and she was thinner—not thin, mind you, but her big dress did seem loose. "Mrs. Wickam?"

She turned and the old smile reappeared. "Daniel, how wonderful to see you! How did you get back to Sandwich?" She looked toward the parlour where I heard men talking, and she whispered, "Why did you come back? This is not a good place to be at the moment."

"It's okay, Mrs. Wickam. I can't talk about it now." I gestured with my head to show her that I didn't want to have the soldiers hear about it.

She opened her eyes wide and nodded.

"Is Mr. Wickam in the back?"

"'Course he his. You go on back and after I've finished feeding the men in there, I'll feed you two. How does that sound?"

"It sounds very good to me. I've been dreaming about your bread." That glued the old smile back on her face!

Mr. Wickam was sitting on his bench carving. When he saw me, he put down the thing he was working on and extended his hand for a good shake, which he backed up with soft slaps on the back and a twinkle in his eye.

I figured he would have liked to pull me into a hug and I would not have minded at all, but that's not the way he was.

He saw me eying the box of carvings. "Get the box down and settle yourself, and tell me everything that's happened to you and why you came back."

I took the box from its shelf, sat down on the plank of wood opposite Mr. Wickam's bench and started messing around with his carvings.

I told him about Brownstown. While I talked, I sifted through his circles inside squares and stars inside circles and triangles inside squares. It was not really that I was talking to him, it was more like I was thinking out loud and my words were being heard by a sympathetic ear—actually, two sympathetic ears, because Prophet was lying at my feet. "I was so scared, my fear stunk like putrid fruit!"

We didn't talk for a while

"Your mother?"

"At the moment she's without fear! In the state she's in, she won't even think about tomorrow until it changes its name."

"Did she come from Amherstburg with you?"

"No, she's still there—at least for a while." And I told him about the Major and how she wanted to go to London with him and that she didn't want me along, and that I thought I should go anyway even if she didn't like me very much. I told him about Drummer Jakes, and Mr. Elliott and his sons, and Joseph becoming Deep River. I told him about Lieutenant Mackenzie who liked men, and I told him how mean the Elliott men and Tecumseh were to me. "They made me feel that I was a bad person because I still love Papa even though he has crossed. They said he was a traitor and that I had a more important duty to my country than to my family. Do you think that's right, Mr. Wickam?"

"Guess you got to love family before country becomes important, but they didn't use the word *love*, did they? They were talking about duty, and I think you're a little young to worry about that word, because it's weighed down with a thousand questions."

"I love both my mother and Papa, and I pray Papa will be all right, 'cause I know Mother needs me more."

Mr. Wickam put down his carving, leaned his hands on his knees and, grunting, pushed himself erect. Even if I didn't hear his bones creak, it sure seemed like they did. "I'll make a bed for you in the loft."

On my third day in the loft, I was wakened by Prophet's whines, which alerted me to the smell of smoke. I jumped up, slid down the ladder and ran outside to see what was happening. There was smoke everywhere! Red and yellow flames were screeching toward the sky. Fields were burning, houses were in flames and even the docks were on fire. The town was silent. Nobody was fighting the fires.

The Wickams were on the front porch of the house wafting their hands at the smoke that was making their eyes tear.

I climbed the steps and stood beside them. "What's happening?"

"Hull has gone back to the fort in Detroit. The soldiers are pulling out and burning everything behind them." Mr. Wickam put his arm around Mrs. Wickam's shoulder. "They took the animals and the stores, and they burned the crops."

"People will starve," Mrs. Wickam whispered.

Mr. Wickam pulled her head to his chest. "We'll get through it somehow. We always do." He looked over his Clementine's head at me. "I'm afraid they've burned your father's store and your house and all the other houses in the centre of Sandwich."

I couldn't speak. The fires were my fault. It was 'cause of the lies in the letter I took to General Hull that he was retreating, that Sandwich was burning, that people would starve. It was so horrible I figured I'd best kill myself, 'cause there was nothing I could do to make it better. I didn't know where to go, what to do, or what to say, so I stood there with tears running down my cheeks and pulled out my mirror. I asked myself if when I was dead I'd still have memory.

Prophet nudged my leg and I knelt down and hugged him, collapsed my face into his soft neck and realized I couldn't kill myself and leave behind my mother and Drummer Jakes and Prophet, so I would have to put the guilt in my pocket and try to help as much as I could. Dog's necks are good for decision-making.

It was August 14, the fifth day after the fire. During that time, Mr. and Mrs. Wickam and I had not stopped trying to help in every way possible. The Wickams had made up beds in every room to take in people who had lost their homes, and I joined others scavenging through the burnt-out houses and barns to find anything that was useful: blankets, food, animals, anything at all that would help us get along.

The people with whom I dug through the smoke-smelly rubble often had to yell at me to get my attention, 'cause there was so much going on in my head that my ears were blocked from the inside. I was worried that Mother would leave without me, that maybe I should cross the river to see Papa and that the people of Sandwich wouldn't have enough to eat during the winter. I knew it was all my fault and I couldn't fix anything.

Working alone in the skeleton of a house, I picked up burned scraps I was unable to name, pulled at dirt-black strips of carpeting, kicked aside large slices of glass, found dead dreams in blackened books and came upon an old woman crying over the remains of her family Bible. I put my arm around her waist and coaxed her outside, where I put her into the arms of a woman who had undertaken the job of caring for such people, and I returned to my job not daring to think too much.

I kicked aside the rubble of the burned kitchen searching for a trapdoor that might be hiding preserves or any food that might stave off the hunger I'd caused. I hated myself. "Dear God," I prayed. "Please don't let the people of Sandwich starve, please keep Papa well and please, please don't let Mother go away with the Major until I get back to Amherstburg and can go with her."

CHAPTER 11
AUGUST 1812

▼

Matthew Elliott

"I've 50 militia signatures here sayin' the boy did not drum a retreat, and you know damned well none of your officers will lie for you at a hearing. Furthermore, Tecumseh says he'll appear in defence of the drummer." I slid the paper onto Procter's desk.

Procter stood behind his desk, leaned on his fists and in anger jutted his many chins out at me. "Tecumseh knows nothing of drummed signals, and no officer would dare speak against me."

"I guarantee Tecumseh can translate every drumroll the army uses. Just try him." I softened my voice. "Look, Procter, there was obviously a misunderstanding, but I would suggest with Brock about to arrive, a hearing on the subject would make us all look like damned idjits. Just release the drummer, and we'll forget the whole mess."

His face was so red I thought the man might burst. "I'll decide what's to be done about the drummer! Now get out of my sight, Elliott."

I had sent a boy on a man's mission, a dangerous one that could have terrible results. Although it would not soothe my guilt, I was damned if I was going to leave without fulfilling my promise to him. "'Twould be good if your decision came fast, Lieutenant Colonel." My voice was no longer conciliatory. "Brock is on his way, and you wouldn't want our argument to be publicized, now would ya?" I put my fists on his desk and leaned into him. "And I'll not get out of your sight until you agree to release the boy."

"All right, damn you, Elliott, but this is not the end of it. Quebec has probably received my letter by now. We'll see what they suggest I do about you."

Brock arrived last night and was hardly out of the boat before giving orders, askin' questions, checking maps, writing letters and sleepin' only a few hours before this morning's meeting with all his officers—and me, of course, bein' "the Agent in Charge of Indian Affairs."

Bein' smaller and darker and the only one sittin' around the big table who was not wearin' a scarlet jacket, I was a weed in a flower bed. If anyone had been interested in lookin' hard he'd have seen this weed was old and bent, but the flowers were too busy admirin' themselves to have considered the condition of an old seed.

"The false letter Elliott sent to Sandwich has had its effect," Brock told the officers. "I believe the time to attack is now, before Hull can solidify his position within the fort at Detroit."

Only a couple of us were still lookin' at the General. The rest of them were lookin' down at the table, doodlin' with their pencils or tracing imaginary lines on the wood—each one, I was sure, wondering what to say to convince Brock to slow down. 'Course it was the admirable Lieutenant Colonel Procter who voiced the officers' worries.

"General Brock, you do know, I'm sure, that we are greatly outnumbered by the Americans."

Brock nodded.

"It seems logical, therefore, that we should proceed with more caution." The man's voice simpered when talking to his general! It shivered my hackles, it did, but Brock listened with civility—which, I s'pose, was the reason he was a general.

Major Muir added with more respect, "We all think, sir, that we would be better served if we had more information to deal with, more supplies brought forward and more Indians to help us. Would it not be wise to be less precipitate?"

This was followed by grunts of agreement from the mouths of the other "cautious" officers.

With that, I stepped into the fray. "I kin guarantee 600 Indians."

"And half of them will be drunk," Procter snarled.

I slammed my hand down on the table, which jerked a lot of the slackers to attention. "Tecumseh's warriors have sworn an oath not to touch alcohol until the battle is won. I've told you that before."

Procter shook his head in disbelief.

"Do you believe him, Elliott?" Brock asked.

"He's a man of his word, General—and I'd like to add, sir, that it will be difficult for him and me to hold all the various tribes here if we do nothin'."

"I've heard both sides of the argument, have chewed on them while you talked and have decided that surprise outweighs caution. We will cross the Detroit as soon as possible, and I ask—no, I *command*—you to support my decision with all your capabilities. Tomorrow we march to Sandwich and from there we will cross the Detroit."

He turned to me and said, "You and Tecumseh meet me at your home in an hour."

I was in my office with Brock, who was pourin' over a map, when Tecumseh made his entrance. He and Brock sure were different. General Brock was a big man—tall with reddish hair—and his white pants were tucked into shining boots. Lookin' at him, you felt the power of the British Army. Tecumseh was short and wiry and equally dangerous, but his power sneaked through the woods on tiptoes. He was dressed to kill, Tecumseh was, with deerskin pants so damned soft there was not a wrinkle to be seen, tucked into moccasin boots decorated with porcupine quills. He had silver in his nose, wampum around his neck and a soft leather jacket with fringed sleeves, but it was not the getup that impressed, it was his ramrod straight posture, his determined expression and his intelligent eyes. I could tell that the General and the Indian liked what they saw in each other.

With me actin' as translator, we discussed the approaching attack, each man concentratin' on the other's words. On the map, Tecumseh pointed out the town of Detroit, the fort, the forest that could be used for camouflage and the methods he suggested for keeping the soldiers and warriors supplied.

Once the decisions were made, Tecumseh left and as Brock wound up his maps, I said, "'Tis a big gamble, sir, to attack when we're outnumbered and outgunned. I'm with you all the way, but then I'm a gamblin' man."

He started for the door. "You're right, Elliott, but the gamble is going to work. I feel it in my bones."

CHAPTER 12
AUGUST 1812

▼

Daniel

Sandwich was like a dog chasing its tail: while carts and horses struggled along the corduroy roads toward the area where soldiers were putting up tents, the regular citizens were pushed aside as they tried to retreat down the same destroyed road carrying all their remaining possessions. To the tune of bellowed orders, soldiers were putting up tents in an area of green grass sheltered from the river by trees and away from the fields of ash. Pounding hammers and screeching saws building a battery added to the confusion.

I was on the middle of a seesaw again: Papa and General Hull were on one end struggling against Drummer, the Elliotts, Tecumseh and Joseph, and I was praying a hopeless prayer that neither end would touch the ground.

General Brock, Tecumseh and the Elliotts were standing on the shore. I went down to try to speak to them, but a soldier wouldn't let me get near, so I started off for the Wickams'. "We want to see you later, Daniel," Mr. Elliott called after me. "Be at General Brock's tent at six this evening."

I had to go through a neat row of soldiers' tents to reach the General's headquarters. Some men were dragging a cannon to the almost completed battery, which was screened from the river by a stand of large oak trees. Soon they would have the monster gun pointed right at Fort Detroit and my father.

I approached the large tent of General Brock with my hand deep in my pocket, massaging my mirror. The reflection would not have been nervous.

A soldier standing guard outside the General's tent stopped me. "Are you Daniel Brownell?"

"Yes."

The soldier pulled aside the entrance flap and I went in. I might have felt proud about having been invited into the General's tent, but I'd learned that important people always had their reasons to include unimportant people, and it was never good for the lesser man.

The three Elliotts, Tecumseh, Lieutenant Colonel Procter, General Brock and a number of officers were standing around a table studying a map. Tecumseh was doing the talking and tracing lines on the map.

I coughed to get some attention. They all turned at once and stared down at me. I was a worm that wanted to squirm. "You told me to come, Mr. Elliott?"

"I did, Daniel. General Brock would like to ask you some questions."

The General looked down at me. He didn't like kids, I could tell. "I understand you delivered a letter to General Hull."

"Yes, sir." I figured I'd better not get into the fact that I was forced to do it.

"You met General Hull?"

"Yes, sir."

"Tell me about it."

"What do you want to know?"

"Everything you can think of, young man."

"Well, he is old, and he's fat, and I think he is a good man."

"What do you mean?"

"He asked me a lot about the Indians. I think they scared him, and he was worried about the safety of the people in the fort."

"Did he say that?"

"I don't remember, but that is what I felt."

"Can you think of anything else?"

"Well—" I was not sure I should say what I was thinking.

"Well, what? Out with it, boy, I don't have much time."

"I think the other officers don't like him very much."

"Explain what you mean!"

"Can't you feel it when someone is mad at you? I can. It's like there is ice in the air, and it makes everyone's expressions stiff."

The men all looked at each other as though I'd said something interesting.

Brock nodded his head. "Good, thank you, young man. You can go now." The men all turned back to their maps.

I crossed the tent slowly and listened to their conversation.

"My men have scoured the countryside," Brock said, putting his hands on the base of his back and stretching to his full height, "and have roused every available man to form the militia. We've given them cast-off crimson tunics to make Hull think our force of regulars is twice the size." He looked at Mr. Elliott. "You can still promise me 600 Indians?"

"Perhaps a few more than that," Mr. Elliott said, and he looked at Tecumseh with a question on his face.

Tecumseh grunted agreement. He was a man of few words, that was for sure.

"I want you to cross over tomorrow and take positions in the flank and the rear."

Tecumseh grunted again.

When I got to the opening, Mr. Elliott called to my back, "The Drummer is in his tent, Daniel."

I turned and nodded. He didn't deserve a smile.

Outside, I breathed normal air and figured I was lucky to have escaped without having been forced into anything else. I asked the soldier on guard where the drummers would be billeted, and he pointed me to the correct tent.

Drummer Jakes was sitting on his bed in his socks and cleaning his boots. When he saw me, he smiled. "Hello, friend."

I sat down beside him on his camp bed and watched as he continued to work on his boots. "What happened after they dragged you off?"

"They threw me in a cell all by myself, which I figger was a good thing. There were some pretty rough men starin' out from the group cell."

"How long were you there? Were they mean to you?"

"Jist one night, and they brung me a real good supper. Somehow they knew I was innocent. Can't say I slept much, though, 'cause I was damned scared." He put one boot down and picked up the other. "How'd it go with the letter delivery? Mr. Elliott told me when he got me out of jail. Said you paid for my release by deliverin' that letter." He looked down at the ground. "I've never had a real friend before, so I'm not sure how ta say thanks."

"Doesn't matter." It made me feel warm to be called a real friend.

"Anyway, how did it go?"

"'Twas okay." I sat in silence for a minute. "General Hull's an old man. I thought he was nice."

Drummer picked up the other boot and started shining it. "I guess we're goin' to attack that nice old man."

"Tomorrow, I think."

"How d'ya know?"

"I had to report to General Brock about delivering the letter, and I heard him say so."

"Music left my feet after the last battle, I tell ya!"

"You afraid?"

"'Course!"

"Me too." I took out my mirror and asked myself: *When tomorrow is over, will it become another bad memory?*

I left Drummer's tent when it was beginning to get dark. There was one thing I wanted to do before the morning attack, and it took me to the Indian camp. It was a frightening sight. I knew there were 600 of them because I heard Mr. Elliott say so, but it seemed like there were thousands. They had many fires burning, were dressed only in breechcloths and were leaping and screaming in the firelight. All of them were painted one colour or another and as the vermillion and blue and black and white bodies leapt and screamed around the flames, they seemed like devils in hell! How was I going to find Joseph, now Deep River, in that madness?

I stood at a distance and watched, and then Joseph saw me and came from out of the crowd. His face was half black and half red; I'd not have recognized him except for the downturned mouth and distinct walk. It was funny how walks had such definite personalities. He crouched down to my level and waited for me to speak.

"Mr. Elliott and Tecumseh and General Brock promised that if they win tomorrow, Papa would not be treated as a traitor!"

He waited.

"But they don't know what he looks like! Only you know that! I want you to make sure he's recognized." I looked straight into his eyes. "If you do that for me, I will make sure Papa saves you if the Americans win!"

He didn't smile. "You man now? Make man treaties?"

"Will you do it?"

He stood up straight, took my arm in an Indian handshake and nodded his head.

"Thanks." I turned to go and then turned back to him and gave him a half smile and a "Thanks, Joseph" and left quickly. I could feel his eyes on my back but didn't turn.

Everyone knew that the letter Brock sent across the river to General Hull demanding his surrender would be refused, but they considered it a good ruse in any case because in the letter Brock said he wouldn't be able to control the Indians if fighting broke out, which was meant to frighten General Hull.

The cannonade started the minute the men who delivered the letter returned with the message that Hull refused to surrender. Cannonballs screamed across the mile-wide river—tearing down trees, ripping into walls and destroying rooftops. The Americans threw back as much as they received and the fire across the water went on into the night.

It was dark. I watched the Elliotts, the Prophet, Tecumseh and all the Indians slip into canoes and paddle downriver, out of range of any possible shelling, before starting across, and I found a place on the bank downriver where I sat clutching my knees and shivering with every explosion. An explosion on either side could kill a person I loved.

My hound lay beside me, shivering. We stayed on the bank all night, which was pretty stupid, because being miserable on the damp earth and being eaten by bugs was not going to help anyone or anything, but I couldn't leave and Prophet, my dog, wouldn't.

It was dawn, the morning of August 16, and as the troops climbed into boats to cross, the rising sun threw the jiggled reflections of their crimson jackets on the clear water. I saw Drummer climb into a boat, waved to him and sent thumbs up . . . and then I waited and waited and waited.

Mr. Wickam found me on the bank staring across the river. He had brought some bread for me. "Not much sense in staying here. Why don't you come back to the house, Daniel?"

"Can't," I mumbled. "Waiting's the only job I have."

"You can wait at the house."

I couldn't turn my head away from the river. "It's not the same."

He didn't answer that. I guessed he understood. For a while, he stared out at the river and the shelling, and then he brushed my head with his hand and left.

As I watched the river, thoughts buzzed inside my head, and they were as desperate as a trapped fly. *If Papa is killed, I'll go to England with Mother, even if she doesn't want me—maybe she's gone already—how horrible of me to even think that Papa might be dead—Joseph had better save him from being grouped with the traitors—if Papa is a prisoner, what will they do to him?—if Joseph is hurt, the Shawnee will take him away and I'll never see him again— Drummer had better be okay—what if he gets shot or loses an eye or is killed and scalped?—what if the Americans win?—what if the British win? Stupid war!*

Suddenly the bombardment stopped. I stood up, wondering what was happening. Other people walked down to the shore and stared in curiosity. And then we saw it: a white flag had been raised at Fort Detroit! Could the Americans have surrendered? No one cheered, as it was too unbelievable.

Hours later, a soldier returned and announced that the Americans had really surrendered. He said that all the documents were to be signed as soon as they solved the negotiations about the treatment of traitors. Hull was trying to get them leniency, but Brock was drawing the line.

His announcement burdened my waiting with a whole load of fear. The body of the fear was Papa's fate, and the tentacles were more self-centred. What was I going to do?

I knew nothing more would happen that night and that I should go to the Wickams to sleep, but I stayed where I was, hugged my dog and stared at the river, waiting for the rest of my life to paddle across to me. Mr. Wickam came with blankets and food and sat down with me. Without talking, he put his arm around me and pulled my head to his shoulder.

We sat and stared out at the river, and my eyes began to droop.

I wakened to the noise of troops disembarking from boats and watched them empty other vessels of cannons, barrels of gunpowder and armloads of muskets. Some even had cattle and pack animals and provisions from stores. Now the people on the other side of the river would go hungry, and I bet it was not the soldiers but innocent citizens of the town of Detroit who would suffer just like the innocent citizens of Sandwich who had been clobbered by the fires of war. War was an animal that sniffed out the innocent. I knew that already.

Troops began to come back across the Detroit, some escorting prisoners who were forced out of the boats at gunpoint and taken away. I waited and watched. No Papa, but then I saw Drummer and ran down to the shore to meet him. "You okay?"

Smiling, Drummer nodded.

I waited impatiently as the arriving soldiers formed up and were dismissed, and then I joined Drummer. "Tell me everything that happened."

"We pulled into shore out of sight of the fort, and Tecumseh was there waiting for General Brock. He was sitting on a white horse and had another horse for the General."

"I wonder where he got them."

"Flummoxed if I know!"

We walked to his tent, and Drummer threw himself down on the bed. I perched on the bed opposite. "General Brock told Tecumseh that he would wait until dark to march," Drummer continued. "But then a scout arrived and said that reinforcements were on their way to help Hull, so Brock drew up the troops and made the spaces between the columns larger so that it looked like we were more than we really were."

"That was smart."

"Yup, the General's a real smart man, I guess. Anyway, we started marching along the road that runs beside the river while the guns from the battery in Sandwich and from the two British ships on the river fired over our heads. There was so much noise my drum couldn't have been heard!"

"Weren't they shooting at you from the fort?"

"That's the strange thing. They weren't. When we got in close, Brock had the troops turn left into a ravine where we were protected; then, you know what happened?"

"What?"

"Tecumseh marched his Indians across a meadow that was just out of range of the American guns and then went into the forest, circled around and repeated the march through the meadow again so that Hull would think there were many more Indians than there really were. He did it three times!"

"Poor General Hull!"

"Why do you say that?"

"I think he's more scared of the Indians than he is of the soldiers."

"Guess you're right, 'cause he surrendered without a fight."

"Were any Americans hurt or killed?"

"Some by the bombardment, but not many."

"I sure hope Papa wasn't one of them." I had another thought. "Do you know what they're doing with the prisoners?"

"I know they're sending General Hull and his officers to Quebec, but I don't know about the rest of them. I kinda think they let many of them go, but they aren't allowed to fight anymore." He looked straight into my eyes. "They're going to hang the traitors, Daniel."

"Papa isn't a traitor! He's an American. Anyway, I made a deal with General Brock."

"I hope he remembers."

I returned to my blanket on the bank to wait and see if anything more would happen that night. If there was no news of Papa by morning, I would go to Mr. Elliott and find out what happened to him. Maybe Joseph saved him and he escaped.

Boats lit with flames went back and forth across the water, but they were scattered and the people who landed on our side could not answer any questions or would not. I grew heavy-eyed, and I guess I fell asleep, 'cause next thing I knew someone was shaking me. It was Joseph.

"Is it Papa?"

"Ungh."

"Is he all right?"

"No—he bad." He took my hand, pulling me out of the blankets and toward the canoe. He and another Indian paddled me to Bois Blanc. I sat in the canoe and shivered. "How bad is he?"

"Bad."

On Bois Blanc, Joseph pulled the canoe up on the shore, took my hand and pulled me along a path through the woods past a clearing where night had made huge trees into black monsters through which streaked jittering shadows of wild dancers celebrating victory by the flames of huge fires. It seemed forever that I was stumbling along with Joseph. Finally we arrived at an open field well away from the noise where there were three Indian huts, in front of which there burned a huge fire tended by a woman.

Joseph pulled aside the flap of hide covering the door of the first hut and gently pushed me in. Papa was lying on a bed of evergreens covered with a deerskin. An old Indian woman was wiping his brow and his eyes and his cheeks with a damp cloth. His breathing squealed.

I knelt down beside him and took his hand. "Papa?" I couldn't keep the tinge of hysteria from my voice. "Papa, it's me, Daniel."

His eyelids seemed locked closed, but there was movement behind them and then they opened—kind of. He tried to talk, but I could see it really hurt him. He whispered, "Son."

"Don't die, Papa!" I put my hand over my mouth and squeezed my nose; it stopped tears.

"Your mother?"

"She's in Amherstburg—I think."

He opened his eyes wider when he heard my quavering *I think*. "Come closer." His breathing was tortured.

I leaned into him.

"There's a woman who lives in York. Her name is Belle Fontaine." He stopped. I thought he was not going to go on, but then he took another screeching breath. "She's my sister. Remember the name. She'll take care of you if you need her."

I nodded my head. I didn't know Papa even had a sister, but I couldn't waste his breath demanding an explanation.

"Say the name!" he whispered.

"Belle Fontaine in York," I answered.

His eyes rolled up in his head and his mouth fell open.

"Papa, don't go!" I shook him. "I love you, Papa!" It was too late; he didn't hear me. I shook his shoulders. "Papa, don't go! Please don't go!" I needed him. He couldn't leave me now. I knew he was dead, but I couldn't stop shaking him and crying.

Joseph pulled me away and crushed my face into his chest. "He free now—no cry—you cry tears for you—not him."

I knew Joseph was right, but it didn't help.

I looked up at Joseph through my tears. "What now?"

"We bury."

I looked back at Papa. His cheeks had sagged, the bones on his face stuck out and his lips had lost their elasticity and fallen open, exposing his teeth. His eyes were still open. I bent over him and shut each lid; it was like I was turning off life. "Someone has to tell Mother."

Joseph and the Indian women wrapped Papa in birchbark. "Wartime. No skins to wrap bodies. Tomorrow we bury."

He left me in the teepee, and I lay down and fell into an exhausted sleep with my arms on top of my father's bound body.

In the morning, Joseph and two Indians dug the grave. I sat with my arms around my legs and rocked and watched.

Tecumseh came and shovelled two loads of dirt. "Your family should dig the grave of your father. Since you have no one, we will be family, young one." After two shovelfuls he said he had to leave. I stood up to thank him. He nodded once and left.

At noon, I was still sitting and rocking by the grave when Alexander Elliott arrived. He was alone. I turned my cheek onto my arm, sad before I even asked, "Where's my mother?"

"I'm sorry, Daniel, she's gone."

"Did she know Papa died?"

"I really don't know."

I supposed I was expecting it, but that didn't make things better. What was I to do about her? About me?

He sat down on the grass beside me, so close that our shoulders were touching. We both stared at the grave. "My father had to meet with Brock and Tecumseh, but I'll stay with you to bury your papa."

When the grave was dug and lined with wood, some Indian musicians surrounded the hole and sang sad music to the rhythm of their skin drums and gourd rattles. Papa, wrapped in bark, was lowered into the hole. Poles were laid on top of the grave and bark was placed over the poles, and then Joseph and his friends covered the bark with the earth they had taken from the grave. I tried to remember a Christian prayer, but my mind wouldn't wrap around one. I thanked God that Papa was with him and was free of worries about Mother, about me, about roots and war and prejudice and money and patriotism and all the other incomprehensible things of life. "Thank you, God," I said and looked up at the sky.

I don't know how long I stood there shivering before Alexander lifted me up and carried me to a canoe. He wrapped a blanket around me and pushed off. "We'll go home and put you to bed."

I looked down into the shadows of the deep river and saw death and couldn't look away.

He carried me in through the kitchen, up the back stairs to the second floor and into the room Mother used. "Now let's get those clothes off and get you into bed." He pulled up my shirt and I undid my shoes, pulled off my socks and pants and climbed into the bed, but I was sure I wouldn't be able to sleep because I could hear glasses clinking and men laughing and yelling.

"What's happening downstairs?"

"It's a victory dinner. They're all there: my father and brother, Tecumseh, Brock, Procter and the other officers."

"I'm sorry I kept you away, Mr. Alexander."

"I wanted to be with you to send your father on his way, Daniel, so don't be sorry."

"Where do you think he went?"

"He went to the place his soul chose. Perhaps it was the Christian heaven."

"Maybe it was the blue sky in a place higher than the clouds."

"That's certainly possible."

"Or his soul could have chosen to dance in a sunbeam or swim into the indigo in a rainbow or just rock inside a dangling dewdrop."

"Wherever it is, Daniel, he'll be at peace." He tousled my hair and tucked the blankets around me. "Now you go to sleep."

I didn't like being in the bed Mother used because I knew the Major shared it with her. I turned the pillow upside down thinking maybe their heads didn't touch the bottom side; it didn't help. Sleep was probably not going to come to me no matter where I was, but it surely wasn't going to arrive in that bed, so I decided to talk to Papa before his soul travelled too far away.

"Papa, there's no one left to love me. Mother can only love when she stops twirling, and that isn't happening very often these days." I tossed in the bed. Mother was not supposed to interfere when I had so much to say to Papa. I shook my head hard to try to control the words that played around in my skull. It didn't work, so I just looked at the ceiling and spoke to Papa about the whole situation. "When she feels better, I know she'll be sorry she left me behind, but by then it'll be hard for her to get back here to collect me, what with the war and all, so I guess I'd better go after her. You'd agree with that, wouldn't you, Papa? Who else understands her extremes? How will I find out where she is? If I can figure that out, I'll figure out how to find her. I'm sure Mr. Elliott will help me. Yes, Papa, I remember your sister—Belle Fontaine in York—but first I have to find Mother."

The sun woke me. I guess I fell asleep in spite of myself. I put on my shirt and pulled on my socks and britches, which were filthy. I wondered if

Mother left my clothes behind. She probably did; it would lighten her load. The morning didn't feel quite so sad because I had a mission, which I was undertaking for Papa as well as myself. I dumped water from the pitcher into the washbowl, washed the sand out of my eyes and went downstairs to find Mr. Elliott.

CHAPTER 13
AUGUST 1812

▼

Matthew Elliott

"I sent a man to the River Raisin with an order for you and Tecumseh to return to Detroit and you refused. You deserve to be court-martialled!" Procter screamed.

"You'll not court-martial me, Procter! You need the Indians too much, and they sure as hell won't do anything for you if I'm not around!" We were in his office in the barracks, and the son-of-a-bitch had left me standing while he had his fat ass plunked in a chair.

"It's because of those damned Indians I needed you. They were stealing horses and raiding houses, and it was your job to control them."

"'Course they were raiding houses and stealing horses. They were the winners, weren't they? That's what winners do, and don't tell me soldiers weren't doin' the same thing."

"Not under my watch, they weren't."

"Then you weren't watchin' too well."

"It doesn't matter what my men did, they aren't dangerous savages."

"In battle, we're all savages who cut and maim and burn and kill, and if you think otherwise you're deceiving yourself!" God, how I despised this idjit!

"White men don't rape and scalp!"

"The Indians did no such thing! Tecumseh ordered them not to touch alcohol nor to attack a woman or slice a head, and they damned well didn't!"

Procter banged his fist on the desk and stood up. "No thanks to you!"

"Nor to you!"

"You're too old for the position of Indian Agent. When I hear from Quebec, it will give me the greatest of pleasures to see the last of you!"

"Go ahead! Try to solve your goddamned problem with a pen and see how far it gets you." As I stomped out, I swung the door too hard and it banged against the inner wall, causing some things to clatter to the floor. I didn't look back.

I was so angry at that pissin' Procter that when I got to my office and told Alexander and Boy of our conversation, I couldn't hold myself back and kicked the desk before throwing myself in the chair. "Jaysus, Mary and Joseph! What was Brock thinking when he put that man in charge?"

The boys knew enough to keep quiet and let me seethe.

Finally, Boy picked up the chair and put it back on its feet. "You have to show him your strength with actions, not words, Da."

"And how would you suggest I do that, my brilliant son?"

He stared at me and, without any expression on his face, said, "Hold Tecumseh and the Indians back. Procter will soon know he can't do without them."

I thought about the consequences. "Not a bad idea. Harrison is gathering troops to the south, so 'twould be dangerous to do it for too long, but a short withdrawal might prick his confidence." I grabbed my coat. "I'll go across the river and find Tecumseh and see what he has to say."

Alexander grabbed my arm. "Let Boy go. It was his idea."

I looked down at my favoured son with a frown. "You don't think I'm up to it?"

"It's not that, Da. I just think Boy should get out of the house for a while." He looked over at his brother. "He's been around your children so much they are going to think he's the father."

Boy glared at Alexander, and I saw a tension between my two sons that I'd not noticed before. Maybe Alexander was right. I should be around the house a little more. "You go then, Boy. Explain to Tecumseh it would be for just long enough for Procter to recognize the value of having the Indians at their back."

"Mr. Elliott?" Young Daniel was standing at the door. I didn't know how long he'd been there. "Do you know where Mother went?"

The question threw a net over my anger. I stared at the boy, tryin' to absorb what he had just said and decide what to answer—not an easy thing when I was busy percolating on my own anger. "She went off with the Major. I'm sorry, Daniel."

"Do you know where they went?"

"First ta York. The Major's after gettin' his pension straightened out and then ta Europe." I walked over to him. "Ya can stay with us, Daniel. Sarah and me'd be happy ta have a strappin' young sod like you around the house."

"Thank you, sir. Can I think about it?"

"'Course ya can!" I leaned over to put my arm around his shoulder, and a hot poker of pain streaked down my back and into my leg. I was not sure I could straighten up.

"Mm-mm-mm, that's good, my lass, but could ya go a little lower! Now a little to the right—that's it! The only good thing about this damned lumbago is yer massages." The pain had driven me to my bed, where I'd remained for the past three weeks.

"You're an old fool, Matthew. If you continue riding around the countryside corralling Indians, fighting battles and camping in the wilderness at your age, you'll soon be bedridden permanently"

"'Tis probably true! Could ya rub a little lower, my Sarah?"

"Get away with you! You're a sick man, Matthew Elliott!" Bein' on my stomach, I couldn't see her, but there didn't seem ta be much of a smile in her words. "Now tell me why the military gets so angry with you and the Indian department."

"They ask the impossible. Not only do they expect me to recruit the Indians, they expect the Indians to act accordin' to the military standard of discipline, which just ain't the way the Indians make war." I rolled over on my back, making peter more available for massage, but he was ignored.

"But they can't blame you!"

"Ah, but they do! I'm the head of the Indian department, so it's all my fault. Doesn't matter that the tribes are most unruly when they receive liquor from the soldiers." I leaned over on my elbow and shoved my feet over the edge of the bed. "Now help me up, my Sarah, I'm expecting Major Muir to come by."

Sarah pushed me back in the bed. "You'll not get up yet, Matthew Elliott, and you needn't worry about Major Muir. I told him your lumbago was bad and sent him on his way."

"Sarah!"

She ignored me and stomped out the door.

Sarah's Diary

How could I ever have considered leaving? Matthew needs me now more than ever. He's almost crippled with lumbago, and without my restrictions and ministrations he would destroy himself.

For better or worse, I, Mrs. Matthew Elliott, am his wife until death do us part, and I will remain with him. I will give him my ear into which he can vent his emotions, vomit his opinions and put his mind back into working order, but God forgive me, I cannot sleep with him, even though I know it would be a gift of kindness.

When we're together, Boy and I act without thought. We can't leave each other alone: we're savages who mount and scratch and explode together in divine pain. I can't resist his golden body—nor, it seems, can he resist me. But when it's over, guilt tears at us with an opposite, excruciating pain, and we lie to ourselves that it will never happen again.

Alexander is suspicious. I've warned Boy to be careful. He says not to worry, that he will take care of it, which worries me even more. I'm helplessly drawn to the unstable streak that dwells within this man, but that very same ferocity that makes our loving so incomparable is very, very, dangerous.

CHAPTER 14
AUGUST 1812

▼

Daniel

"I'm sorry about your Pa. I wanted to go over but they wouldn't let me off."

Drummer Jakes and I were leaning against the cannon where we first met. "It's all right. Tecumseh came, and Mr. Elliott and Alexander Elliott and Joseph were there too."

"Lieutenant Mackenzie wanted to go too, but he couldn't get off either."

"You've talked to him?"

"Ya, he ain't so bad. Just a little light on his feet is all. He found me 'cause he wanted to know about you and what was happening with your pa and all."

"I appreciate that."

"Yup. I think it's nice for him that we like him, even if he is the way he is."

"Doesn't make any difference to us, really."

"Did you know when we ship out for Niagara tomorrow, he'll be leaving for York in the east?"

"You're leaving?"

"Yup, that's why we ain't had no time off. Brock wants us on boats tomorrow so we can get to Niagara without any holdups."

"I'm going to leave soon too. I just have to figure out how."

"Where're you goin'?"

"I'm going east too. I want to find Mother before she does something foolish."

"What might she do?"

"Almost anything. She has real highs and lows, and when she peaks or bottoms it's a bad thing to see." I kicked the ground and turned to look down the river. Drummer didn't ask any more questions. He seemed to know it was a subject that became even more soiled by curiosity. I guessed one of the reasons I liked Drummer is that he understood this. "When I go east, I'll stop in Niagara and try to find you."

"That'll be good."

"But if I don't get there, and you end up in York, you can find me through Belle Fontaine, who has a house there."

"Who's she?"

"My father's sister."

"Belle Fontaine, in York. I'll remember." He reached down and patted Bruno. It made me sad that I'd left Prophet in Sandwich with Mr. Wickam.

"What're you going to do with the dog?"

"Lieutenant Mackenzie is going to take him when he gets out. I was hopin' you could keep him until then. It'll only be a few days."

"'Course I could."

"I gotta go back now."

We both stared at the ground, not knowing what to say.

"Well, bye for now," I said.

"I'll see you in Niagara!" he answered and walked off toward the parade ground. Then he stopped and yelled over his shoulder, "You should see if you could go east with Lieutenant Mackenzie!"

Since I was at the fort, I decided I'd visit Lieutenant Mackenzie right away. I knocked on the door of the officers' barracks, and when a man opened it, I could see Lieutenant Mackenzie leaning on his hands over the desk in the main room talking to another officer. He looked over his shoulder to see what the interruption was and smiled. "Hello, Daniel. I'm glad you've come. I want to talk to you. Go on in to my room, and I'll join you when I finish here. No, no, not with the dog. Leave him outside."

His room was still overstuffed, and there was nowhere to sit but on the bed. Looking at all his possessions, I figured it would take a lot of space in a boat just for his trunks and all the extra paraphernalia. 'Course, he probably wouldn't need the snowshoes or skis anymore. Maybe he'd give them to me. I would just ask him if there was snow where he was going and see what he said.

He opened the door, came in, sat down beside me on the bed and put his arm around me.

"I'm sorry about your father, Daniel."

Sympathy sure pumped up the tears. "Thanks." I was not sure I could say much more on the subject.

"I wanted to go over to Bois Blanc to help you bury him, but no one was allowed off base."

"I know, Drummer told me."

"Was it terrible? His death, and the burial?"

"I got to talk to him before he died." I looked away. "Only thing was, he was so busy giving me instructions I had no time to tell him I loved him, and that's keeping me awake at night, that's for sure." Lieutenant Mackenzie gave me his handkerchief. "But he was buried with respect, which doesn't always happen these days." I was thinking of bodies still rotting on the battlefields.

"What were the instructions your father gave you?"

"He told me he had a sister in York and to go to her if I needed to." I crumpled his handkerchief in my fist. "My job now is to find my mother. She went off with the Major. They're supposed to go to England, but I suspect Mother won't make it."

"Why do you think that?"

"The Major will see under her skin before they get too far. And one of two things will happen. He'll leave her behind, or she'll leave him."

"You seem sure of that."

"I guess I am. My mother's either moving faster than a ferret or she's so miserable she has to stay in a dark room for weeks on end. When the Major sees this, he'll run from her fast as a skunk from a bear."

"That's sad. She's such a beautiful woman."

"Yup. I guess God wouldn't let her have everything." We sat quietly for a while. I guess he didn't know what more to say. "Drummer says you're leaving soon."

"I am."

"Where are you going?"

"I'm going east. I haven't yet decided whether to take half-pay and land here in Canada or return to England. It will depend on what I find in the east."

"How do you go?"

"By boat, of course."

"Can I go with you? I need to get to York. Maybe Mother is there, and if she isn't, I can stay with Papa's sister."

"Of course you can go with me, but I'm not free until the end of September."

"That's not far off."

Bruno lay quietly at my feet as I paddled back to Mr. Elliott's house. My dips and strokes of the paddle created a satisfactory rhythm, and I smiled to myself. Everything was falling into place. I had a friend who would take me east, and I was sure I would find Mother, I felt it in my bones.

PART 2

CHAPTER 15
OCTOBER 1812

▼

Daniel

We boarded the ship at Fort Malden. It would take us to Fort Erie and from there Lieutenant Mackenzie said we would go by coach to Niagara.

Mr. Elliott and Mr. Alexander Elliott came down to say goodbye. Mr. Elliott shook my hand. "Come back when you can, young Daniel. As long as our house is standing, there will always be a bed awaiting you."

I didn't much like the "as long as" included in his words.

Mr. Alexander gave me a box that held paper, pen and inkwell. "Write when you can, Daniel. I will worry about you until I know what is happening."

"I will, sir. If you don't receive my letters, you will have to blame the war, not me."

He gave me a hug and then pushed me toward the gangplank. When the anchor was lifted and the ship pulled away from the dock, my stomach fell. I was floating away from friendship and affection into the east where I knew no one. Of course, there was no question I had to do it. Who else would look out for Mother?

When we passed Bois Blanc, Joseph was standing on the shore waving. That was the saddest moment of all. I figured Deep River, the warrior, was saying goodbye to the last person who knew the gentle, grumpy Joseph, and it was as bad for him as it was for me. I loved Joseph, and he was gone too.

We were delayed in Niagara because Lieutenant Mackenzie was forced to take to his bed with a bad case of gout. I tried to continue on by myself, but all the transportation was reserved for the military and other important people, and a 12-year-old kid didn't fall into any of those slots. It was the first time I'd said to myself that I was 12 years old. Nobody else knew about it.

The falls in Niagara showed God more than the inside of any church I'd ever visited, not that I'd visited very many. The power of the water bellowing over the cliff could crush any human who got in the way, and yet there was beauty in the rainbows it collected in the steam created by the crashing water. I spent hours staring at the spectacle and heard God screaming instructions: "Love me!" and "Thou shalt not kill!" and "Fear me!" and "An eye for an eye!" and on and on until I was so confused I had to leave the place. Once I threw a stick into the falls, and it tumbled this way and that, up and down, in and out, over and under as the awesome falls had its pleasure with it, but the stick finally reached the river in one piece and floated happily on its way, so maybe there's hope for me too.

When you're scared, yesterday and tomorrow disappear, making *right now* so huge it eats you up. From the upstairs window, I saw tongues of flame shooting across the Niagara River. Cannons screeched and boomed from both banks, and the explosions mixed with thunder, rain and streaks of lightning. "They're going to come and get you soon, sir. They're putting bedding in the wagon now and someone will help you down."

Lieutenant Mackenzie was wrapped in a blanket with his left foot bound and elevated on a stool. His fair hair was stringy and fell over his eyes, and his illness sweated a stink that was like unwashed clothes, forcing me to breathe through my mouth so I didn't gag. He couldn't seem to lift his head from the back of the chair, and he looked really pale.

"The war seems to be chasing us, Daniel."

"Yes, sir, we're going to evacuate the house and move to MacNeil's farm. I'll see you there. I'm to take one of the horses."

"Go carefully, young Daniel, I don't want to lose you."

"I will." I ran down the stairs and into the kitchen where servants, their hair and clothes drenched from the downfall, were running in and out of the house with supplies that they were throwing into wagons. They were so nervous they were adding a time-wasting flurry of steps and gestures to the packing and carrying.

The war noise had blocked my ears, imprisoning the screams of the cannons inside my head where they were twirling and clashing with the flashes of fire and the stink of smoke. How could I escape this disaster? Every minute here wasted the time I had to find Mother before she disappeared entirely.

Mrs. Hamilton, the lady of the house, was at the door with a list in her trembling hands and anxiety in her eyes as she peered over half-glasses, trying to keep track of the confusion. She saw me standing in the door. "Daniel, take one of the horses and go on to the MacNeil farm. We'll follow as soon as we get Lieutenant Mackenzie down."

The front window crashed to bits. Something came hurling through the room. We were statues frozen in place. A servant shrieked, "It's a cannonball!" The back wall shattered and the world exploded, throwing us to the floor. The cannonball had gone right through the room and landed in the garden.

Mrs. Hamilton was the first to come to her senses. "Go, Daniel."

I grabbed my slicker and ran through the storm to the stables, where a stable hand had a horse saddled and waiting for me. He helped me up and slapped the rear of the horse, making my head jerk as the horse took off.

Less than 10 minutes had passed, but the pelting rain blinded and almost choked me, and I wasn't sure where I was, and I couldn't turn around, and the horse was slipping, and I was sliding off the saddle into the mud, and the horse was running away, and I stood up and screamed at it but it did no good, and I didn't know whether I was yelling or crying, and I didn't know what to do, and I didn't know whether the water on my face was rain or tears. There was nowhere to go, and the guns were blasting below, and I'd failed in my job, and my face was covered in mud and snot.

The noise below the cliffs got louder. I rubbed my messed-up face with my sleeve, wrapped my rain slicker around me and with the help of an overhanging branch pulled myself all the way up a huge boulder where I could peek over the edge of the cliff while I lay flat with the branches above hiding me.

Scores of large boats carrying hundreds of American soldiers appeared and disappeared through clouds of smoke billowing from the fire-spitting cannons on both sides of the river. Some boats were being dragged downriver by the current; some had been hit, dumping bodies into the cold water, but I could see hundreds of soldiers landing just south of the cliffs.

Below me, an infantry company was spread out on the crest of the hill above the redan, which had a cannon on the point of its V and was returning so much fire it made the cliff look like it was spewing flames. On the shore below the cliff, hundreds of British redcoats shot from long straight lines, one line behind the next, forever changing places so that the firing never stopped. I could recognize Drummer Jakes by his height, the angle he tilted his body and his knee-raising step. *Please God, don't let anything happen to him.*

I was so far above the fighting that I couldn't see blood. When a man in one of the boats fell into the water or a soldier on this side left a hole in the line, it was like I was looking at a picture book. It didn't have the stink of Brownstown. I was floating above the battle and looking down on it and asking *Why? Why? Why?* I ducked under my slicker to muffle a cough and stayed there with my hands over my ears and my eyes squeezed tight shut, and I rocked back and forth, not wanting to see any more of the horrible game that grown men were playing.

There was a noise in the bushes on the left that made me pull my slicker over my body and lie as still as possible.

"It's Brock," I heard a soldier from below whisper.

I peeked out of my carapace and saw below me the white plume on an officer's hat. Brock and his officers were climbing the hill, leading their horses so they wouldn't slip like mine had. They were muddied, but they made it to the redan and the officers rushed back and forth behind the line of soldiers using telescopes to look down at the battle from different angles.

"We need reinforcements down below," Brock said to the sergeant. "Move these men down."

I thought I heard shuffling in the woods to my right, but the noise of the guns below was so loud I wasn't sure. I crept up the boulder and peered over. Americans! They'd climbed the cliff and were going after the cannons from the rear. I had to warn the soldiers, but if I stood up and yelled the Americans would hear me. If I didn't, they'd capture the cannons. Maybe I could yell and then run. I stood up and screamed, "Watch behind you! Americans!" Nobody heard, not Americans, not British. I took my slicker and waved it, but in the smoke and the dust nobody could see.

The Americans were on the cannons. They attacked with muskets and knives, and the British cannoneers had no protection since General Brock had sent the infantry away, and they didn't even have time to reach for their guns to use the bayonets. A head exploded; a man with a dead leg dragged himself to the edge and tumbled down the cliff; bleeding bodies fell over the cannons, and the Americans pushed them off the cliff. There was stink and confusion and screams of pain, and it was not a picture book anymore.

Brock was on the redan below. His men were spiking the big 18-pounder. I screamed again, "Hurry! The Americans are turning the cannons on you!" This time they heard. Brock saw I was right, and he and his men slid over the cliff before the first shot was fired.

The Americans fired on the British below, holding them down so their boats would be able to land without interference. I forgot myself and stood staring down at the debacle, convinced that it was the beginning of our defeat. Too late I saw a soldier pointing his gun at me.

I woke up with my face pasted to the rock. My head screamed with pain, but I felt only a lump, no blood. I must have dropped down in time and knocked myself out.

On my stomach, I pulled myself up the rock to try to see what was happening below. Queenston was on fire. The Americans were still bombarding the soldiers beneath them, but to my left the British were storming the cliff trying to rescue their cannons. Brock was out in front and with his tall hat and its big white plume he was a perfect target. I saw him fall and soldiers carry him down. Now surely the Americans would win and maybe I didn't care, maybe I just wanted it all to stop.

It was not over! The British were trying again, and this time they made it to the top, but the cannons and the muskets were mowing them down. Bodies fell on bodies, dead ones could be smothering live ones, and soldiers were retreating over the injured, often tripping and pushing their hands into the prone bodies without even looking to see if they were alive. The Americans chased after them. Where was Drummer?

I wanted to get out of there, but the woods behind me exploded in bloodcurdling screams. Screeching Mohawk Indians crashed through the trees, waving tomahawks above their painted bodies as they tore past me, shooting and slashing and screaming and scalping. I peed my pants again.

The Indians couldn't fight cannons, so they ran back into the woods. Maybe there was time for me to get out of there.

But no! The British were arriving from both the left and the right. They must have circled up behind the cliffs, and they were gathering on the big field below me. It looked like a thousand men were forming into military lines with the Indians on one side, the militia bringing up the rear, and the drummers drumming an advance, which I recognized 'cause Drummer Jakes taught me. He had to be down there.

They were like one giant monster moving forward in a thumping rhythm. There couldn't have been more than 300 Americans waiting to join in battle. I guessed the fighting at the water's edge and the reinforcements being bombarded and the screaming Indians had scared off most of the militia, so it was just real soldiers who were standing strong waiting for the advancing massive body of red.

The tall American general waved his sword with a white piece of material attached.

A British general accepted the surrender. A bugler sounded the ceasefire, but the Indians were back and weren't paying any attention. They were screaming and slashing and throwing soldiers over the cliff! They scalped and bit and gouged, and their painted bodies wove in and out of the smoke. Some carried flames on sticks that they smashed into the faces of soldiers, and it was not just the Indians who were butchering, British soldiers were joining them.

The American general was screaming at the British general, probably telling him to stop the slaughter, and the British general made the bugler repeat his call, and the man-animals didn't hear, and the British general threw down his hat and jammed his sword into the ground.

Finally the Indians disappeared into the woods, and the British soldiers were brought to order by their officers, and I turned on my back on the rock in time to see hundreds of birds shoot out of their hiding places and fly through the smoke, up into the clean sky away from all this evil. As I watched their escape, I wished I could join them. Something hard rubbed against my bottom, and I realized it was my old mirror. I took it out and stared at it without looking in it. It was cracked.

CHAPTER 16
OCTOBER/NOVEMBER 1812

▼

Matthew Elliott

An adventuresome fly could have had a grand slide startin' between Procter's eyes, zippin' down his nose, landin' on his protruding chin—which at that moment was quivering—and then slippin' from chin to chest to bloated stomach without once hitting an indentation! Procter was pacin' in my parlour. "I've ordered the Indians to cross the Detroit, but they refuse."

"Kin ya blame them? We retreated at Macaqua and left them alone at Fort Wayne. They don't have a hell of a lot of trust in the British, and I can't say I blame them!"

"I'll deal with that later. Now the problem is provisions for the Indians! I want the tribes to winter at the old gathering place at the foot of the Maumee rapids. There's enough corn left behind by the Americans, and cattle are running wild in that area. It should be enough to keep the tribes fed throughout the cold season."

"'Tis a good idea."

"They won't go without you."

"Shows ya still need me, don't it?" There was somethin' about his "official" accent that made me want to prick his balloon whenever I could, which was not very smart. Still, it felt good to know he couldn't manage the Indians himself, so good that I'd figure out how to go in spite of my back.

"Once the Indians are fed you can send out parties to annoy Winchester."

"Love had some kinda concoction that she'd rub on my back when things were real bad. Maybe I kin get one of the Indian doctors to treat me when I'm down there."

Sarah didn't answer, and her hands stopped rubbin' my back for a minute. I was lyin' on my bed bein' attended to. "Perhaps you can." Her tone made me think she was not concentratin' on my words. I was expectin' her to complain about my departure, but she was givin' me the silent treatment instead.

I turned my head to the side so I could get a view of her face. The mouth was turned down and her eyes were ice. "I've got to go, lass. I'm needed. The Indians won't stay together much longer if they can't fill their stomachs, and they won't go to the Maumee, where there is food available, without me."

She stood up from the bed and, with hands on hips, stared down at me lookin' as though she was close ta tears. "I know I can't stop you, Matthew Elliott, but let me tell you a truth you won't hear from anyone else. You are too old for this. Neither your brain nor your body is quick enough for war. You should leave it to the young and the strong."

"What do ya mean, my brain isn't quick enough?" I couldn't argue about my body.

"Just what I said. You don't realize it, but everyone practices a hell of a lot of patience waiting to hear what your decisions are."

"That's not old age, that's 'cause I'm wise enough to consider all the options!" I was yellin' 'cause her words cut.

She stared at me for a cold minute and then her eyes softened. "You are testing my patience, Matthew Elliott!" She took a deep breath and pursed her lips as though she had more blather to throw at me but was biting it back. She shook her head and left the room, shuttin' the door quietly behind her. My Sarah didn't tolerate bein' yelled at.

Didn't she understand that my body and my brain screamed to be released from these responsibilities, that all I wanted was to sit by a warm fire and watch my babes at play? I knew I had slowed down, and I could feel Boy and Alexander's patience as they waited for my ground-out decisions. Sure, didn't I know how slow I was in mountin' a horse or climbin' a stair? But if we lost this war, there would never be that moment in front of the fire, and if we lost the allegiance of the Indians, we'd sure as hell lose the war. So these old bones would have to stay glued for a while longer.

There weren't many leaves left on the trees, and those that were still holdin' on had turned from red to rust, yellow to brown and green to black. The Maumee River ran fast and cold, and the air already nipped at fingers and toes and nose and ears, and 'twas just the beginnin' of November.

"Da, where do you want me to pitch our tent?"

"Over by them rocks would be out of the wind." Thank God Alexander was with me. Not only did I love havin' this smilin' son near me, I was not sure I could have managed the whole winter here on the Maumee without him.

Shawnee, Delaware, Potawatomi, Miami and Wyandot had set up camps well separated one from the other. The area was quickly takin' on the look of a village. Smoke rose from the crux of teepees that were grouped accordin' ta tribes, and while children, ignorant of the upheaval in their lives, ran about playin' innocent games, the squaws did all the work: some haulin' water and others wood while their sisters mashed the corn and cooked it over small fires. Normally the Indians separated into family units, makin' surviving the cold winter easier, there bein' less hunting and fishing necessary 'cause there were fewer to feed and clothe in warm winter garments. 'Twas war that had changed the world for these men, and sure as hell it was going to be tough work to keep them all together throughout the whole damned winter.

Each day more Indians arrived on horseback. "By my count, we've over 200 already, and they're still coming," Alexander told me, havin' done the rounds.

"Sure there'll not be enough provisions for the whole damned winter, 'specially as 200 pounds of supplies got ruined by the waves. We'll have to send a messenger to Amherstburg askin' for more supplies. I hope ta hell Procter will help us, 'specially as the gunpowder got soaked too."

"We do have the corn, Da, and beef from the escaped cattle and the supplies we brought. Couldn't we hunt and fish for the rest?"

"'Course we'll have to do some of that, but, I tell ya, Alexander, our Indians—and by that I mean them that's willin' ta fight with the British—now expect to be fed and clothed and armed by us and are much less willin' ta go out and hunt and fish for their food."

"In a way, we can't blame them. They'd never be in this situation if it weren't for us."

"'Tis true they wouldn't be here, but they wouldn't be on their own land either, it havin' bin overrun by the Americans. No matter the reason, we still have the same problem, that being, how in fekin' hell are we going to keep them fed? If the man we sent to Procter doesn't succeed, we'll have to start winter raids on farms and small villages. Not something I'm interested in doing."

Heavy snow made our world so damned silent that not even the birds had energy to sing, and when a limb broke or the ice cracked, the noise thundered throughout our haphazard settlement with a sound that wasn't unlike a cannon shot. We spent most of the time in our huts around fires made in mud chimneys, and when forced out into the cold we moved slowly on snowshoes and bundled ourselves in fur blankets so damned heavy we were all hunched like bunch of cripples. Alexander and I moved from campfire to campfire talkin' up Tecumseh and the British army.

Not long after our arrival, a Wyandot scout rode up to his tribe's campfire where we were talking and jumped off his horse. "Winchester and Harrison are marching this way."

'Twas hard to believe anyone would force their troops to go forward in this freezin' weather.

Their chief stood up and pulled his beaver blanket tight around his shoulders. "We will move north."

"You can't," I insisted. "This is where the food is. If you move north, you will starve." I couldn't really blame them, as they had no real attachment to the British and were frightened they might be on the losin' side. "They'll not get here until the thaw."

While we were tryin' to convince the Wyandots, the rumour spread through the camp like a burning ash in the wind.

The moment the Delawares, who had only recently been convinced to join the British, heard the news, they began to pack up. I rushed over to their camp. "Harrison is still in Ohio. His troops cannot make it here until the thaw, and we'll be able to leave before then."

Their chief, who had been directing the packing up, answered, "The Long Knives have a huge army. They will beat the redcoats."

I shook my head. "You are making a mistake. And remember, even if you fight with them and they win, you will lose. The British don't want your land; the Americans do."

It worked for the moment, but 'twas goin' to be a long winter.

Alexander said he wanted to take some Shawnee to check out the exact location of the American armies. I was against his departure for all the reasons any father would spout to argue against his son ridin' off into danger, but Alexander, recognizing the impracticality of my reasoning, embraced me and set off.

Something was wrong! Alexander should have been back. I could feel the dread in my bones, and I could do nothin' but wait and worry.

I heard horses and crawled out of my tent into the deep snow, keeping the bear hide wrapped around me to disguise the shiverin' that wasn't caused entirely by the cold. Other Indians heard the horses' snorts unaccompanied by any chatter amongst the returning Shawnee and came out of their tents to watch silently as the procession of straight-backed warriors rode toward my tent. *Let it be because I'm the Indian Agent; let it be because they must tell me first; let it be the loss of a skirmish; forgive me, God, please let it be someone else's son!*

Expressions frozen, they stopped in front of me. The leader was pulling a travois behind his horse and on it was a skin-wrapped bundle. "My son?" I asked, and the leader nodded. I unwrapped the bundle enough to see Alexander's face.

"We met some Delaware west of here. They said your other son was coming from the north with more men. We Shawnee did not want to turn north. We did not believe those Delaware. They were not from our camp. We did not trust them. Alexander said we must go; we must meet Boy. We followed those Delaware into an ambush. Indians who fight with the Long Knives were waiting. Alexander, he was killed with the first arrow. Two more died. The battle was long and we were few, but we fought our way out and escaped into the woods. From there we waited and watched. When they were gone, we went back for the bodies."

If he said more, I didn't hear. He'd bin scalped. His face was dead. All life had left him. Alexander, my Alexander, my pride, my loved one, my child, Love's child: I fell to my knees, wrapped my hands around his body and moaned.

It didn't matter what they said, I was goin' ta take my son home even if we had to row around ice floes, and I'd do it myself if no one was willin' to help. I attached the travois to my horse and then mounted and started toward the river

My tears were icicles piercin' my soul. Nothing existed but the body I was pullin'. Nothing mattered. I was pulling dead love. I squinted in the winter light, a frozen, empty man. I had no idea how long Round Head, Tecumseh's friend, had bin here or when I had handed him my horse's lead, nor did I care. "We're goin' home ta Amherstburg, Alexander, home to burial in a place you deserve. Ah, lad, I'm sorry, I'm sorry!"

We rowed around clumps of ice. The wind bit and the Erie was a heavin', churnin' caldron. It was rainin' buckets. The boat rose on each wave and slammed down in the troughs. Alexander's body flew from my arms and slid into the freezing water. "Get him out! Get him out!" I leaned into the water and grabbed at the wrappings, pulling with all my strength. If I couldn't get him in, I'd join him in Erie. Two of the Indians helped, and we dragged the sodden bundle back into the boat.

It kept thunderin' and rainin' buckets, and I vomited over the side, almost fallin' in. An Indian pulled me back onto the flooded floor of the boat, and I lay there wantin' ta scream my lungs out.

Round Head, his wet hair whipping across his face, pulled me onto a seat and screamed through the noise of the storm, "You will die on the floor."

I tried to fight him off and slide back down on the floor to die in the place where Alexander's shrouded body was rolling back and forth, but he held me, and I didn't have the strength to fight him. My head fell back against his chest and I wept.

Boy and Sarah pulled me out of the boat.

"You take care of Alexander, Boy, I'll take your father to the house."

Boy lifted me on to the shore and handed me to Sarah.

"It's because Alexander is Love's child! Love's and mine!" I lashed out. "That's why you don't want to deal with the body!"

"Shh, shh, my dear." Sarah wrapped me in a dry bearskin and, with her arms around my heaving shoulders, pushed me up toward the house.

"I'm sorry, Sarah, I didn't mean it."

"Yes you did, Matthew, but it's all right. I understand."

Sarah's Diary

Matthew will never recover from the loss of Alexander. My only hope is to help him package his misery into a manageable memory and return to we who are left living, who love and depend on him. I do love the old boy, and God knows we all depend on him.

I don't know how I'll get him out of his bed and into a room with light, but I will do it. I have to do it.

Boy returned only a few days before my husband. He, too, was accompanying Indian tribes to winter quarters and making forays into occupied land to attack small groups of soldiers and their Indian allies. He could not possibly have had anything to do with his brother's death . . . could he?

After putting my husband to sleep, I went to Boy's room. I told him we could not meet. I told him that the world was falling apart and that his father was needed more than ever. I told him I had to devote my efforts to getting Matthew back on his feet. He smiled and attempted to take me in his arms. I resisted and tried to fight him off, but I'm weak and he can make me do anything he wants.

Chapter 17
January/March 1813

▼

Matthew Elliott

"Come, Matthew, you can't stay in bed forever. It's the New Year; time to look ahead. Don't look at me like that, my dear! I know it's difficult, but you'll have to manage it. You have to get up and live for those of us who are left alive. Here, let me help you up."

"Ah, Sarah, my mind runs round and round in a circle of tears, always stoppin' at Alexander. 'Tis like I've been held together by an invisible shape that I knew nothin' about, till it left my body and now I'm not sure I can even stand."

"Of course you can! Give me your arm, and we'll sit you up. Good! Now, onto your feet! Don't worry. I have hold of you. There! You can sit in the chair for a while, and I'll come back with some tea."

"A bottle of rum would serve me better," I grumbled.

Boy arrived with two glasses and a bottle and pulled up a chair across from mine. He slithered like his Indian ancestors and was just as inscrutable. I'd bin a right bastard not to realize that he, too, had suffered a big loss.

"Thank you, my son." I leaned over and massaged his knee, which appeared to be a mistake since he pulled back and looked away. "'Tis a hard thing, Boy, and I've bin no help to you at all. Forgive me, please."

"Not much you could have done anyway, and I know how special Alexander was to you."

"No more special than you, my boy," I lied. "Just different, that's all."

My son knocked back a slug. "Guess I'm the Elliott future now, at least until the babies grow."

"And proud I am that you carry the mantel," I whispered and took a slug myself. I thought it best ta change the subject. "Tell me what's happened here since I've bin gone."

"Since the cold and snow and ice have set in, things have slowed down. I've emptied the warehouses, sending the rest of the food to the Indians on the Maumee."

I banged my glass down on the table. "Emptied the warehouses? You charged the military, I hope."

"Procter said he'd pay."

"But he hasn't, has he?"

Pushing his chair back violently, Boy stood up. "It was vital to keep the Indians from starving, and at least they're staying in place. You should be grateful for that."

I looked at the icicles hanging down in front of the window. "If I thought we could win this war, perhaps I'd feel feedin' the Indians was worth it and that Alexander died for a good cause, but I think the situation is damned hopeless."

"Why do you say that? We won Detroit and Queenston Heights, and right now the only Americans on Canadian soil are prisoners."

"Sure, 1812 goes to our side, but think about it. The American army has 17,000 soldiers to our 7,000."

"We have Tecumseh and at least 2,000 Indians."

"Pray they stay with us."

"And there's the militia."

"There is that, and on both sides they have had no training and aren't worth 10 soldiers except to stand in front of bullets and save a real soldier from dyin'."

How can the military believe in a twit like Procter? He'd done it again: turned success inside out. When Winchester attacked Frenchtown on the Raisin River, Procter gathered every soldier he could find and crossed the river, even draggin' his cannons across the ice, and his troops overwhelmed Winchester, forcin' the American general to surrender. That was the good part, but as usual, the idjit made a fekin' mess of the aftermath.

He promised the American officers he would guarantee the safety of their wounded and sick but instead left the poor buggers guarded by Indians and only one officer, sayin' he had to take his own wounded across to Amherstburg and would return in the morning to collect them. Didn't he realize that Indians who had been at Tippecanoe and Fort Wayne would recognize some of the soldiers and, in revenge, slaughter every one of those poor souls? I'm told 'twas was so bad that when the citizens of Frenchtown dared to come out of their houses, they found hogs had bin eating the corpses and were dragging off arms, legs, intestines and skulls in their slathering jaws.

Why did Procter leave them? He's as useless as a tit on a bull! What did he think would happen? Does he not realize that revenge fuels the most dastardly acts of war? I kin hear the battle cry already: "Remember the Raisin!" those Kentuckians will scream when next they attack, and those memories will be on the tips of their knives and the edges of their bayonets.

I have just bin told that a general order has been issued from Quebec stating, "On this occasion, the gallantry of Colonel Procter was most nobly displayed in his humane and unwearied exertions in securing the vanquished from the revenge of the Indian warriors. And has been promoted to brigadier general." So they've honoured an ignorant ass for something he did not do! Jaysus wept!

Sarah's Diary

I tried telling Matthew we should leave, that he was too old to return to the battlefield, and the dear old fool said, "No, my dear, much as you'd like to, you can't run away from war, 'cause it'll chase ya right into yer hidey-hole, if not with guns and cannons, then with theft, with robbin' you of your possessions, with words that change your laws. While we're tryin' to escape their fekin' war, they'd settle on our land, leavin' us with nothin'." He stroked my cheek and looked into my eyes with a beautiful but wan smile. "I'm a lucky man to have reached old age, my Sarah; there's many a young warrior around here who the Battle God will take before he's had a chance ta love, and I've bin gifted with two great loves, which is damned wonderful for an ugly old bruiser."

God forgive me!

CHAPTER 18
MARCH 1813

▼

Daniel

Six months after the battle at Niagara I still couldn't remember how I got to MacNeil's farm. Everyone blamed it on the bang on the head I'd suffered, but I'm not so sure. I think my memory just couldn't pack any more bad experiences into my thick head, so it protected me by shutting down. When I did arrive at the farm, I was put to bed, and for a week I was so sick with fever that memory did not have a chance to return. When I was able to get out of bed, I found Lieutenant Mackenzie still suffering with gout and fever. It took a long time for him to recover. Finally, in March we were able to set off for York, and I worried that we had left it so long Mother might have left for England, but Lieutenant Mackenzie said the winter would probably have held her back. I prayed he was right.

As there was still some ice on the lakes, Lieutenant Mackenzie had hired a coach to take us to York. The ride was so bumpy, I had to hold on to the strap to keep from slipping across the seat.

Bruno was sitting on the seat beside Lieutenant Mackenzie, who seemed to have become quite devoted to Drummer's dog. I was facing away from the direction we were going, and it felt like I was running from everything I had seen but couldn't escape. I stared out the coach window to try to stop thinking, but every time I saw something interesting, the coach passed it so fast my eyes kept getting left behind, and when that happened I couldn't stop the remembering, even if I shook my head to push bad thoughts away, so I looked up at the sky to try to catch the memory of a good time.

I woke up with a jerk and tapped my breast pocket to make sure my mirror was there. It felt good to have it sitting over my heart. I pulled it out and stared at my reflection, which was harder to see because of the crack.

With a delicate hand, Lieutenant Mackenzie swished his fair hair from his eyes. "We're almost there."

We both leaned out the window to see the beginnings of York. The fort was bigger than Amherstburg, and there was a lot of activity, with wagons bearing food and guns lined up waiting to go through the gates and soldiers everywhere, some marching toward the battery, others lining the walls, while still others checked the squared bundles sailors were bringing up to the fort from ships at the docks. "It feels like they're expecting an invasion, Lieutenant Mackenzie."

"As I said before, Daniel, the war is chasing us."

The carriage took us along the road lining the shore, where we passed the fort and arrived at the beginnings of the town of York. I leaned out of the window to stare at all the boats on the lake. There were barges, boats with large hulls and a single sail, giant timber rafts that had smoke coming out of shacks built on their flat surface and three schooners, each with two billowing white sails. A docked schooner had her skirts pulled up and porters carrying luggage scrambled up and down her runway.

Past the dock was a busy open market where farmers were selling their foods to a crowd of well-dressed men and women. On the other side of the road were large houses with windows looking over the lake, and behind those houses I saw simpler homes lining muddy streets and behind them thick forest.

"What are you going to do in York?"

"First we'll get you settled, and after that I'll find some sort of accommodation and then go back to the fort to find out about my pension or half-pay and land."

"How are we going to find my father's sister?"

"Nothing easier, Daniel. We just ask." We were on what I guessed was the main street, 'cause stores lined the wooden boardwalk, and there were lots of people going in and out of the inn, the apothecary and the general store. A group of men were standing in front of the tavern. "One of them must know," he said, knocking on the seat of the driver to tell him to stop. Leaning out of the window, he called, "Excuse me, gentlemen." The men stopped their conversation and stared at my friend. "Do any of you know where the home of Belle Fontaine can be found?"

The men smirked at each other as though there was some secret we didn't understand. "'Course we do. Everyone knows Belle." One of them dropped his cigar and ground it out with his heel. "She lives down yonder, right here on Yonge Street, but she's retired, you know. Everyone's tried to get her to go back to work, but she'll have none of it." He leered at the other men as though he had said something funny, and they seemed to think he had.

"That doesn't matter," Mackenzie answered. "Thank you." He tapped the seat to get the driver to continue.

The house was set back, with a wide veranda running across the front. We climbed out of the coach. "Wait for me," Lieutenant Mackenzie instructed the driver. He put his hand on my shoulder and pushed me toward the picket fence that lined the property.

On the veranda, a large lady was pulling herself out of a wicker chair and coming down the steps toward us. Her hair was a very strange colour of red and orange and black, kinda like the flames in a fire. I stopped and looked back at the Lieutenant. "You're not going to leave me, are you? Please don't!"

"We'll see how this goes and then decide."

We opened the little gate and walked toward the lady. Her head was cocked to one side with curiosity. "Can I help you?" Her voice was deep and gravelly and comfortable, and her smile made her eyes crinkle.

Lieutenant Mackenzie shook her hand. "I've brought Daniel Brownell to you. I believe he's your nephew."

She put her hands on my shoulders. "You're Ezra's son?"

I nodded. "He's dead." I hadn't meant to say that so fast, but it just popped out.

The shock of my words made her eyes freeze, which told me that her mind had gone elsewhere. Was she remembering Papa? Maybe she couldn't believe my words, or maybe it was too much to put together all at the same time—meeting a boy she didn't know who was supposed to be her nephew, who brought news of her brother's death. Her eyes returned to us, and before I knew what was happening, she pulled me into her arms, which was a bit suffocating but not unappealing.

"At Detroit," Mackenzie added. He didn't say that Papa was on the American side, for which I was grateful.

She pushed me back from the hug so as to see my face better. "And your mother? Where's Margaret?"

"I don't know." I was looking at the ground. "I hope she's here in York. I've come looking for her."

She nodded her head as though she understood. "Well, don't you worry, you can stay with me for as long as you want."

"Will you help me look for Mother?"

"Of course I will." She looked at the Lieutenant. "Will you come in and have a cup of tea?"

"I think I'll leave Daniel with you for the moment, but I would like to come back tomorrow if that is all right with you."

"Of course." She pulled me in to her side. "Daniel and I look forward to it."

Lieutenant Mackenzie crouched over. "You don't mind if I go, Daniel?"

I shook my head. I felt like my heart and my mind were floating in a stream that was emptying into a big river and that I could let go and be swept along by the new current. Maybe it was because this lady and I had some of the same blood. "No, I don't mind, but you'll come back tomorrow?"

"Of course I will."

Belle Fontaine walked Lieutenant Mackenzie back to the coach, saw him into the cabin and came back to me with my travel sack. "Now then, lets go sit on the veranda and get to know each other." She took my hand, which should have bothered me since I was 12 but for some reason didn't, and we walked up the stairs and along the porch to a pair of wicker chairs. She put down my bag, squeezed into one chair and gestured for me to take the other, but I stood at the railing and looked out at the street. Without looking at her, I told her about Papa and Joseph and Brownstown and Niagara and Mr. Elliott and Lieutenant Mackenzie and Bruno, and I went on and on and I couldn't stop. "The very worst thing is that Mother has run away with a British officer who has no idea what she's like, and I have to try to find her but I'm scared she's already left for England."

"Come here, Daniel," she interrupted.

I turned to her and she beckoned with her hand to come closer, and when I took her hand she pulled me right up close so I was touching her knees, and then she took hold of me at the top of my arms. At first I tried to escape, because I knew her sympathy was going to do me in, but her grip told me she'd probably wait till my wisdom tooth grew in before letting me go, so I just tried to look at any place but her, but she wasn't going to have any of that either, and still holding tight to one arm, she grabbed my chin, turning my face until I couldn't look anywhere else. Her eyes were like honey. I could see she knew I was not nearly as brave as I pretended to be. Her knowing made my face crumble. I squiggled up my eyes to stop the tears, but it just made sobs burst through my lips even though I was holding them as tight shut as I could. Stuff came out of my nose too. It was really messy, but Madame Fontaine didn't care. She pulled me into her shoulder, guck and all, and we rocked back and forth, back and forth. She didn't say anything, which was good.

Messy crying doesn't happen when you hurt yourself but know the pain will get better and not when somebody is mad at you but you know it will pass. Messy crying happens when things will never be right again. Once, when I was with Joseph, we watched some Indians trapping beaver. They must have missed the mother, because that night, sleeping under the stars, we could hear her crying for her lost babies. It had the same feeling as messy crying. Even when the messy part is finished, you are still crying inside.

It got to the stage I was sort of sleeping. I could have, I think, if giant sobs hadn't sneaked up from my toes and caught me by surprise.

Madame Fontaine kissed me on the head and said, "Last I heard, Ezra and Margaret were in Ohio." She was talking to herself more than to me, but I answered her anyway.

"I was born there," I sniffed. "We moved to Sandwich when I was two." Sometimes I thought I remembered, but Mother said that was impossible, that I had too much imagination. I thought I remembered stiff arms holding me and long silences interrupted by voices that were held as tight as an anchor rope in a storm.

"Did you like Sandwich?" she asked. She took a handkerchief from her sleeve and handed it to me so I could blow.

"In summer, it smells like peaches." I told her about Prophet, my dog, and Mr. and Mrs. Wickam and more about Joseph and Amherstburg and General Brock and Papa and how careful we were with Mother.

We stayed in that wicker chair until it started to get dark and Madame Fontaine could feel me shivering.

She rubbed her hands up and down my back and arms to try to get me warm. "Life's not fair, Daniel, and having your mother go away without you is like getting kicked by a big old horse, but there is nothing we can do about it, so I guess we'd just better get on with living." She pushed me gently away and then stuck out her hand so that I could pull her up. "We'll find out where Margaret's gone, but it may take a while, so you'll just have to think of this as the middle time, between the time before she went away and the time she returns. Kind of like a picture inside a frame."

"Or a star inside a circle," I whispered as she took my hand and we went inside.

Madame Fontaine put a bowl of soup in front of me. I tried one sip and then put the spoon down. My throat wouldn't open.

"That's all right, child, I've felt like that more then once myself," Madame Fontaine said in a kind voice. "Come, we'll get you settled in your bedroom." She led me to a room in the front of the house that had a window looking out on the porch and beyond it to the street. Madame put my suitcase on the bed to open it, and as she put my clothes in the chest of drawers, I felt like my life was being packed away in a strange place. She pulled out a nightshirt and handed it to me. "Best get yourself ready for bed." She pulled the blanket back. "If you empty your pockets, I can take those clothes away to be washed." I put some coins on the dresser along with a stone from the Detroit River, a smushed handkerchief, half a bright red leaf and my mirror.

She picked up the mirror and looked at her reflection. "The crack divides me in two!"

I nodded my head. "I guess there's some truth in a cracked reflection. One part is good, and the other part can't be counted on."

Still holding the mirror, she looked at me with a question on her face, but I ignored it 'cause I was too tired for any more discussion.

"Perhaps we'll talk about that another day," she said. "Right now, let's get you washed and into bed. You must be tuckered out."

There was a bright moon shining through the window. It made shadows run around the ceiling of the bedroom. I felt like I was floating in a place where everything was strange: the smells, the noises and even the accents weren't the same, and worse yet, there was no one in that place I knew and no one who knew me. I would have given anything to be back in Sandwich, even on one of Mother's bad days. The thought made me so sad I couldn't stand myself, and I got up to go to look for Madame.

The parlour was dark, so I crept down the hall to her bedroom where there was light. At the door, I came to a full stop. She was putting a big white tent over her head. Before it fell, I saw giant breasts with huge brown circles around the nipples. Those breasts were so big that if a kid got his head stuck between them, he would surely suffocate to death. She heard me, and when her head appeared through the hole at the top of her tent gown, she turned and caught me wide-eyed. I didn't even have time to shut my mouth.

"Can't sleep?" She walked over to the bed and threw open the covers. "Come on, then, jump in with Belle for a while."

I wasn't sure that it was such a good idea, what with the possibility of suffocation and all. She got in first and spread across the whole mattress, and then she patted the bed for me to come and join her. It made me realize I was not as ready to die as I thought I was, but I didn't know how I could say no without hurting her, so I took a deep breath, bit on my upper lip to keep it from twitching and climbed in. She put her arm around me and pulled my head toward her breasts, and I knew I was going to die young—that I would never grow a beard, kill a buffalo or see the ocean. It was really scary. Then I got the surprise of my life. She was like a giant soft pillow. My head sank so deep I could hear her heartbeat. She kissed me on the top of the head. I didn't move. "I forgot my mirror," I mumbled.

"It's an unusual mirror," she whispered, kissing my head again. "Who fixed the edges for you?"

"Joseph."

"The Indian you told me about who was Tecumseh's spy?"

"And my friend."

"Tell me about Tecumseh."

"He is the most famous Indian alive. Joseph told me that the very minute Tecumseh was born, a giant meteor streaked across the sky from the north and passed directly over their village, leaving a green-white light that hung there for almost a whole minute. The old people said this meteor was the Panther, a powerful spirit passing over to the south, seeking a hole in which to sleep. That's why Tecumseh was named to the Panther Unsoma."

"What's an *Unsoma?*"

"I think they are like clans. I heard Joseph talking about groups inside his tribe; one that is named after animals with hooves and one that has only the names of birds and one that has rabbits, hares, squirrels and mice, and one that has every kind of turtle, lizard, snake, frog, toad—" It was too long a story. I snuggled into Madame.

CHAPTER 19
APRIL 1813

▼

Matthew Elliott

Fort Miami was a wreck of a place, but the soldiers there were protected from the howling wind and goddamned rain a whole lot better than we were in the Indian camp across the river. The British army wouldn't have for a minute considered invitin' the Indians into the protection of the fort, even though when it came to a fight they would have been ground ta mincemeat if they didn't have these warriors at their backs. 'Twas a way of doing things, I supposed, and naught I could do about it.

I'd come to the fort with Tecumseh, who was in a rage because Procter wasn't ready to attack Fort Meigs down the Maumee River where William Henry Harrison was garrisoned with his troops.

"We'll attack when we're ready!" Procter stayed seated behind his desk with hands squeezing the edge to control his anger. He didn't like Tecumseh any more than the Indian liked him.

"Listen, Father, we must attack now! The more we wait, the more time Harrison has to make the fort strong. The man destroyed Tippecanoe, he burned the villages of the Kickapoo, the Miami and the Ottawa! The blade of my tomahawk thirsts for his head!" He was pacing in furor, and I was translatin' as fast as I could. "Listen, Father, I have challenged Harrison to battle, but he remains burrowed in his hole and refuses to leave." He pressed his fists on Procter's desk and leaned in to his face. "Listen, we must not wait!"

When translatin', I'd bin skipping the "listen, Father" bit for weeks, but this time I hadn't left the words out. They seemed to match Tecumseh's mood.

"We're not ready yet. I've still to pull forward the 24-pounders. When that's done, we'll prepare for an attack, but not a moment sooner!"

"Listen, Father, it will take 200 men all night to pull those guns through the mud. We should not waste so much time!"

Procter stood up. "I have studied the history of military sieges and will go by the book." He slammed his fist on the table. "There will be no more argument!"

Tecumseh and I waded through the mud to the Indian camp. "At least the men you have hidden in the woods around Fort Meigs can keep the Americans from escaping while Procter tries to git it all together," I said, trying to console him.

He bashed his hand down as though he was tryin' to kill my words, and he stomped off to his teepee.

So there I was with water seepin' in under the teepee trying to sleep on a layer of pine boughs. It was cold and damp, my bones were aching, and I was fightin' a black sense of futility. I had to stick it out in the hope of holding everyone together, but I was an old man with not a hell of a lot of hope. In the morning, I would tell Procter that if he didn't get with it, the Indians would go ahead on their own, which, without military backing would be disastrous.

Even with my pleading, it took two days before the cannons started pounding Fort Meigs, but once it started, the noise screamed inside our ears and thick smoke fumes stunk of mould mixed with mud. I rode my horse from Fort Miami to the Indian camp to Fort Meigs tryin' to keep track of the Indians' whereabouts for Procter, but in truth I had no idea where all 800 were 'cause many of them were in small groups that darted in and out of the woods. Tecumseh had kept 500 or so close to the camp, so I could at least honestly report on that number.

Tecumseh galloped past me and yelled, "Come and see!"

I followed him to a hill well beyond weapon range and to an old maple where he and another Indian hoisted me up into the crux of the tree. From there, we could look down at the fort Procter had been bombarding for three days and see that our cannonballs were slapping into walls of earth that the wily Harrison has constructed within the fort, and they were having no effect at all.

"Look!" Tecumseh pointed. "Procter is moving half of his cannons to the other side of the fort! When he shoots at those tents inside the fort, he will find that behind them there is another embankment. We should have attacked earlier!"

"We should tell him."

"There is no time!"

He was right. The cannons had started shooting from the second position, and he was not wrong about the tents either. They'd bin pulled down, revealing a huge barrier of mud into which the cannonballs were thudding. "Now what?" I wondered out loud.

It was day four, and the cannons had slacked off. Tecumseh and I were in the Indian camp, sittin' on stones around a fire eatin' corn mush and sipping sassafras tea. I'd have preferred a good slug of rum, but Tecumseh didn't allow alcohol in camp, which was a good idea 'cause alcohol and Indians didn't mix. "Kin you believe it? Procter sent a man into Fort Meigs under a white flag with a note demandin' Harrison surrender."

"Harrison laughed?"

"Might have. He certainly refused to surrender." We sat quietly wondering what was going to happen next. Things were not lookin' too promising, and even Tecumseh seemed to have bin punched by bad thoughts.

An Indian broke through the underbrush, makin' us forget our dismal preoccupations. "Across the river, many Long Knives are landing."

"Show me!" Tecumseh demanded.

The Indian grabbed a stick and drew the Maumee River, showing the landing place below the rapids.

"Harrison can't get out of Fort Meigs. They must be reinforcements." The noise of the guns drowned out my words.

More Indians appeared through the underbrush, and their leader stumbled toward Tecumseh. "A small number have landed on this side. The real army is on the other side."

Tecumseh took only a minute to come to a decision. "Take your men against the Long Knives on this side. I will cross the river."

Carrying their weapons, Tecumseh's warriors poured in from camps in the woods and gathered in our clearing to receive instructions. How they knew to gather was beyond me. Standing on a rock, Tecumseh addressed the listeners who were so damned quiet that between cannon blasts I could hear a woodpecker choppin' away at a hollow tree trunk. "We must swim the river, flank the British and attack the Americans from behind." That's all he said, but it seemed to be enough, as the Indians slipped through the woods in groups as well organized as any fekin' battalion in the British Army.

Jaysus, Mary and Joseph what was I to do? Swimmin' the Maumee didn't have a grand appeal. I would git to the shore and find a canoe.

Explosions shook the ground, and flames screeched up into the sky. The Americans had destroyed our battery! I was paddling into hell! From the middle of the river, I could see the Americans at the battery— circling, waving their hats and shooting off their rifles in celebration, but the idiots didn't seem to be advancing or retreating. *Keep celebratin', boys, it'll give Tecumseh time to have at you!* I scrambled up on the shore, dashed to Fort Miami and used my position as head of the Indian Department to commandeer a horse.

By the time I reached Tecumseh, the Americans had surrendered, and I'd bin lucky enough to miss the battle. I followed Tecumseh in the chase after soldiers who had escaped into the woods. We spent the whole day rounding up prisoners who we led back to Fort Miami, but when the fort came into range and I heard high-pitched screams streaking over the wall, I slouched in despair, 'cause I could guess what was going on. We spurred our horses into action, and when the wall of the fort came into our view my suspicions were confirmed.

Outside the gate, the Indians had formed a gauntlet, forcing the Americans to run through it before they could get into the safety of the fort. Tecumseh dashed forward screaming at them to stop, and I followed to find dead bodies with exposed brains, bashed in faces and limbs so badly broken the bones were exposed.

Tecumseh's arrival made them freeze the swings of their clubs and rifles. "You shame your race!" Tecumseh yelled. "And you shame me. Stop immediately!"

They backed away, but many grumbled in complaint. The prisoners who could still walk stumbled toward the gate, but as we passed through we were frozen in place. Mother o' God, they were all liquored up! Chippewa and Potawatomi had stripped their prisoners naked, donned their uniforms and were circling the Americans screeching war cries and waving their tomahawks. Other tribes were sportin' officers' ruffled shirts and leather boots and were dancin' wild dances with scalps hanging from their belts. Squaws were stretching human skin on frames, and wild dogs were gnawing at the feet and fingers of the flayed bodies. Two dogs were fightin' over intestines, each with an end clutched between its teeth, growlin' and droolin', back feet anchored and pullin' at the innards till they split, spewing everything that was inside. Ach! 'Twas a frightful scene! I heard the devil laughing.

Tecumseh spurred his horse toward a savage Potawatomi who had shot an American and was scalping him. He shot his gun in the air over the Indian's head and screamed at them all, forcing the hysteria to slow but not stop. The scalping Potawatomi ignored him entirely, and Tecumseh shot the wild Indian. That brought them all to a standstill.

From his horse he yelled, "Brothers, you prance in petticoats and scream like crows while waving weapons over the vanquished. You dishonour the Red Man!" He was standing in his stirrups, and his fury was visible in his taut body, his flaring nostrils and his off-key voice.

I thought he was goin' to lose control to his anger, but no; he sat back down on his horse, rubbed his hand over his eyes and started again. "This is not the way of warriors!" Although quieter, his voice was insistent. "Warriors do not lose their heads when those around them do; warriors do not give way to hate when they know they are hated. Brothers, listen, warriors must meet triumph with dignity and treat disaster the same. We are fighting for our survival and must force every nerve and sinew to serve our purpose. Warriors must ignore the twisted words of the white man. We must be strong when all looks lost. We cannot dance and prance over one small victory. Listen, brothers, warriors must never, ever act like squawking roosters as you have done today. You must be men!"

I returned to the British with a dirty soul and found there was damned little to celebrate, 'cause while we beat the Americans on the right bank, Harrison's reinforcements were successful on the opposite side, having destroyed the British battery and driven off the Indian opposition, giving Harrison time to rearm the fort with guns and ammunition brought up the river by support troops.

Nobody won the battle, and it looked like we were not much interested in continuing the siege. The hung-over Indians had drifted off into the woods, the militia had left to plant the spring crops, the soldiers were in bad shape—suffering from ague and dysentery and just plain fatigue—so it was decided to head for home: Tecumseh to Bois Blanc with his men, Procter and the army to Fort Malden and me to my home and my Sarah.

News arrived that Procter had again been promoted, this time to major general. God almighty! Couldn't Quebec understand the man didn't have the wind for leadership?

CHAPTER 20
APRIL 1813

▼

Daniel

It was morning, and we were going to look for Mother. As we went down the porch steps, a wagon pulled up in front of the house.

"This might take a minute, Daniel."

The man sitting on his cart was twisting the rim of his hat. His hair was slicked down the way the Sandwich farmers greased their hair when they came into town. He had rough farmer-hands, rosy cheeks and a nervous smile on his face. We had to squint from the sun as we went down the stairs and along the path. The garden gate could swing, so I stood on it and waited impatiently while Madame went to the hay wagon. She leaned against the large wooden wheel and tilted her head.

"It's good to see you, Dunc. It's bin a donkey's age," she laughed up at him. "Still maulin' that old hat, I see. Thought it'd be dead by now." Her voice had the sound of whiskey in it. I liked it, all low and rumbly.

"Didn't know if ya wanted visitors since ya, you know, since ya retired."

"Just cause I don't spread my—ah . . . ." She looked over at me. "Just 'cause I'm not working anymore, it doesn't mean I can't see old friends for a drink and a chat."

The farmer twisted his hat into a rope as tight as a stroud of tobacco. "I brung ya a quarter hind of beef. Ya couldn't, kinda, come out of retirement for a quickie, could ya?"

There was need in his voice. I could hear it, but I didn't understand.

"Can't do it, Dunc, but I'd love to have you for a visit. It'll have to be another day, though. I have a new man living in my house." She indicated me with her head. "We're just getting settled."

The man called Dunc looked as though he might cry.

"I know where I can get some good brandy." He sounded like he was begging.

"I'd love to share a glass with you, but that's it, Dunc. I can't come out of retirement. Not even for you."

"I guess I'll come along anyway." He gave her a sideways smile. "We kin talk about old times and maybe after a little juice you might just change your mind?"

"Dunc!"

"All right, all right." He laughed, shook his head and punched his hat back into shape.

Madame and Dunc didn't seem to feel the need for more talk. Madame leaned on the wagon wheel and stared up at the sky. I swung on the gate and looked up too. My eyes froze on the budding maple branches. They were like charcoal lines in the sky. Returning geese cut across the sky, but my eyes felt anchored and didn't follow them.

"The house is lookin' good."

I blinked and turned to look at the house with them. It wasn't very big, but the porch ran across the whole front.

"It is, isn't it?" Madame agreed. "Joe Bradley carved the bannisters, and Ezekiel Daniel put on a fresh coat of paint." She straightened up from leaning on the wheel and put her hands on her back without taking her eyes from the house. "Not bad for a 40-year-old retiree, I'd say. I love the place. My secrets have surely seeped into the walls, but that's as it should be. It feels comfortable to live in a place that knows all my tales."

The noise of the traffic made us turn to the street. High-wheeled carts loaded with soldiers and weapons were barrelling past, forcing other vehicles to the side of the road where they waited like frightened rabbits.

"Just got back to the farm when some soldiers arrived and ordered me to return to York for militia exercises," Dunc said.

"Do ya think they can take Canada?" Madame asked.

"All I can say is we've been damned lucky so far."

I kept swinging on the gate. I thought that this man had not seen war, 'cause I knew *luck* and *death* were not words that could live side by side.

"We drove 'em back at Niagara, maybe that'll make 'em think twice." He threw the well-mangled piece of straw to the ground. "I hear tell Mr. Thomas Jefferson told Congress it was just a question of marching. Guess we showed him and President Madison a thing or two."

"But we lost Brock at Niagara, and I don't believe there are many generals the likes of that man."

"That's the truth."

"Maybe Daniel and I should pack up and head north; there's trouble coming, there's no doubt of that."

"This here's Daniel?"

"Yup. My brother's son."

Dunc nodded his head at me and I gave him a half-wave. I kept swinging on the gate. It was better than thinking about Detroit and Niagara. The big people kept talking, but I didn't hear any more till Dunc said, "Maybe I'll see ya later, Belle." He flicked his reins and the cart pulled away.

Madame beckoned me through the gate, and we walked down Yonge Street toward the centre of town and the lake. She had her hand on my shoulder. "Poor sod! Loretta, his wife, has begun to look like the cows she gets up to milk every morning. All Dunc needs is a little quickie to remind himself that the thing hangin' between his legs hasn't lost all its elastic."

"Elastic?"

Madame laughed. "I must watch my mouth now that you're living with me."

This elastic subject demanded a little thought. I had a suspicion, 'cause the thing hanging between my legs sometimes jumped up when I had to pee. Couldn't Dunc pee? Couldn't his wife give him a quickie so he could pee? Maybe Madame's quickies were a special concoction. I wondered what she put in them. I would ask her sometime, but I had more important things on my mind at that moment.

The sidewalk was wood, and the mud on top made it very slippery, which made us go slowly. When wagons and carriages came speeding down Yonge Street, we stood sideways and took a step back so we didn't get splattered with mud.

"What does *capital* mean?" I asked.

"It means the city where the seat of government is located. York is the capital of Upper Canada," Madame said. She had tight hold of my hand so when I slipped, I didn't fall. Madam didn't slip.

"Seat?"

"The place where they make the laws."

"Why is that called *seat*?"

"Good question. Probably because the people that make the laws like to be comfortable—they're always sitting."

"That doesn't sound like fun."

"Guess they like it."

"Where will we look for Mother?"

"First we'll go to the church and see what Bishop Strachan has to say."

"Mother wouldn't have gone there. She says that a cold building is a foolish place to worship God and that ministers are fools who think they have a special relationship with the almighty."

"I agree with your mother, but Bishop Strachan is such a busybody, he knows about everything that's going on in York."

We went into the side door of the church and knocked on the door that said *Office*. A deep voice told us to come in. A large man with a thin lower lip that pulled his mouth down looked up from his desk and his jaw dropped. He stood so fast I got the feeling he was shocked to see us. "Madame Fontaine. You surprise me. It is the first time I've seen you cross the church's threshold." Standing, he was kind of frightening. He was dressed all in black and didn't have a lot of hair, and his voice boomed.

"I've come for some information, Bishop."

"Ah!" The bishop returned to his seat. "I might have guessed it was not that you were eager to join the congregation!"

Madame ignored his sarcastic voice and jutting chin. "This here is Daniel Brownell, and we're looking for his mother, Margaret Brownell. Has she, by any chance, crossed your path?"

"Margaret Brownell? No, I've not heard the name." He looked at me. "Daniel, is it?"

"Yes, sir."

"You've lost your mother?"

"She came here ahead of me with Major Black, and now that I've arrived I need to find her."

"How is it she came without you?"

"I was to follow with Lieutenant Mackenzie, but he got gout and we were delayed in Niagara." I could tell he didn't like Madame, so I didn't like him, and I was not going to tell him the real story about Mother.

"I'll ask around for you." He looked at Madame. "Where is the boy staying?"

"With me," Madame answered.

"I'm not sure that's a good idea, Madame Fontaine. I'll find other accommodations for him. I'm sure there are healthier places for young boys."

I didn't know why he thought Madame's place wasn't healthy, but I didn't want to leave her. I pushed myself into her skirts.

"The boy is my nephew, Reverend Doctor, and he'll stay with me." Madame glared at Bishop Strachan as he looked down his long nose at the two of us, and she pulled me tight into her skirts.

The bishop stared at me. "There's not a person in York who would approve of a woman like you taking in a child."

"You'd be surprised, sir! I believe there are a lot of important men whom I could convince to protest in my name if you took him from me!" She steered me toward the door. "Just let me know if you hear of his mother."

The way she pulled me out of the churchyard, I could tell she was angry. "Why doesn't he like you, Madame?"

"Don't worry about it, Daniel. The man is just a whirlwind of righteousness. He sticks his clerical collar into everything that takes place in the town of York. He's like the black bantam rooster in my backyard, pecking at everything that he doesn't like."

"Was he looking down at us 'cause he didn't like us, or are his eyes always droopy?"

"Both! And did you see that thin lower lip, Daniel? Never trust a man with a thin lower lip!" If the speed at which we were walking was a sign of how angry she was, I figured the lady was really mad.

I kept quiet and let her stomp off her anger. If the meddlesome minister hadn't heard about Mother, maybe she wasn't here; maybe she went to London with the Major, and if she did, what would I do next? It was better not to think about it. After a few blocks, Madame's pace returned to normal. We were still heading down Yonge Street. "Where are we going?"

"To see a friend of mine."

Through the window of a house on the other side of the street I could see four ladies sitting around a table holding cards. They were staring at us. "Who are those ladies?"

"I call them the Whist Girls."

"Why?"

"'Cause that's what they're doing, playing whist. They're always playin' when I walk past."

They were still staring out at us, so I waved at them.

She pushed my hand down. "No, don't wave." She didn't look up at them.

"Why?"

"Why? 'Cause you don't know them."

"Do you?"

"Nope. I know who they are, and they sure-as-shootin' know who I am, although we ain't never had the opportunity to talk. They are the wives of important men. That's the house of the Chief Justice. They don't have anythin' to do with someone like me."

"Are their husbands the men with the seats?"

"That's them, all right."

There was lots of traffic on the street, soldiers on horses—some in the British red-and-white uniforms and some in the blue jackets of the militia—stringy-haired farmers in wagons, a coach with curtains that had two horses pulling it, and lots of people on foot who were trying to cross the muddy road without getting killed. As we got closer to the lake, there were men and women going in and out of the stores and cafes that were so close to the sidewalk we had to stop a lot to let them come out with their parcels. "How many people live in York?"

"'Bout a thousand."

"That's a lot!"

"A lot for a village, maybe, but not for the capital of a province."

We stomped down the street all the way to the lake, where there was a large store with a sign that said *Apothecary*, and we went in. It was a huge room lined with shelves of bottles that were full of liquids and dried herbs. They were lined up alphabetically and had words like *Anise* in big letters, with *colds* written below. I heard Madame say, "Is Dacana in?" while I stared at some of the bottles. Basil for wasp and hornet bites, betony for the liver, bistort to sweat out venom and borage to expel melancholy. That might be good for mother. I kept walking along the various rows to see if I could find something for hysteria: calendula, damaged skin; corn poppy, insomnia; day lily, orange dye. I passed the Fs and Gs and Hs: there was Jacob's ladder, hysteria. There were so many, it would have taken me hours to read them all. I wondered who owned this place.

"Daniel." I pulled my eyes away from the wonderful collection.

"Madame, look at this! Maybe borage and Jacob's ladder could help Mother!"

"Daniel, I want you to meet Mrs. Dacana Cameron. She's my very good friend and might be able to help us find Margaret."

The lady was so tall I had to look straight up. She was big, too, but not big like Madame. Her kind of big was like a well-proportioned tree. I thought she must be halfway between Madame and me in age, 'cause her kind face had no wrinkles. "How nice to meet you, Daniel. Your Aunt Belle has been telling me good things about you."

Aunt Belle! I hadn't thought of her like that, but of course she was my aunt, and I liked that. "Thank you, but I'm not old enough to have many good things said about me yet. Has Aunt Belle—" It felt funny to use the name, funny but good. "Has Aunt Belle told you about my mother?"

"She has, Daniel."

"Everything?"

"Yes, everything."

"Do you think some of theses medicines might help if we find her?"

"It's possible, but I can't promise anything."

"Who fills all the bottles?"

"I have another building in the back where we do all the work. Would you like to see it?"

"Yes, please."

There was a back door behind the counter. It made me feel important to go through it, like I was somebody special. The second building was only a few steps away and was as new as the apothecary. Inside, there were a number of people working. One was a woman with fading red hair who was small and wiry and was using tongs to remove bottles from a huge vat of water that was boiling in the fireplace. She was putting them on a table where two young Indian girls were sitting. A giant black man was grinding some herb with a mortar and pestle, and the girls were filling some cooled jars marked *Meadow Sweet* and in smaller letters, *for pain*.

"Annie," Mrs. Dacana Cameron said to the little woman, "I want you to meet Daniel. He's Belle's nephew."

Annie looked up with a smile, put down her tongs, wiped her hands on her apron and came over to shake my hand. "And where did you come from, young Daniel?"

"From Sandwich, before the war started, then Amherstburg, then Niagara and now here."

She stood back and nodded her head as though she understood all the things that had happened underneath my words. "Well, 'tis glad I am to meet you." She looked up at Aunt Belle. "And happy I am for you, my friend, to have such a nice young man in your home." She gave Aunt Belle a hug.

"If Bishop Strachan has anything to do with it, he'll not be in my home for long," Aunt Belle whispered.

"Don't you worry about Strachan," Dacana said. "He's trying to be the saviour of all the armies and as such needs my medicines, so I can take care of him if he tries to remove Daniel."

I wandered over to the huge black man who had moved from his mortar and pestle to a pile of herbs that he was pressing into individual pages of a very large book. He was completely bald, and he was wide but not tall. The material in the arms of his shirt looked as though it was stretched to the limit, and it was the same for the breeches on his legs. I stood and watched while he pasted. "I'm Daniel," I told him when he looked down at me.

"Dey call me Black Henri." He had a French accent. "I am a friend of Dacana."

"She's nice." I looked back at the big lady.

"Yes, and she is good."

"I guess good is even better than nice." I wasn't really sure that *good* and *nice* were virtues that were going to succeed in these times, but I kept it to myself.

"What are you doing?"

"Dis is to know de story of each flower."

"Do you write words on each page?"

"Annie, over dere," he pointed with his head so that his hands could keep working. "She does de writing."

I recognized some of the dried herbs. "What does lavender do?"

"For de pains in de head after a cold."

"And this horseradish?"

"For de worms in de children."

"I thought flowers were just to look pretty. I guess I was wrong."

"*Oui*, nature, she is wise, but we are children who do not always listen."

"So that's why you're making a record?"

"*Oui*."

Aunt Belle and Dacana were whispering and looking over at me. I wandered back to see what they were saying.

"I'll let you know what I find out," Dacana said to Aunt Belle.

"Do you know something about my mother?" My voice was quivering.

"No, Daniel," she said, patting my head. "But I'll do my best to find out. Meanwhile, you should get Belle to take you down to the docks to see the ship that's being built." She looked at Aunt Belle with a teasing smile, and my aunt looked embarrassed. Adults were certainly peculiar animals.

The ship sounded interesting, but it would be time wasted. "Shouldn't we keep looking for Mother?"

Dacana touched my shoulder. "I have a lot of connections in York, and I'll send out searchers immediately. You go with Belle and see the ship."

"You'll send someone to find us when you know something?"

"Of course I will." She pushed me gently. "Now off you go."

The black flies—Aunt Belle called them *moustiques*—were bad close to the water. They especially liked the place behind my ears, and I had to keep swishing them away.

At the dock, we stood below the unfinished frigate, which already had the name on its bow. It was called the Isaac Brock! "Boy! Look at that! The General's only been dead a month, and he's riding the bow of a boat!"

"'Twon't be the only place. I'll not be surprised if the name becomes braver than ever the man was."

"He was very brave. I saw him die, but I think he was a little stupid too. Marching up the cliff with the white plume sticking up out of his hat made him a perfect target."

"That was the man, this is the name, the myth, and this is what Canada needs now, a hero, not a flawed human being."

The ship made a shadow all along the dock and up the hill. I felt like I was an ant and it could step on me whenever it wanted. There was a web of raw wood wrapped all around it holding it up in the air. "It looks like it's in a prison," I whispered.

"That's called the scaffolding," Aunt Belle said. "It holds everything together till they've finished building the ship."

Scaffolding. I liked the word. Held up by scaffolding, you would breath more easily, but I was sure that giant ship could break all the scaffolding just by letting out its breath.

"Belle, I'm up here."

There was a man leaning over the unfinished railing yelling down at us. "Bring the boy around to the other side and up the gangplank," he shouted with his hands cupped to his mouth.

"That's my friend, Donald Bradley," Aunt Belle said. She waved at him and nodded her head that she understood, and we walked around in the dark shadow of the Isaac Brock until we found the planks that let us climb to the deck. I was happy to go first, because the narrow planks began to wobble under Aunt Belle's weight.

Mr. Bradley must have been a very good friend of Aunt Belle's, because he gave her a huge wet kiss right in front of me. Then he bent and shook my hand. His hand was wide with great big knuckles, but I liked him right away because he held my hand for a long time, and he didn't squeeze too hard, and he smiled showing his yellow teeth. The rest of him wasn't big like his hands, and he was a little bit crooked all over. He could have done with some scaffolding himself.

"Mr. Bradley is a carpenter, Daniel," Aunt Belle said. "He and other carpenters have built this ship."

"You built all this?" I asked. It was hard to believe that just a few men could make such a giant thing.

"Yup," he answered. "What do you think of it?"

"I think you must be a very happy man!"

Mr. Bradley didn't move. He still had his smile but it was quieter. "Why do you say that, child?"

"I guess because a ship is kind of magic."

He thought about that and asked, "What do you mean?"

"'Cause a ship lets us do the impossible: travel on water. Who else helps us with the impossible? Soldiers don't. Storekeepers don't. Not even ministers." Then I had another thought. "That's if the ship floats. It will, won't it?"

"Sure hope so," he answered. He rumpled up my hair, and I tried to smooth it down again.

"Can I go below deck and see?"

"It's too dangerous for that, I'm afraid. We're not far enough along for you to be climbing up and down."

"Tell us how you made it, then," I pleaded. I didn't want to go down from the ship yet. I liked the feeling of it under my feet, and I liked looking over the side at the shadow it made a lot better than standing below in that shadow.

He steered us to an overturned box on the deck and helped Aunt Belle sit down. "We start with the skeleton. There's a spine that goes along the bottom of the boat and then ribs that go out from the spine, and they join other pieces that run parallel to the spine. Can you picture it?"

"Yes, sir!" While he talked, I imagined myself becoming the most famous shipbuilder in the whole world and welcoming the king onto the ship I had just built for him. It would be the biggest ship ever made.

"The ship has an inside skin and an outside skin," Mr. Bradley said.

I guess we all did. Mother certainly did, and I know I did, but I didn't want to think of that. *Back to shipbuilding.* My ship would have many masts. "How many masts will this ship have?" I asked.

"She's a frigate, that means she's three-masted," he answered.

My ship will have five masts but no guns. "How many guns will the Isaac Brock have?"

"A single gun deck carrying 24 to 50 guns. I'm not sure of the exact number."

The king will not want guns. There will be peace in his world.

"The Isaac Brock is the first frigate on the lake," Mr. Bradley said. Then he turned to Aunt Belle and, out of the side of his mouth, added, "I sure hope it's finished in time."

"You mean before the Americans invade?" I asked.

He looked at Aunt Belle with a lifted eyebrow, which was an adult way of talking without words. It could mean, *How does he know about that?* or *Should a boy of 12 have to worry about such things?* or *Who's been talking to the boy?*

Aunt Belle rubbed my shoulder, which told him she knew that I knew about the war.

I turned away from them and climbed onto an exposed beam, leaned my arms on the unfinished siding and stared out at the lake where I could continue to build my king's ship without interference. Their words became mumbles and mixed with the gentle waves. I thought I'd paint my ship the same colour as the water I was staring at; that way, the lake and the ship would become one. I heard Aunt Belle saying Mother's name.

"Could be she's at the fort," Donald Bradley was saying. "I heard something about them having a madwoman in their jail."

I stepped down from my dream and turned slowly. There was a pain in my chest, because I knew the woman must be Mother.

"We don't know if it's Margaret, Daniel. Don't get upset until we find out more."

But we did know; both of us knew. How many madwomen could there be around York and of them, how many would have to be put in jail?

"Can we go and see?"

"'Course we can."

"Now?"

"Right this minute." She turned to Donald. "I'm sorry, this isn't the visit I'd planned."

He put his arm around her. "Don't worry, Belle. There's time for us. Take the lad to the fort." He kissed her again and looked down at me. "I hope it's not your mother, Daniel, but if it is, you can count on Belle and me to be your friends."

"Thank you." I was not paying attention as I pulled Aunt Belle down the plank. My mind was running ahead.

Aunt Belle hailed a buggy and we climbed in. "Take us to the garrison, please."

At the garrison, Aunt Belle explained to a soldier at the gate why we'd come, and he made us wait while he sent someone in to ask for information.

We waited holding hands and staring into space, each isolated in private worries. "If it's her, what will we do?" I whispered.

"Don't know, Daniel. We'll have to see what it's all about first. See if it really is Margaret and if it is, what she's said to have done."

We waited for a long time, and didn't move. Finally, a tall grey-haired officer appeared. His age made me think he must have been in charge of the fort. He asked, "What can I do for you?"

"We understand you have a woman in your jail and worry that she might be this boy's mother. Is her name Margaret Brownell?"

The officer answered, "There is a woman in the jail. We don't know her name, but I'll take you to her." His voice was sympathetic. "Why do you think the woman could be your mother?"

"Because she's disappeared and because sometimes she goes a little crazy." There were tears in my voice. Aunt Belle squeezed my hand. We followed him to a low wooden building that was being guarded by two soldiers each at front and back.

The front room had a desk, and a soldier behind it stood at attention and saluted the officer, who acknowledged the salute. He then spoke to the soldier in a low voice. Their whispers blew fumes of fear, making me fall against Aunt Belle. She squeezed my shoulder. As our officer spoke, the soldier listened and stared at us, and then from his desk he took a set of keys from the drawer.

The officer turned to leave. "This soldier will take you to the woman. I hope she is not your mother, but if she is, he'll show you to my office, and we can talk about what is to be done."

We followed the soldier through a door to another room that was lined with cells, and in the one straight in front of us my beautiful mother was lying on a pallet with her hands crossed over her chest, her legs drawn up to her hands, her hair down and dirty and covering her face. She was humming and rocking.

"Is she your mother?" the soldier asked.

I nodded my head. "Can I go in?"

"I'm not sure that's a good idea, son. When anyone tries to go in, she attacks like a witch and tries to claw at faces, all the time screamin' like the world's comin' to an end."

"She won't attack me."

"Can't you keep an eye and let him go in?" Aunt Belle asked. "The woman's his mother. She won't attack him."

"She may be his mother, but she's a dangerous, violent woman. She murdered an officer of the British Army." He lowered his voice and whispered to Aunt Belle, "If the officer's friends have anything to do with it, she'll soon be swinging from a rope, and if some in the army get their wish, they'll have her branded with a hot iron to make her suffer before she's dangled."

He whispered too loud, letting me hear everything he said, and it made me furious. I hit the soldier in the stomach and tried to get his chin with my fists but he backed away. "She's not a witch and she's not dangerous. She has spells that change her. It's a sickness and she can't help it!" I was swinging my fists fast and hard, and when the officer grabbed my hands, I kicked out at him but all I get was air. Messy tears covered my face.

"Back off, boy." The soldier pushed me against the wall.

He was still holding my fist so I couldn't wipe my face. I turned my head to the side. "Please let me in, she's my mother."

Aunt Belle put her hand on the soldier's shoulder. "Let Daniel in there. You can keep an eye out, and I'll help if things go awry."

"You ain't seen this creature when, as you say, things go awry, but all right. I'll let him in, and we can stand watch."

"Thank you, soldier."

The minute he opened the cell door, I pushed past him to go in and sit beside Mother, close enough to be able to push the hair out of her eyes. "Mother, it's me, Daniel." She didn't respond at all. I leaned over and kissed her on the cheek. Her eyes seemed to focus and she gave a vague smile, took my hand in hers and pulled it to her chest, but then she went away again. I sat on the edge of the pallet and waited. There was a barred window up high through which the sun threw particles of dust at us. The walls were covered with scratches and writing. What did the prisoners use, fingernails? "Mother, please talk to me." Without releasing my hand from her grip, I leaned over to try to get my face in her vision.

"Daniel?" Her free hand searched for me—it was as though she was blind. "Son."

Her eyes focused. She knew I was there. I felt her hand squeezing our old message, *I-love-you*, and I squeezed back, *I-love-you-too*. "He promised to take me to London, but it was a lie. He started to count out money for me to go back where I came from. Money, a broken promise, shame, war, the stupidity of life, a black cloud, and I don't remember anything more."

We hugged each other, and my messy tears wouldn't stop.

"Don't let the world overtake you, Daniel, it hurts so much." Her words were cut off by the sound of cannons exploding and rifle fire and musket fire.

"What the hell—?" The soldier turned toward the door where the officer had appeared.

"The Americans are landing!"

Both men ran out of the room and probably out of the building, leaving the prison door open.

"We have to get out of here, Daniel!" Aunt Belle grabbed one of Mother's arms. "Help me with your mother."

An explosion made my ears scream. I was hit in the back and the world disappeared.

Chapter 21
April 2013

▼

Daniel

What happened? Where am I? It was dark and I was in a hole, but there was light above me if I could reach it. I clawed myself out onto the pile of bricks and iron and wood that covered me, and I peered through smoke into a changed world. Where was Mother? Where was Aunt Belle? I saw Belle's dress peeking through the pile. My fingers were bleeding, but I kept pulling the debris off until I could see all of her. Her eyes were shut. I wiggled her chin back and forth. "Belle! Belle!" She opened her eyes.

"What happened?"

"Don't know. Have to find Mother. Are you all right?"

She struggled to a sitting position and wiped dust from her eyes and her hair. "I'm fine. Give me a minute and I'll help you."

There were more explosions and things were flying through the air, and there was so much smoke I could hardly see. On the side of the pile I found the pallet and blanket. "Mother! Mother!" I screamed and clawed away the pallet. Bleeding nails, running nose, blocked ears, stinging eyes didn't matter, I had to find Mother. I grabbed and threw aside things that were as heavy as I was. "Mother! Mother!"

It was all right, her head was there. "I'm here now, Mother." I pulled away the piece covering her body, but it wasn't there. Where was it? I didn't understand. Her head was there, but there was no body. I vomited and everything turned black.

"Daniel, Daniel, wake up! We have to get out of here!"

"Mother!" I screamed.

"I know, Daniel, I know, but we have to go now!"

Aunt Belle pulled me to my feet, and we staggered, along with others who were reeling through the smoke, over charcoaled bodies, stray arms and legless men; through screams of pain, explosions of muskets and rifles and cannons; through the stink of burning flesh; and through this horrible dream. *I must not trip. I must not think. I stare at nothing far away from here. If I blink I'll vomit.* Aunt Belle pulled me on.

"It looks like the British set the battery on fire to keep the Americans from getting it."

I didn't answer. I didn't care.

We sat at the shore and I cried hopeless, messy tears, and Aunt Belle held me. Maybe I slept.

"No!" Aunt Belle cried, shocking me erect. "The Isaac Brock's on fire! Poor Donald!"

No mother, no father, no ship to let us sail over water. "What are we going to do now, Aunt Belle?"

"I think we should stay here for the night and go to York in the morning and find Lieutenant Mackenzie and Dacana. I hope they're all right."

It was getting dark and cold. Wounded birds staggered along the shore, wings flapping. We lay down and hugged each other, trying to stop our shivering, but we couldn't sleep because the war was still screaming and we knew the explosions were messages of death.

In the morning, we followed the route taken by the American army along the shore road to York, stopping at the wharf where the Isaac Brock was being built, but all that was left of the dock were a few burned beams jutting out into the water, holding nothing, and all that was left of the ship were planks of wood tossed into a jam against the shore, rocked there by the waves of the great lake. The place looked like I felt.

"Belle!" Donald Bradley came running along the road we had just taken. He threw his arms around her. "By God, I'm glad to see you. I've been looking all over and feared the worst! Are you all right?"

"We're fine, Donald, but Daniel's mother was killed in the explosion."

He let go of Aunt Belle and crouched down next to me. There was nothing he could say that would help and he saw that, so he pulled me into his rough shirt and wrapped his arms around me. I couldn't feel, I didn't cry, I didn't talk, and I didn't hug back.

"What's the news of York? What's happened, Donald?"

"It was General Schaeff who had the Isaac Brock burned so it wouldn't fall into the hands of the Americans, and then he marched the army out of York and left the surrender to the militia. I've heard the Americans are furious that the army and our other ship escaped, and Bishop Strachan negotiated the surrender."

"That's somethin' I bet the bantam rooster would be good at!"

"You're right. When he saw the militia wasn't negotiating effectively, he stepped in. He couldn't save the stores or the public buildings, but private homes haven't been touched, which is a blessing."

"I hope Lieutenant Mackenzie laid low," Aunt Belle mumbled. "And I wonder if they went after Dacana's store. We'd best go and see."

There were flames in the distance! York was burning! Aunt Belle, Donald Bradley and I hurried along Front Street. The apothecary was burned to the ground and the back building too.

"All those medicines that could be used for the sick!" Aunt Belle cried.

"Where would Dacana go?" Donald Bradley wondered.

"Could be she's at my place," Aunt Belle said, "if she hasn't gone north to her husband. Let's go see."

It was like I was frozen, and everything was happening outside me. Aunt Belle's house was still standing, and Lieutenant Mackenzie was on the porch leaning his slender body against the railing, watching our approach.

We climbed the stairs, and Black Henri came out.

Aunt Belle stopped in her climb. "Are Dacana and Annie all right?"

"Dacana, she has a little burn, *mais elle est bien*. Annie, she was not hurt, that lady she is never hurt."

Lieutenant Mackenzie looked as though he wasn't sure what was going on. "I came because I was so worried about you, Daniel. It's good to see you're all right." But he didn't take his stare away from the street. "Bruno disappeared when the shooting started. I've looked everywhere." He pushed himself away from the railing and went down the stairs and along the path to where his horse was hitched. As he mounted, he said over his shoulder, "I'm going to look a little more."

"Be careful!" Aunt Belle called to his back.

"Dat man," Black Henri said, "he been smacked by de shock. He don't know what he doing."

Inside, Dacana was sitting on the couch, and Annie was putting compresses on her leg.

Aunt Belle went over to them. "I'm sure glad you're both all right, and I'm so damned sorry you've lost the apothecary!" She leaned over and looked at Dacana's leg. "That's a hell of a burn! What happened?"

"I needed to save our medicine book. It has all the mixtures written in it, and without it I'd have a terrible time starting up again."

Aunt Belle leaned over and gave her a hug. "That's why I love you, Dacana. All of York's government buildings have been burned, all the stores have been emptied, you've lost two big buildings and you already talk about starting over."

Mrs. Dacana Cameron smiled. "There is no logic to moaning over ashes, and goodness knows we've been lucky in the conditions of our surrender. The militia has been released, private homes have been left standing and the American soldiers have not been too violent. I understand they're already rounding up their soldiers in preparation for departure."

I was slouched in a big chair in the corner in the darkest part of the room. Dacana's last sentence made Aunt Belle look nervously over at me and say quietly, "We were at the fort when it was bombed by cannons and awful firepower that killed many people. Daniel's mother was one of them." As she talked she came to me, sat on the arm of my chair and took my hand in both of hers.

Her words silenced the room. Black Henri and Annie came too, and Annie kissed and hugged me while Black Henri just stood in front of me shaking his head with sadness pasted all over his face.

Dacana lowered her burned leg to the floor and limped across the room. Black Henri put a chair in front of me for the big lady to sit down. She took my hand from Aunt Belle. "We all know how much you loved her, Daniel, but even your unselfish love would not have saved her from her desperate flailing through life. You have to believe she's relieved of suffering and all the other horrors her mind threw at her."

I guess I knew that, but it was horrible! Even though I was frozen inside by the desperate loss of my mother, relief tweaked at the edge of my brain, which was certainly not unselfish love, and it made me feel miserable. *Please, God, let her have died without pain.* I grabbed my head to try to erase the image of my mother's head in a pile of rubble. I didn't want to look at anyone, I just wanted to be alone, which they seemed to sense because one by one they returned to the centre of the room and resumed their conversation.

Donald Bradley came in from the porch with Lieutenant Mackenzie.

"Did you find the dog?" Annie asked.

"No, I don't know where he could have gone. I hope he wasn't hurt in the fighting!" He came over to me in the corner. "Mr. Bradley and I went back to the fort, Daniel, and there was nothing left. The buildings and all that was in them were burned to the ground. There was no sign of your mother's body, but we brought you some ashes from the site thinking perhaps you could bury them in your mother's memory." He handed me a finely made wooden box about a foot square.

I took the box and put it beside me on the chair. "Thank you, Lieutenant," I whispered, and I wiped my hand across the smooth surface of the box, which made me look up at Mr. Donald Bradley. "Did you make this?"

He nodded his head. "I made it a long time ago, but there was never a good purpose for it. Now there is."

Kindness can sure choke up a kid.

"I know the perfect place to bury those ashes," Dacana said. "Under a magic tree that's on our property up in the North Country. It would be a good idea to get out of York for a while anyway, and we could all go: There's room in my home for everyone. As soon as I can walk we could leave. What do you think, Belle?"

"Yes, it's a good idea."

Burying a box of ashes that came from a killing field should seem unimportant, but somehow it felt right. I guessed that maybe ceremony put a period after the word *misery* and began a new sentence with the word *memory*. How did Donald Bradley and Lieutenant Mackenzie know this?

The noise of footsteps pounding up the stairs and across the porch stopped conversation. Black Henri opened the door to that busy clergyman, who looked unnaturally pale in his all-black outfit.

"Bishop Strachan," Aunt Belle said. "Your first-ever visit to my house! War sure does destroy the order of things, doesn't it? Come in. Would you like some tea?"

"No, I'm here to speak to Mrs. Cameron."

Dacana said, "Please come and sit over here, Bishop Strachan. I'm afraid I'm a little incapacitated."

He sidled past Aunt Belle without looking her in the eye and hurried over to Dacana's sofa. "I need medicines for the injured!" He sounded like a general ordering a common soldier.

"I'm sorry, Reverend, we lost almost everything in the fire, but we did manage to save some dried herbs, and Annie and Black Henri are going to work with a mortar and pestle right away."

"What can I do to hurry it along?"

"We'll need oil to bind the herbs."

"I'll see what I can do, but I'm afraid we'll not find anything in York. They took everything." He collapsed in the chair beside Dacana and looked so upset that I figured he was probably a good person but with a personality that would make even a dog growl. "The soldiers are in rags; half are suffering from dysentery and many from war wounds. I'm at my wits' end as to how to help them."

"From what I've heard, you've done a lot already," Dacana said. "They say it was you who negotiated the surrender."

"If the army had stayed to fight, we might not have been forced to surrender!" I could tell he was angry, because his brogue was getting thicker. "I can't believe the actions of Major General Schaeffe! First, he should have attacked the Americans as they were landing—even *I* know that it's a principle of war that an amphibious landing should be attacked at the shore before troops have a chance to form, but he dallied too long letting the Americans disembark without interference and then he decided to burn the batteries and the Isaac Brock and remove his troops from the area rather than fight. Now the Americans have confiscated all the materials for building ships, and that means they're bound to win the battle of the lakes. It was the act of a coward!" He slammed his hand down on the edge of the chair.

"Perhaps he thought he didn't have enough men to fight the invaders," Lieutenant Mackenzie said quietly.

"Not enough? He had 300 regulars, just as many Indians, and the militia as well! No, I tell you, his defensive attitude to warfare will ruin the country!"

Silence reigned. I figured they all understood there was no value in arguing with the Reverend Bishop Strachan, 'cause he knew himself to be right and figured he had God on his side of an opinion.

"As far as medicines," Dacana said, changing the subject, "I think the Indians would be your best source. They have many remedies available and I'm sure would be willing to help."

Bishop Strachan got to his feet. "I'll try anything to assuage the screams of pain that pour out of the hospital tent."

He left some of his energy and power floating in the room when he went out the front door. We sat enveloped in it.

"Well!" Aunt Belle said. "Shows the man is desperate to help if he'll come to *my* home."

If I'd had the energy, I'd ask for an explanation, but I was too tired and too sad.

"And into a room full o' Catholics. He'll have to fall on his knees over that," Annie laughed.

"He's a strange person and fast becoming the most powerful man in York," Dacana added. "The citizens won't forget the strength he's shown in the last few days, but I'm wary of the man. He is too opinionated, and he's ingraining those opinions into the young men he teaches in his Anglican schools."

"I think he believes his words have a special shine to them," Aunt Belle added. "When used on me, they're meant to skewer, and I can't deny they hit home."

"I'm told that from the pulpit, his words do shine, but when he preaches hatred of the Americans—claiming them to be degenerate and rapacious— he is fomenting hate, which helps no one, and his prejudice runs against other religions as well." Dacana moved to make herself more comfortable.

How could they be talking about dumb Bishop Strachan or anything else when my mother was dead, her head separated from her neck, her arms and her legs and her musical body in pieces buried under stinking burned rubble? Why didn't they stop nattering? I plugged my ears, pulled my knees up to my chest and tried to rock the horror out.

Chapter 22
May 1813

▼

Daniel

Dacana's leg had not healed, so we weren't able to go north yet, and Aunt Belle's house was overflowing. She had three bedrooms: Lieutenant Mackenzie and Mr. Bradley shared one, Annie and Dacana another, Black Henri slept outside under an overturned canoe and I shared Aunt Belle's bed, where she hugged me when I cried, left me alone when I didn't want to talk and listened when I did. "I love you, Belle, and I love the Wickams, and Drummer and Lieutenant Mackenzie, but it's not the same as loving Mother and Papa. With blood love, you're kinda helpless."

She rubbed her cheek on my forehead. "We have some of the same blood."

"That's right!"

"And I don't have a choice about lovin' you."

I snuggled into her, put my arms around her big waist and squeezed like a desperate puppy.

Lieutenant Mackenzie returned from another search for Bruno with a black eye and a broken arm. We all knew something must have happened because he was, as Drummer called it, "light on his feet," and some ruffians decided to fix him. It was sad to watch him stand on the porch all day long as though he expected the dog to come marching up the stairs any minute. I suspected the beating he had received shook him a whole lot and since he didn't want to talk about it, he poured all his agonies into worries over the lost Bruno. Everyone was gentle with him, and Aunt Belle said he'd be better soon, but it was sad to watch.

It was difficult to purchase food in York, so Black Henri had traps set up in the woods to the east and from them brought us back meat. Donald Bradley and I caught fish in the streams that ran off the big river. I caught the biggest pickerel of all, and it almost fed the whole group for one entire meal. Donald Bradley's smaller fish had to be included, but it was mostly mine! Annie was an expert when it came to all the wild herbs that were beginning to pop up, and she knew how to mix them into excellent sauces, which sure made the food taste delicious. Of course, my pickerel only needed to be fried in a little lard, 'cause it was so tender. They all said it was the best fish they'd ever eaten.

Major Cameron, Dacana's husband, arrived from the North Country. He was a very large man, which was good considering the height of Dacana, and he was quiet in a strong man's way that made me feel peaceful, but since he spent most of his short visit in the bedroom with Dacana, I couldn't say I knew him very well. What I saw, I liked: he lifted heavy things for Annie, questioned Black Henri about his hunting and trapping, joked with Aunt Belle, conversed with me as though I was already a man and, for some reason I didn't understand, talked about Indian medicine with Lieutenant Mackenzie, who appeared surprisingly interested. Major Cameron's kilt looked good on his large body, and the muscles in his big arms seemed to balance him out.

The women were all in the house and Black Henri had taken Lieutenant Mackenzie and Donald Bradley in his canoe to fish on the big lake. I was sitting with Major Cameron on the settee on the porch.

"Well, lad, it looks like we're not needed around here, what do you think?"

"I don't mind, sir. I like looking at the leaf-buds on the trees; they're kind of like a halo of promise, 'cause we know that no matter what happens, the green always returns and the world goes on."

With his hand draped over the back of the settee, he stared out at the trees with me. "Dacana tells me you've had a nasty war." He reached down and gently massaged my shoulders with his long fingers.

"My mother and father were both killed. Now the only person with my blood is Belle. If anything happens to her, my leaf will fall off the tree before it opens."

"Nothing will happen to Belle. She's a woman with sinews, and now she has you to see through to the future."

"I bet she didn't expect to be strapped with a kid when she retired from the elastic business."

I seemed to have confused him. His silence held a question that he didn't appear to want to ask. "Elastic business?"

"Yes, giving men medicine to put more elastic in the thing between their legs. Didn't you know that was her job?"

He didn't answer for so long I looked up at his face, and he was biting his upper lip as though he was trying not to laugh and to figure out what to say. All of a sudden stars went off, and I understood the "elastic business," Bishop Strachan's dislike of Aunt Belle, and the man with the twisted hat who wanted her to come out of retirement. My mouth formed a silent *Oh!* I slouched back in the chair, crossed my arms and chewed on my new knowledge, searching for a bad feeling that might change my opinion of Aunt Belle. I could find nothing: She was good and strong and funny, and she was my blood, and her job made people happy, so it was all right, I could still go on loving her. I sat forward and changed the subject so that Major Cameron could escape embarrassment and I could too. "Your turn at war is coming now?"

"That's right, lad. I'm an officer in the militia, and we've been ordered to the Niagara Peninsula. I leave tomorrow."

There was already a battle going on down there. Even though we were 40 miles from the west end of the lake, we could hear the boom of cannons. "It takes a lot of courage to march into the middle of a battle."

"I'm told you've been quite courageous yourself."

"Oh no, sir. Courage is when you know what you're getting into and still march forward, I was maybe a little bit brave, which is more idiotic, 'cause it's when you forge ahead because you're too stupid to realize what's waiting for you."

"You don't give yourself enough credit, young Daniel."

Annie and Aunt Belle prepared a special dinner, which we ate at a table on the front porch and tried to drag out, knowing that when we finished, Major Cameron had to go. All of us had seen more war than he had, and we knew that he'd return with secret memories that would change him forever. It was hard to smile, but we all tried to ignore the shadows lurking in the napkins and send him off with love and a song.

Dacana was very brave as she watched him close the gate and give a final wave.

I stood beside her and watched her decent, upright husband leave. "I'm sorry he has to go."

Leaning over the porch rail with her burned leg extended, she looked over her shoulder at me. "We've been given no choice, Daniel, no alternatives, and I hate what we must do preserve our nation." She put her arm on Black Henri's shoulder and hopped back to a chair.

Major Cameron had been gone for a week. We were all trying to keep busy. Lieutenant Mackenzie spent his days wandering around York looking for Bruno. His black eye had turned yellow with streaks of blue, his arm was still in a sling, and his preoccupation over the dog had stepped across the line that defined what was normal. Annie was busy grinding the dried herbs to make medicines, Black Henri went off every morning to check his traps and do some fishing, Aunt Belle ran the household with me a willing errand boy, and Dacana sat on the porch with her leg up pretending not to worry, but I saw her flinch at the sight or sound of anything unusual—like the moment Bishop Strachan and another man appeared in front of the gate driving a horse-drawn, high-sided wagon that seemed to have a bundle of blankets in the back.

As Bishop Strachan barrelled through the gate looking like a black bolt of bad news, the other man, a uniformed soldier, climbed in the back and slid slowly out carrying a bundle of blankets. A dog jumped out after him. I jumped up. "It's Bruno!" I ran down the stairs to hug Bruno but was stopped by the realization that the bundle the man was carrying was a blanket wrapped around a person. It was Drummer, and something had happened to him!

"Belle!" Dacana called. She could see there was something wrong, and she couldn't get down the stairs to help.

Bruno and I followed the procession. Aunt Belle came out with a towel over her shoulder and immediately saw what was happening. She removed the cushions from the back of the wicker settee, and the soldier placed Drummer down gently. My friend moaned in pain.

"Is he all right?" I asked, afraid of what the answer might be. "What's happened to him?"

"I'm the army surgeon." He opened the blanket to show us that Drummer's right leg below the knee was gone: It was a bandaged stump.

"There was no other solution," the doctor said. "If I hadn't amputated, he would have died, and he's not out of danger yet. There's still a chance of infection." While he was talking, he gestured to Aunt Belle for a pillow to put under Drummer's head and another for under the stump. "He's been only semi-conscious but he kept muttering, 'Belle Fontaine in York, Belle Fontaine in York,' so I investigated and Bishop Strachan told me there really was a 'Belle Fontaine in York'! I decided to bring him here where he has more chance of survival than in a medical tent where infections are rampant."

"How did he know my name?" Aunt Belle wondered.

"I told him." I knelt down beside Drummer. "This is my friend Drummer Jakes, and I told him he'd find me with you." We were all whispering even though Drummer's eyes were open.

"God, Daniel! It feels like my leg is sittin' in a fire!"

"Where? Which leg?"

"The ghost leg, the one that's gone!" He moaned and twisted with pain.

"Annie, can you brew the boy some special tea?" Dacana asked Annie, who had joined us on the porch.

"Right away." She turned back into the house.

"They'll get you better, Drummer," I told him. "These women know more about medicines than even the doctors."

"I sure hope they can get rid of the pain. I don't think I can stand it much longer." He tensed his body, tossed his head and grimaced.

"They will. They will." It hurt me to watch the pain chew away at my friend. I wished I could do something.

Aunt Belle brought water and a cloth to cool his head, the back of his neck and the crooks of his arms. "We'll get you better, young Drummer, don't you fear." Her soothing voice seemed to calm his tossing.

Drummer was the only friend of my age I had. He had to get better. I needed him, and I think he needed me. I would do all I could to get him on his feet . . . no, I guessed I'd have to say *foot* from now on.

Annie brought out the tea and Aunt Belle lifted Drummer's head to help him sip it.

"What is in your tea?" the doctor asked.

Without turning from her task, Annie said, "Alfalfa leaves, chamomile leaves, ginger root and crushed willow bark."

"We need that and other herbs for the soldiers," Bishop Strachan insisted.

"We're working on it," Annie answered. "We'll get it to you as soon as possible."

"The wound must be cleaned every day and the dressing changed," the surgeon said.

"We'll take care of him, doctor," Aunt Belle assured the man without looking up from her ministrations.

Finally the tea took effect, and Drummer's face collapsed for the moment. Donald Bradley lifted him gently and carried him into the bedroom he shared with Lieutenant Mackenzie. Bruno followed.

The doctor flopped down in a chair looking exhausted. "I should get back," he said without conviction.

"You just sit a minute, and I'll bring you some tea," Annie ordered. "You'll be no good at the hospital if you don't lift your feet for a short time." She shoved a stool under his legs. "Lift now!"

He smiled at me. "Does she always act like the commander in chief?"

"You'd best do what she says," I told him. "It's not a good idea to disagree with her."

He lifted his eyebrow and then looked at Annie, who stood with her hands on her hips, making him shake his head, smile and lift his feet onto the stool.

"That's right! Now I'll get tea."

We were all quiet for a minute. I was thinking about Drummer, and this poor man was probably thinking about the hundred others he had to doctor. I asked him, "How did Bruno find you?"

"I can't tell you how he knew about the boy, but the damned animal has been whining around the medical tent for days. They've thrown stones to try to get him out of there, as his squeals were very disturbing for the patients, but he always snuck back. Yesterday we found him at the foot of Drummer's bed. The damned dog had dug his way under the tent!"

"Lieutenant Mackenzie will be pleased," Dacana said.

I hoped so.

Now that Drummer was asleep in the bedroom, they began to talk about the war.

"The Niagara Peninsula has fallen to the Americans! All is lost!" Bishop Strachan paced the porch.

"Tell us." Dacana's voice had fallen into the back of her throat.

"Let him tell you," Strachan said, gesturing at the doctor with his head. "He was there."

"For goodness sake, Bishop, I thought I was to relax for a moment." The surgeon threw his head against the back of his chair.

"Please tell us," Dacana croaked.

He shut his eyes but I could see they were moving beneath the lids. "The Americans landed in Crookstown, protected by the guns from their ships, and the British met them at the shore. The two lines were no more than 15 feet apart, firing at each other at point-blank range." The surgeon shook his head. "I've never witnessed such devastating carnage. The British were forced to retreat, leaving many dead and even more maimed. It was then that the drummer was shot."

"Losing Niagara and Fort George means we've lost the war!" Bishop Strachan moaned.

"Not necessarily," the surgeon said. "The British blew up the magazine before retreating along the Queenston Road, and damn me if they didn't march away in perfect formation. For some reason, the Americans chose not to pursue them." He wiped his hand over his tired eyes. "No, I believe we still have a chance."

"Do you know anything of the York volunteers? Were they in the battle?" Dacana's question was afraid of an answer.

"They were."

Dacana pushed herself to her feet and limped to the other end of the veranda away from the gathering. I went, put my arms around her from behind, rested my cheek against her large back and said, "He'll be back and we'll all go north together, away from the war."

Lieutenant Mackenzie took over the dressing of Drummer's leg. He said the incision looked healthy, but the stump was still swollen. Caring for Drummer was a cure for the Lieutenant who took to doctoring so easily I believed he had missed his calling. He moved from Drummer to Annie, whom he questioned continually about all the medicines she was making.

I was out on the porch helping Donald Bradley repair some of the window shutters so we'd be able to close them when we went north.

Lieutenant Mackenzie came out with a cup of tea and plunked himself down in the wicker chair. "Annie has ousted me. She insists I'm sucking so much information out of her that she feels like she's becoming a dried-up old prune!"

"Git out of the way, Bruno!" Drummer hopped out on the porch on crutches, almost tripping on Bruno, who wouldn't get out from underfoot.

"Come here, Bruno." Mackenzie snapped his finger at the dog. "Give the boy a chance to sit down." Drummer collapsed on the wicker couch, and the

Lieutenant helped him lift his legs up and put a pillow behind his back. "The leg looks good, but it's still swollen."

Donald Bradley stopped hammering, took the nails out of his mouth and said, "When the swelling goes down, I'll make you a leg, and then you'll be able to get around better."

"What happens when I grow?"

"I'll make you another if you're still around."

"What about you? Will you still be around?"

Donald Bradley smiled a secret smile. "I suspect so."

"If I could get rid of this ghost pain, I might get me some sleep, which would help a whole lot."

"I have an idea!" I ran into the bedroom, fished around in the drawer Aunt Belle had given me and pulled out my mirror, which I took out and gave to Drummer. "Maybe this will help."

With a questioning frown on his face Drummer took the mirror. "How?"

"Maybe if you shine it on your stump and your brain sees that there is nothing below it, it won't make pain."

Drummer looked unsure. "I guess I could try; can't hurt." He aimed the mirror at the ghost leg. "I remember this mirror. You used to pull it out all the time. How'd it get cracked?"

"I had it in my pocket and fell on it." There was no sense in telling him I was knocked out while watching the battle at Queenston. He was there and wouldn't want to talk about it.

Donald Bradley came and sat down with us, and we all watched Drummer play the mirror over his stump.

The late June sun was shining; the trees stood straight and tall, showing off their new leaves with flutters in the summer breeze. A letter had arrived from Major Cameron telling us that the Niagara Peninsula was once more in British hands and that he would be home in a week.

"Major Cameron should be back any day," I said. "It looks like we'll be going north soon."

"How're we getting' there?" Drummer asked.

"Black Henri has found two North West Company canoes and some of his friends to paddle them. Dacana will rent them for the day."

Lieutenant Mackenzie looked over at Drummer Jakes. "Will we all fit in two canoes? This boy will take a lot of space."

Drummer sat up with the mirror still in his hand. "Don't worry about me." He pointed to his stump. "This doesn't take any room, and I can tuck up my good leg." He shook his head and grimaced away his pain. "You gotta stop thinking of me as a patient. I'll be fine."

CHAPTER 23
AUGUST 1813

▼

Matthew Elliott

There she was: my home! She sat quietly on a rise overlookin' the river, untouched by the battles I'd seen, and the sight of her loosened the ties that had bin holdin' me together fer the last few months. The Indians pulled the large canoe up to my dock and I was helped out, which I feared was necessary. The lawn leading up to the house seemed longer than ever. Finally I was in the kitchen, past the servants who greeted me and into the front of the house, where I followed the beautiful sound of an innocent child's laughter.

Boy was lying on the floor tossing the toddler in the air, and my Sarah was smiling at him from her chair where she was bouncing the babe.

I leaned against the doorjamb and watched, remembering myself tossing Alexander with Love beside me feeding Matthew and the most damned beautiful sensation of flawless happiness that accompanied it. It made me jealous of the sight I was beholdin'. It took a minute fer them to see me.

"Matthew!" My Sarah put down the babe and ran into my arms. "I'm so glad you're back. I've been worried about you."

Boy got up from the floor and stood there with the toddler on his hip. "Welcome home."

No touchin' from that one.

Sarah stood back to absorb the whole of me. "You're exhausted, my dear! Here, come and sit down, and I'll get rid of the children and bring you some tea." She steered me to the sofa, pushed me down and enveloped me with a hug. "From the looks of you, I do believe I'll not have to insist that you stay at home with me, at least for a while."

She was not wrong. I couldn't have left even if I'd wanted to.

"I'll take the children away and be right back." She kissed me again. "It's good to have you home, Matthew."

"I'll help you," Boy said and followed her out with the toddler on his hip.

"Thank you, dear," Sarah said over her shoulder to my son.

So Boy was "dear" now. 'Course he should have a special name in the family; it showed how much he was loved. It shouldn't have scratched my soul, but it did a little.

Boy came back and sat in the chair across from me. "You've been gone since the beginning of May. Tell me what's happened, Da."

I let my head drop back. "Nothing good, my boy." Between yawns, I told him of Procter's failed siege on Fort Meigs. "That goddamned William Henry Harrison is a wily son-of-a-bitch and an impressive soldier. Makes our man look pathetic."

It took more energy than I could muster to tell him the whole story. I closed my eyes, pretendin' to fall asleep. There was no need to share the horror of what had followed, but I couldn't get it out of my mind. Tecumseh and I should'a bin there! 'Twas our fault the captured prisoners were forced to run the gauntlet. If we'd bin there, 'twould never have happened. I heard Boy leave the room and opened my eyes. How could a man return to the delights of daily life when he was burdened with vile memories?

We were eatin' dinner in the ante-kitchen, where Sarah knew I felt more comfortable, but I didn't converse, just shovelled food and relived the last months, becoming more and more furious as I thought about them.

After spendin' two months roundin' up Indians who had spread out all over the country, Tecumseh and I arrived at Amherstburg with about 600 Indians.

Tecumseh and I reported immediately to "Major General Procter," who carried his new title with an offensive tone of voice that told us muck-savages that he was the master of our universe.

"Without Tecumseh, we'd never have convinced so many to return," I told him, hoping the Shawnee warrior would receive some recognition.

"Good," was all he said to that, as though our two months of scrambling were nothing more than a notation on his grand plan.

Tecumseh stood forward. "I will not be able to keep the tribes together if we don't do battle. We must go up the Maumee and attack Fort Stevenson."

Procter didn't like being told what to do. "The Americans have almost finished constructing a new fleet of ships on Lake Erie, and our ships are not close to being finished. We have to strike their shipyard before the Yankees win the lake."

"First, Fort Stevenson," Tecumseh insisted. "No Fort Stevenson, no warriors."

Procter rapped his knuckles on the table and considered the threat. "All right, take your Indians, and I'll send my troops to join you."

The boat and the horse did nothin' for my old bones, but we arrived at the fort, set up camp and waited for Procter. And waited and waited.

Tecumseh was in a furor. "The Long Knives know we are going to attack. Every day we wait gives them more time to prepare their defences."

'Twas a week before Procter arrived with 500 regulars. "We'll get this done as fast as possible. I've no intention of conducting a siege. Harrison is too close and would come to their aid."

"We must attack now," Tecumseh insisted.

The two men were opposing magnets. They had a savage hate for each other. And there I was translatin' the words. Poison floated in the air.

Procter was not to be told how to do battle. "First our artillery and gunboats will shell the fort to weaken the walls, and then we'll attack."

Tecumseh didn't argue. "Give us scaling ladders to use when we attack."

The look on Procter's face did not need words. There were no scaling ladders. Tecumseh slapped his sides, turned in a circle with disgust and stomped off.

The bombardment continued on and on. Cannon booms, artillery screeches, and rat-a-tat-tats of bullets flying, but with little effect. The walls were holding fast. I crouched with Tecumseh and awaited the order to attack, and when it came 700 Indians and 500 soldiers moved forward into total silence. No one was shooting from the fort. 'Twas frightening. Then a hundred yards out, they opened fire with cannons and guns, mowing down hundreds of Indians and soldiers.

Procter had the bugler call a retreat.

Away from the fort, he announced, "This is hopeless. I refuse to put any more men in danger. We will withdraw to the ships tonight."

I stayed with Tecumseh and after dark joined the Indians in retrieving the bodies of their comrades. 'Tis a horrible undertaking to drag young, muscular bodies slippery with blood through the wet mud of a battlefield. The moon was bright, and the Americans could have shot at us, but they left us to our morbid chore, which we achieved in dead silence.

An Indian spy who had been in the fort during the battle later told us there were only a hundred soldiers in the fort and a 21-year-old officer leading them.

'Twas a defeat Procter would not easily live down

I could see from his carriage that even Tecumseh was giving up hope, although knowin' him, he would fight on till the bitter end. I s'posed we all would.

I was in bed with Sarah, too damned tired to do anything but talk, and talk we had to. "You'd best start loading the wagons, my Sarah. I've not much hope that things are going to get better."

"I'll start in the morning and send the babes ahead with the servants."

"No, you go too. Life here is only goin' to get worse."

"I'll not go without you, Matthew Elliott!"

I pulled her into my arms. "'Twould be worse for me to have you stay, my Sarah, 'cause I'd be so damned worried about you all the time I wouldn't be able to function."

"You'll not be able to function without me, I'm sure. No, I'm staying no matter what you say."

I was too tired to argue and anyway, deep down, I wanted her with me. I shut my eyes, hopin' to fall asleep.

"If you insist on staying, we could send Boy with the babes."

Did I sleep and was wakened or had I not gone off yet when Sarah said, "Are you afraid to die, Matthew?"

"'Spect I am," I mumbled.

"I suppose I am too."

Sarah's Diary

Boy followed me out of the room and pushed me into the closet in the hall and with his free hand pulled me to him and kissed me hard. There we were, with a child on his hip and a babe in my arms, forgetting ourselves.

Matthew suggested Boy take the babes away. Is he suspicious? Maybe it would be good. I hate myself.

Matthew is drained; he cries in his sleep. He won't tell me what he's witnessed, but I imagine it was horrible.

I understand, perhaps more than he, that deep down he knows he has soiled his soul for the sake of his Indians and for Canada, and his deeds have deprived him of any escape from feelings of guilt and responsibility. He has had to put aside his humanity and attend to the rules of force, which separate men from the laws of moral life.

The poor man, how will he live with it all?

CHAPTER 24
AUGUST 1813

▼

Daniel

Before we got to the canoes, we had to travel 33 miles up Yonge Street in two wagons. Major Cameron had the women in the first wagon and the men were in the other one with Black Henri in the driver's seat and Donald Bradley beside him. Lieutenant Mackenzie and I were in the back with Drummer, who was feeling better

"I never thought that danged mirror would do any good, but it works!" He took it out of his pocket and tilted it so that he could see below the stump. "When I see there's no leg there, I don't feel pain. Yer real smart to have thought of it, Daniel!"

"I figured a mirror threw a person back at himself. It helped me a whole lot, but I wasn't sure it'd help you though. I'm really glad it did." I kinda missed the mirror, but I guessed that made it an even better present.

"How'd it help you?" Drummer asked.

"My friend Joseph said the reflection was only an echo without feelings, but I think it's like looking through a window at myself and seeing the truth I don't want to face."

Drummer's eyes hadn't left me, and he nodded his head. A huge bump in the road made us forget about mirrors.

"Ow-w-w-w!" Drummer held his stump in the air to keep it from banging.

"One of these days, they'll lay something smoother than side-by-side logs, but for now these corduroy roads will have to suffice." Lieutenant Mackenzie tucked a blanket under Drummer's stump to protect it from the bumps.

"How much farther to the canoes?" I asked

"Not long now."

"Do you think war will follow us?"

Lieutenant Mackenzie looked up from attending to Drummer. "I hope not. I believe we're going far enough north to escape it."

Drummer Jakes banged the side of the canoe. "Whoo-ee. Clean air, good food and sleep! D'ya think it's possible?"

"I'm hoping so," I answered, "and I'm really excited to see this magic tree Dacana's talking about. She says the Indians have ceremonies around it and that it's probably the biggest sugar maple in the whole country!"

Drummer leaned back on his elbows. "What's magic about it? Will it grow me a new leg?"

Lieutenant Mackenzie shook his head and laughed. "No, but it might help you accept that you'll have a good life with a wooden leg."

"I know that already. 'Specially when I have an expert carpenter ta fashion the wooden leg." He turned his head to the seat in front. "Isn't that right, Mr. Bradley?"

Laughing, Mr. Bradley looked back at us. "Right you are, my boy."

"Dat tree, it has de magic!" Black Henri added to our conversation. "If you 'ave a bad worry dat grows inside you or a bad dream dat keeps you awake in de night, or if you cannot throw away de sadness, all you got to do is sleep under dat tree, and de tree flutters its leaves and calls to de wind to blow away your troubles, and you wake in de morning and all your worries, dey have floated away. I know dis to be true. Dacana knows dis to be true, and de Indians know it too."

His description silenced us. The others were probably, like me, thinking how wonderful it would be to be cleansed of memories that scratched and scraped deep in our souls. Could the tree really help us?

At Holland's Landing, the voyageurs had two large and one small canoe awaiting us. The big canoes would easily hold all of us, but Dacana pushed the small canoe into the water herself, saying, "I'll go ahead and get things ready." She stood in the front of the canoe and paddled away, swooping her arms through each great stroke with such ease she flew across the water.

Major Cameron stared after his wife. "Amazing!" he said with wonder in his voice. "The first time I saw her, she was paddling through heavy waves, screaming at me and my men to put down the axes with which we were about to chop down her sugar maple. I'll never forget the sight!"

"Why were you going to chop it down?" I asked as we settled into the two canoes.

"I was sent from Scotland to clear the land bought by a rich landowner and mistakenly thought the sugar maple was on his property, which it wasn't. Dacana owned the small cabin and an acre around the tree. It was lucky she arrived in time, because I think she might have turned the axe on me if I'd cut down the tree!"

"Is that where we're goin'?" Drummer asked. "Will all of us fit in the cabin?"

Major Cameron laughed. "No, Dacana offered the absent landowner a lot of money for his 800 acres, so we own it all. I'm in charge of the farming and the building while Dacana runs the apothecary in York."

"Where did Dacana get the money?" I asked.

"Her father, Jean-Luc Brossard, was a partner in the North West Company and left her a substantial sum, with which she bought this property, more property along the water in York and the land on which to build the apothecary."

"She must be rich!" Drummer exclaimed.

"Land rich, money poor, but perhaps someday the investment will pay off." Major Cameron looked over the two canoes. Everybody was settled in, and he nodded to the voyageurs to set off.

The water was so clear I could see the rippled sand on the bottom and the fish that swam under the canoe. There were huge cedar trees bordering the lake, which seemed to be quite shallow for some distance from the shore. Indians stood in the shallows with spears, especially where the small rivers ran into the lake, and when we passed shoals there were a number of canoes fishing with nets.

Gliding along on silk-smooth water in air so clean it tingled, I knew this place could never have been burdened with the black fumes of war.

I was sharing my canoe with Annie, Drummer, Aunt Belle and Black Henri, who was paddling in the back. There was one voyageur in the front and two in the middle. Aunt Belle was grunting and twisting a bit. "Are you all right, Aunt Belle?"

"I'm fine, Daniel."

It was like her not to complain, but I could see her bulk did not sit easily on the floor of a canoe. She was directly in front of me, and I put my hand on her shoulder. "It sure is peaceful here, isn't it?"

She took my hand and kissed it and then she put it back on her shoulder without releasing it. It felt good. "We're in luck with the weather,"

Annie was talking to the voyageurs in French.

I was sitting in the back almost on top of Black Henri. "What's Annie talking about?"

"She is asking de man about her husband, Emil. He was a voyageur, too, but he died in de north. She has a son, Louie, and soon he will meet her at de farm."

"I didn't know Annie was ever married!"

"*Oui*! For *beaucoup des années*! Louie, her son, is *plus o moins* the same age as Dacana, and he is a voyageur *tambien*. We were all together in de North Country, and dat Annie, she has many tales to tell."

"You must have too."

"*Oui,* but Annie, she tell dem better."

We'd been paddling for a long time. "When will we get there, Black Henri?"

"*Bientot,* soon! Dis lake, she is a big one."

We all fell into silent reflections lulled by the rhythm of the paddles—dip and pull, dip and pull. The voyageurs treated the water like it was precious and sliced their paddle blades into its silk with as little disturbance as possible. Aunt Belle searched for my hand and gave it another squeeze. I squeezed back and shook my head to erase the memory of Mother's *I-love-you* squeezes. Could it be that if I slept under the sugar maple, I'd be able to get rid of the tears that ached in my chest?

"There it is!" Drummer yelled. "D'ya see it?"

On a point that jutted out into the water, the giant tree sat quiet and confident, like it was the mistress of the lake.

"De Indians, dey believe dat de history of de people from de very beginning, it flows in her sap."

Close to shore, we had to get out of the canoes because the water was shallow, and with our weight they would scrape on the bottom.

"You stay in, Drummer," Lieutenant Mackenzie said.

"Not on yer life!" my friend answered. "I have my crutches, and even if I fall it won't hurt."

Indians on the shore helped to pull in the canoes. They had horses waiting for us too, but we all wanted to visit the sugar maple first.

"Let's join hands and see if we can surround it!" I cried, running ahead of them all. We formed a circle around the tree, and six of us joining hands didn't even make it!

Annie laughed. "Every time someone new comes, we've got to do this again. Seems to me it makes the tree real happy to be so appreciated!"

"Can Drummer and I sleep under it tonight?" I asked.

"We'll see," Aunt Belle answered. "Let's get settled first."

There was a dirt path leading away from the tree into the interior, and Dacana appeared with a wagon into which we piled our belongings. Because there weren't enough horses, a number of us climbed into the back too.

The path led to a wider lane, which was bordered by fields, some of which had corn growing between the stumps of what must have been very large trees, and in better-cleared fields there was wheat. Around a curve, we arrived at a clearing that had a number of log buildings. The biggest was long and low and had bright flowers tickling its base. Behind this building were three log cabins, a well with a pump, a cooking pit and some sheep that were keeping the grass short and fertilizing it too!

Drummer and I were in the men's cabin with Lieutenant Mackenzie and Donald Bradley. Aunt Belle and Annie shared the women's cabin, and the third cabin was for the Indian help. Dacana and Major Cameron had a room in the big house, and Black Henri preferred to sleep outdoors.

We dumped our things, washed our hands and faces at the pump and went to the big house.

The main room was furnished with homemade furniture that held cushions covered in hide and surrounded a big, low table with legs made of logs. There were antlers on the wall above a shelf where books were lined up. I wondered where all the boots and coats and things were. They must have had a special room for them, which left this room feeling unusually clean and organized. I was torn between investigating the books and asking about the sugar maple.

"Kin we sleep under the sugar maple tonight?" Drummer made the choice for me.

"It's a good night for it. No wind and a full moon," Dacana replied. "But first you must eat something."

We could hardly get our food down, we were so excited about our night out under the branches of the great tree. Black Henri made us beds of pine boughs, covered them with hide and left us bearskin blankets in case it turned cold.

We lay side by side and stared through the gentle curves of the sugar maple's branches at the clear sky where stars twinkled and boasted that we were not important enough to understand their secrets.

"Kinda makes ya think of God, don't it?" Drummer had his hands behind his head.

"Yup, I wonder what's up there."

"Don't know, but I sure as hell don't believe there are angel ladies with wings and God sittin' on a throne directin' things."

"What do you think happens when we die?"

"Don't know that neither, but I'm sure somethin' must happen. I can't believe we just disintegrate into nothin'."

"Why not?"

Drummer turned on his side facing me, picked at a piece of grass, looked out on the lake and said, "'Cause that would mean God made human beings so perfect that there was nothin' left to do but blow 'em away at the end of life. You and me, we've both seen how wrong that is, and we're not even full-grown. I figure life is one long education."

"Education for what?"

Drummer returned to his back. "That's the problem. No one knows."

"I like it that the Indians think the sugar maple carries knowledge of all life in its sap."

"Unh-hun."

Drummer was snoring. I rolled on my side and looked out at the sleeping lake. Where did it all come from—the water, this tree and those stars? There had to be a God. I was drowsy, and I could feel the roots of the sugar maple under my bed. They were pulling poison out of me, not the memories but the poison that accompanied them—Mother's cutting words; her severed head in the muck in the middle of screaming missiles and choking smoke; Papa's Indian grave on an island on the Detroit River halfway between the two countries; Brownstown and its mud, blood, savagery and pain; sad, drunken, gentle Joseph who I loved but who was now Deep River, a violent and hopeless Indian warrior who I couldn't love. The sugar maple's roots sucked out all the misery and even though it felt as though my innards were being torn out of me, I knew it was positive pain that would make me lighter.

Too bad the tree could not predict the future and tell me what would happen to Drummer Jakes and me, two penniless orphans with no home to go to and no ideas about where we should go or what would happen to us. I guessed we would just have to let the future pull us along and figure out things as we went.

I rolled over and shut my tear-filled eyes.

CHAPTER 25
SEPTEMBER/OCTOBER 1813
▼

Matthew Elliott

Sarah and I stared out from the widow's peak of our house tryin' to see what was happenin' out on the lake, but the ships were too far away to make any sense of the battle. We heard the screams of explosions from cannons and could see flames spit from the decks of ships that wove in and out of clouds of black smoke. There were moments the smoke cleared long enough ta view one vessel tilted toward the water and another with sails in flames, but we couldn't make sense of it. "I'm damned if I can figure out who's who and what's happenin' out there, but I tell ya, my Sarah, if it's the American Navy that's winnin' and we lose Lake Erie, it'll mean we've lost the war on the lakes."

Sarah kissed me on the cheek as we watched our fates bein' determined by outside forces.

"You've got the wagons ready, Sarah?"

"Too many. We've filled nine wagons, Matthew. The silver plate alone takes up one whole cart, and do you really want to move 30 horses?"

"Could be those wagons will hold all that's left of the good life, my Sarah, and the horses I'll need for trade if we're still alive and havin' to deal with defeat. We may be forced to leave some possessions behind later on, but for now we'll try'n take it all."

We stared down at Erie's unnatural and uneven waves burstin' toward shore burdened with the rubble of war.

Fearin' he would lose the Indians' support if they knew of the disaster, pissin' Procter lied to Tecumseh about the outcome of the sea battle, but Tecumseh was no fool and when he saw the British fleet limp into Put-In Bay, 'twasn't difficult to learn that we'd lost the battle on Lake Erie. There were 15 ships went at each other, and Admiral Perry defeated the one-armed Admiral Barclay of the British Navy. I was told 'twas the first time that the King's Navy had been captured intact by the enemy.

Procter started to dismantle the forts at Detroit and here in Amherstburg, and only an idjit could miss what was happenin', which was not a description of the furious Indian chief pacin' in my kitchen.

"The General is a coward! He is afraid to meet the enemy. Now he runs like a dog with his tail between his legs. He leaves the Indians to fight. I say now, if he does this, I will call my followers to a council and there I will bring out the great wampum belt and cut it in two! I will break our friendship, and I will attack the British forces!"

"Look, you know my opinion of Procter, but we gotta try to see things from his point of view. Half his troops were on those ships and now they're prisoners; no support is arrivin' from the east, and he can't defend the forts from William Henry Harrison's army 'cause now with our loss of the lakes, Harrison can land anywhere." I never thought I'd be defendin' the old ball bag, but what could I do?

"We must swat the bees as they land, not wait for the swarm. We Indians will not run away with the Great Father Procter! Here we must stand and fight!" Tecumseh's furor was akin to an eruptin' volcano.

Obese Procter was not the man we wanted in this place at this time. He dilly-dallied when he should attack, he became unnerved when he should be decisive and he didn't even let his underlings know what he was thinkin'. 'Course, I had an extra complaint, that bein' that when anything went wrong, he blamed the Indian Department. Still, he was the card we'd bin dealt, and we'd best try to work with it. "Before you break the wampum belt, let's call a meeting of your council, and I'll make sure Procter attends."

Hundreds of Indians squatted on the parade ground. Procter and his officers stood to the side. I followed Tecumseh to a rock perched on the edge of the river, which he mounted as I stayed at his feet to translate.

"Father," he began. "Listen to your children! You have them now all before you. The war before this, our British father gave the hatchet to his red children when old chiefs were alive. They are now dead. In that war, our father was thrown on his back by the Americans, and our father took them by the hand without our knowledge; and we are afraid that our father will do so again at this time."

My translatin' wasn't perfect, but Tecumseh was angry and talking very fast.

"Summer before last," he continued, "when I came forward with my red brethren and was ready to take up the hatchet in favour of our British father, we were told not to be in a hurry, that he had not yet determined to fight the Americans."

Procter lifted his hand to try to answer Tecumseh but was ignored.

"*Listen!*" Tecumseh demanded. "When war was declared, our father stood up and gave us the tomahawk and told us that he was ready to strike the Americans—that he wanted our assistance and that he would certainly get us our lands back, which the Americans had taken from us."

Procter again tried to answer but was again silenced.

"*Listen!* You told us at that time to bring forward our families to this place, and we did so; and you promised to take care of them and that they should want for nothing while the men would go and fight the enemy; that we need not trouble ourselves about the enemy's garrisons; that we knew nothing about them and that our father would attend to that part of the business. You also told your red children that you would take good care of your garrison here, which made our hearts glad."

The Indians cheered in confirmation.

"*Listen!*" Tecumseh continued. "When we were last at the Rapids, it is true we gave you little assistance. It is hard to fight people who live like groundhogs.

"Father, *listen!* Our fleet has gone out; we know they have fought; we have heard the great guns but know nothing of what has happened to our father with one arm. Our ships have gone one way, and we are much astonished to see our father tying up everything and preparing to run away the other without letting his red children know what his intentions are. You always told us to remain here and take care of our lands. It made our hearts glad to hear that was your wish. Our great father, the king, is the head, and you represent him. You always told us that you would never draw your foot off British ground; but now, Father, we see you are drawing back, and we are sorry to see our father doing so without seeing the enemy. We must compare our father's conduct to a fat animal that carries its tail upon its back, but when affrighted it drops it between its legs and runs off."

The Indians were stomping on the ground and yowling.

"*Listen*, Father! The Americans have not yet defeated us by land; neither are we sure that they have done so by water; we therefore wish to remain here and fight our enemy should they make their appearance. If they defeat us, we will then retreat with our father.

"At the Battle of the Rapids, last war, the Americans certainly defeated us; and when we retreated to our father's fort in that place, the gates were shut against us. We were afraid that it would now be the case, but instead of that we now see our British father preparing to march out of his garrison.

"Father! You have got the arms and ammunition, which our great father sent for his red children. If you have an idea of going away, give them to us, and you may go and welcome; for us, our lives are in the hands of the Great Spirit. We are determined to defend our lands, and if it is His will, we wish to leave our bones upon them."

It was sad that Procter and his officers had to hear his speech second hand. Tecumseh was a real orator; his voice was powerful and it seeped into the minds of his listeners. The Indians were so damned worked up, some of them went after the British waving tomahawks, but Tecumseh called them off.

Then it was Procter's turn, and I had to somersault in my translatin'. Getting up on the rock wasn't so easy for the fat, fleshy-faced idjit, but with the help of his officers he made it.

"I've heard the complaints of my red friend and promise that we are not going to leave you. In four days, I will call my own council to explain the plans of your white father. Until then, I ask you to be patient."

Finally, we were meeting in the fort's council chambers. 'Twas three days later than planned, which meant Harrison's army was three days closer. Tecumseh was still in a furor and rightly so. Pissin' Procter had to get it together or we were all done for.

Again I translated for Tecumseh. "Father," he said to Procter, "we must meet them at Amherstburg. You attack from the front and my warriors will flank the Long Knives. If the attack fails, we will retreat to River aux Canards and fight again."

Procter shook his head. "That's impossible!"

Tecumseh couldn't contain himself. He screamed, "Your words are those of an old squaw. We must stand and fight or we die!"

There were some pleasurable moments in the translatin' business!

181

Procter's face turned purple, but he bit his tongue and rolled out a map of the area. He moved his finger along the Detroit River, pointin' out the island of Bois Blanc and the fort at Detroit. "If the American gunboats come up the river, they will cut off Bois Blanc, and your warriors will be unable to cross and fight. Furthermore, they could move their boats all the way up Lake St. Clair and approach the army from the rear, which would cut off all possibility of retreat."

Tecumseh followed Procter's finger. "What do you plan?"

"Here," Procter pointed, "at the forks of the River Thames we will fortify our position and together face the army of the Long Knives."

Tecumseh drew his finger along the map of the river. "What do you think, Elliott?"

I surveyed the map. "There's a logic to his plan."

Tecumseh grunted. "I will speak to my chiefs."

I could tell he was not completely convinced, but I detected a sense of inevitability in the man.

Within hours, he returned and agreed to the plan. "We will follow you into the country we do not know and from which we may never return."

The past week had been a disaster! Some 10,000 Indians from Bois Blanc, whites from Detroit, women and children from Sandwich and Amherstburg, all retreatin' along the one corduroy road or massed on the shore waitin' for one of the limited number of boats to take them up the Detroit River into Lake St. Clair. You would have thought such an accumulation of human beings would create a cacophony of noise, but it was worse than that. The silence of defeat made the heavy trudge of their steps one of the saddest sounds I'd ever heard. Everyone was wantin' to take as many of their belongings as they could, fearin' that we'd never be able to return to this part of the world, but as the miles went on the load got heavier, and the sides of the road became littered with kitchen goods, bedding, suitcases and tools.

Before joining Tecumseh, I found Sarah and the family, who were in the wagons well ahead of the big exodus. I couldn't wait to dismount before leanin' into my Sarah, who had stood to greet me. Our kiss was full of unsaid words and we broke to look in each other's eyes, each recognizin' in the other that the kiss was more delicate, more fragile and a damned sight sadder than usual.

"I love you, Matthew Elliott."

"And I you, my Sarah." There was naught more to be said. Removin' my arm from her shoulders, I dismounted and went to the innocents, givin' each of them a kiss.

Boy sat beside my Sarah, holding the reins of the horse team. He was starin' straight ahead to grant me my private moment with Sarah. I reached up and patted his leg, but he pulled away—he was that sad. "Take them to Burlington, Son. I'll follow as soon as I can." He nodded, flipped the reins and geed the horses. I'd done it all arseways with this son, leavin' him ta manage home while I went off fightin' for and with the Indians. There was so much to say to this young man and no time to say it. When I returned, I would not leave it any longer.

The troops had to offload all their equipment and lug it over a sandbar at the place where the Thames River met Lake St. Clair. Tecumseh and I watched the disorganized bottleneck of activity. "Another mistake," I grumbled. "Procter should have ordered the unloading on the shore of the lake where the boats could dock with ease."

Tecumseh sat on his white horse, his back stiff and his face without expression, the very absence of which told me the man was deeply worried. "The Ottawa and Chippewa have sent chiefs to make peace with Harrison. Wyandot, Miami and Delaware may go too. I am sure of only 1,000 warriors."

I had no answer for the man. We both knew the approachin' battle would be critical and without voicing it understood we were not prepared.

Together we rode three miles down the Thames River where Procter had agreed to make a stand and found nothing but confusion and no pissin' Procter! We dismounted and pushed our way through the milling soldiers to Warburton, Procter's second in command. Tecumseh confronted the officer nose to nose. "Where are the fortifications? Where is the turtle Procter?"

Warburton backed away from the furious Shawnee and looked at me to translate, which I did.

"Procter's gone upstream. He's not told me what he wants to do. I've sent messages but heard nothing."

Sure Tecumseh could sense the desperation in the man's voice even without the translation.

"We must make a stand here without him."

Warburton turned in a circle and wiped his brow. "I can't do anything without orders."

"I don't understand any of this," I added. "Why the hell haven't ya ordered the building of a fortification and a battery?"

"I did!" Warburton cried. "But all the tools have gone with Procter!"

"We must stand and fight before all my warriors leave," Tecumseh insisted.

Warburton was about to answer when a horse came galloping up with a soldier carrying a message from Procter. Warburton opened the orders. "We're to move up to Bowles Farm, the head of the navigation route, and destroy all the ships and any stores that must be left behind."

Procter had chosen the site to do battle. He had the Thames on the left where he'd placed the regulars and a heavy marsh on the right behind the militia. He and the other officers were reviewing the placement of the troops.

I was with Tecumseh who had led his warriors to the other side of the swamp where we planned to attack through the woods. We had final words before hunkering down in our hiding places. Each of us knew that the approaching battle held scant hope for the British and even less for the Indians. "It is bad to have our fate in the hands of a turtle, Elliott," he said with a heavy voice. "We will fight because we must, because there is no choice, but I feel a shadow on my shoulder, and I cry for the loss of our rich soil, our hunting grounds and the freedom of the Indian way."

We embraced and turned to the warriors and final preparations. I hid amongst the trees with the painted men, listening hard and jumping at each strange sound. Tecumseh appeared behind my shoulder. "My scout is back. Harrison is close. His line of soldiers is three miles long." And then he was gone. We waited in silence in the shadows of the forest.

"March the troops to their positions," I heard Procter order his officers.

From my spot, I could see the soldiers march forward and hear them ordered to form a line, but it was obvious there were not enough of them to stand shoulder to shoulder. Even pissin' Procter could see that!

"Face them about and march them back to the woods where they can hide between trees!" he ordered.

Back they marched, poor sods, and about-faced once more. Then we waited. And waited. And waited. There was grumblin' from the other side of the swamp, but the Indians were silent. I could see many of the soldiers squatting or sitting on whatever was close at hand, but there was a lot of listenin' too, and if they were like me, their minds were flarin' open wide enough to suck in the crisp air, the sun-blessed autumn sky, the flamin' fall leaves, the frothing river, the robin's chirp and the echo of the woodpecker's hammering—each sight, sound and smell isolated and exaggerated.

The bugle blew. Rifles on both sides fired. Kentuckians charged, bellowing, "Remember the Raisin!" I saw American horsemen break through our line, wheel and charge from behind. British horses bucked and screeched in confusion, adding dust to the tumult of booming cannons. The British line was broken. Infantrymen fought hand to hand, using bayonets and knives. Indian, British and American screams of pain mixed together and broke through the veils of smoke piercing the ears of all in the field. Cannons spouted fire, noise and destruction. Flames chased flames, the arson of war. Pieces of shattered bodies were flung beyond the battlefield. A soldier spittin' blood crawled toward the swamp pleading, "Finish me off! Please, finish me off!" No one dared make the final shot, so I did it.

"Sound the retreat!" Procter ordered the bugler and then he turned his horse and dashed off through the woods. Where the hell was he going?

Tecumseh ordered me back into the shadow of the woods. "You are too old for this, my friend." His warriors were shooting down all attackers, but for every one that fell another appeared. I ignored Tecumseh's order and shot my way through until I was by his side. Then we were fighting hand to hand with tomahawks and knives and pistols. The blood-curdling screams of the body-painted Indians were matched by the inhuman bellows of the Kentuckians, and we were all so entwined I wasn't sure what was happening, I just kept slashing away with my big knife, staggering through the dust and shadows. Beside me, Tecumseh threw a tomahawk that split open the head of his enemy and with his knife in the other hand followed the throw with a dash toward another soldier.

How did I isolate that rifle shot? How did I know it had hit Tecumseh? I ran forward. He lay on dead leaves, a bullet hole in his neck. His face was calm, as though he had exhaled the cares of the world and for the first time his muscles and sinews were at rest. Warriors surrounded the body 10 deep and fought off all attacks as the other chiefs surrounded his body, their shoulders slumped in defeat. Round Head, the Shawnee chief and a friend of Tecumseh, looked up at me with tears running down his cheeks. "Our hope is dead."

'Twas probably true, but I couldn't show what I felt. "Not yet, Round Head. We can fight again, but right now we have to back out of here with as little loss as possible"

"We must take Tecumseh's body to a place the white man cannot find."

I knew he was right about that. If they found his body they'd strip the flesh off and sell it in pieces as a memento of the great man. "Do it!"

Once the chiefs were out of sight, we battled a retreat into the woods, away from the Americans.

Our rearguard galloped up to say that the Americans were hot on our heels.

We joined the retreating troops who staggered along grumblin' and in rags, many of them shoeless and all disgusted with Procter, who was nowhere to be seen.

Death walked with them as they trudged through the mud, half of them asleep on their feet, all of them deaf to orders and drunk with exhaustion. At the end of the long line, oily water seeped into the mud-made footsteps and sat stagnant, swirling corrupted reds, yellows and blues.

Round Head pulled his horse alongside mine. "The Americans have stopped their chase. They have made camp."

"They've probably outrun their supply lines." It gave us time to make our escape, but neither of us felt relieved.

We continued on in miserable silence. "Many will leave," Round Head said of his warriors. "The British have lost our land. There is nothing to fight for."

"Stay with me, Round Head. I promise I'll make sure yer fed for the winter, and I'll fight for land where the tribes can settle here in Canada. There's nothin' out there for ya if you split up and go off in different directions."

He spread his hand, indicating the shuffling soldiers and warriors, weak from hunger and bent by defeat. "It is better to be alone in the woods than to run away like frightened animals. Many will go."

"But you, Round Head. Will you come with me?"

"To keep my people from starving, I will come."

Sarah's Diary

Tecumseh's death means the collapse of the Indian confederation. His words were the scaffolding that held the tribes together. The disbursement of the tribes weighs heavily on my husband.

Marauding soldiers took everything—the silver, the horses, even our trunks of clothes. They held guns to the heads of the children and threatened to shoot them if Boy tried anything. We were left with only our wagon, and that was simply because there weren't enough of them to deal with everything.

The defeat has caused Matthew to bend. Until now, although old, he was virile and upright, but this has done him in. He still plans skirmishes with the Indians, but I'm not sure there is enough juice left in him to work up the energy to even mount a horse. His eyes are clouded and he spends hours looking inward. Perhaps the babes can draw him out.

What is that Greek myth about the god who is tied to a rock and an eagle pierces his stomach and eats his liver, which grows back each day to provide the bird with another repast? Will Boy and I be equally damned? Why can't we stop??

Chapter 26
September/October 1813

▼

Daniel

I hadn't realized my muscles had been tight till we got here and the knots loosened. The sun was playing with the reds and yellows of the fall leaves, the wheat was gold in the fields, the air had a bite and the swish of the lake's waves were an accompanying rhythm. It seemed we'd all exhaled. If only this peace could continue forever.

On this day I was helping Mr. Bradley make Drummer a leg. He had chosen a white pine log 'cause it was straight and tough. "They use this wood for the masts of our ships," he told us as he sawed a hunk off the log.

Drummer, who was sitting on a log watching, grabbed his crutches and jumped up. "I gotta get out of here till yer finished with the sawing! That screechin' noise is all I heard when they chopped off my leg: *screech! crunch! scream! plop!* I dream the pain almost every night, and it makes me feel sick to my stomach!"

Mr. Bradley stood up straight and watched Drummer retreat. "I should have thought of that. It was damned insensitive of me!"

"Don't worry, sir, I figure it's good if Drummer can vomit the memory of all that pain."

He sat down on Drummer's vacated log, filled his pipe and lit it. "And you, Daniel, how are you dealing with memories?"

I sat down cross-legged and poked around the grass for pebbles that I could throw while I thought. "This stupid war has sure tripped me up." I threw a stone as far as I could. "That's why it's good to be here. It's so fresh and clean."

Mr. Bradley sucked on his pipe and nodded his head up and down.

The leg was finished, and Drummer was being fitted with a piece of sheepskin around the stump and then straps to hold the leg up. We were all outside the big house, quiet as the final finishes were achieved.

"There," Mr. Bradley said. "Let's see you walk." He had to hold Bruno off, 'cause the dog wanted to join the excitement by nipping at the base of the new leg.

Drummer, still dressed in his oversized, faded-red drummer's uniform, held on to Lieutenant Mackenzie's arm for a few steps and then took off on his own, wobbling at first but becoming steadier with each step. The smile on my friend's face would have fallen over the edges if it could have! He practically ran into the arms of Black Henri, who lifted him up in his arms and twirled him around in celebration while Annie and Lieutenant Mackenzie patted his back with the pleasure of it. Dacana and Major Cameron stood arm in arm calling out hurrahs, and I was huddled in the middle of an embrace between Aunt Belle and Mr. Bradley, the comfort of which made my smile almost as big as Drummer's.

"You should be real proud of yourself, Donald." Aunt Belle kissed him on the cheek.

"I'll say!" I added. "I want to be a carpenter just like you!"

"Why thank you, son. It's a satisfying profession, but I warn you, you'll not get rich by it."

"I guess that depends on what you mean by *rich*. I figure that as long as I have somewhere to sleep and something to eat, there would be nothing nicer than to spend every day sliding my hands over the grains of different woods and from the beautiful textures make useful things that give pleasure to others. I'd rather make things than circles in squares and stars in circles like my friend Mr. Wickam carves."

"Do you know why he makes them?"

"I've thought about it a whole lot, and I think it's kind of like me and my mirror. We're both trying to balance opposites so the teeter doesn't totter, if you know what I mean."

A noise interrupted our celebration, making us turn to the road where five Indians appeared from around the bend, led by a person with a painted face who was dressed in a squaw's long dress but walked like a man.

Dacana and Major Cameron went to greet them, and Dacana surprised me by talking to them in their own Algonquian language, the same language spoken by the Shawnee.

"What are they saying?" Aunt Belle whispered.

"They're telling Dacana that they will be having the 'Fall of the Leaf' ceremony the night of the full moon," I reported.

Dacana turned and said, "Daniel, come here, will you?"

Curious, I joined the group.

"This is the boy I was telling you about," she said to the leader. She turned to me. "In the 'Fall of the Leaf' ceremony, they celebrate their love for their ancestors and dance a final farewell to those who have died this year. I thought it might be a good time to bury your mother's ashes at the base of the sugar maple. What do you think?"

I nodded my head in agreement because my voice had creeped to the back of my throat. I turned looking for Aunt Belle, and she came up and stood behind me with her hands on my shoulders. I guessed it was 'cause we had the same blood that she knew I needed her support without me having to say a word. 'Course, could have been that the look on my face was a bit desperate.

While Dacana turned back to the Indians, I leaned into Aunt Belle and explained, "When the moon's full, we're going to bury Mother's ashes under the sugar maple."

"It's a good thing, Daniel. I can't think of a better place."

She was right, of course. That old sugar maple would suck her ashes into its sap and carry her memory for hundreds of years. I bet that its roots would spit the bad memories into the lake, where they'd be diluted and washed away.

"I've been wanting to talk to you about something else, Daniel. Maybe this is a good time." Aunt Belle turned me around, held my shoulders and looked into my eyes. "I've come to love you like a son," she choked. "I know I could never replace your mother and I'm a fat old lady with a questionable reputation, but there is nothing, nothing in this world that would make me happier than to have you come to live with me and be the son I've never had."

I kinda took for granted that Aunt Belle would "take me in," but her words told me it would not be from a sense of duty—which, of course, brought on my dumb tears. All I could squeeze out was, "Thank you." I wanted to say a whole lot more, but I was not entirely sure what.

She kissed me on the top of the head. "There's more."

I pulled back and looked up at her.

"If you don't like what I'm going to say, I'll rethink the idea." Her eyes crinkled up in pleasure, and she looked into the distance over my head. "Donald Bradley has asked me to marry him so we'd be a real family."

"Mr. Bradley will be my adopted father?"

"If you don't mind."

"Mind? I think it's wonderful!" I gave her a big kiss. "When will you marry?"

"Before we leave here so that we can go back to York as a family."

"You don't want Bishop Strachan to marry you?" I teased.

"Fortunately, we're Catholic, so he couldn't even if he wanted to, which he wouldn't. There's a priest who travels the lakes, so when he comes here we'll tie the knot."

"Hey, Daniel," came Drummer's voice, "we need some translatin' over here!" Drummer was sitting on a log with his wooden leg tucked tight in his arms, and the Indian man-woman was kneeling and checking the scar on Daniel's stump. Lieutenant Mackenzie was looking on.

As I joined him, Drummer looked at me over the Indian's head. "This guy is maulin' my leg, and it's makin' me real nervous,"

"The scar is clean," the Indian mumbled as he twisted and turned Daniel's stump. "What medicines you use?"

Lieutenant Mackenzie answered and I translated. "Soap and alcohol and a mix from various herbs."

"Why's this man dressed like a woman?" Drummer asked, trying to lean away from the Indian's hands.

"He's a *berdache*, or at least that's what they're called west of here," I explained. "They're men who become shamans and medicine men because they aren't hunters and warriors. Sometimes they dress like women and sometimes like men."

"Do the tribes accept them?" Lieutenant Mackenzie sounded really interested.

My eyes met Drummer's, and we silently acknowledged that Lieutenant Mackenzie's question was loaded with more than an informal curiosity. "Yup! I've seen lots of them out west."

The *berdache* studied Lieutenant Mackenzie. "White man use one medicine, yellow man other medicine. Better if white and yellow share. You come to island. You teach me."

Lieutenant listened to my translation. "Will he teach me about his medicines?"

The Indian grunted in agreement.

Our friend swished back his falling hair as he thought about it.

"Hey! Not so fast!" Drummer tightened his grip on his wooden leg, but the Indian pulled it from his grasp and, still crouched, smoothed his hand over the peg leg and the rounded cup, grunting in appreciation.

"Little soldier's leg, how make so smooth? How stay on?"

"Ask that man." I pointed to Mr. Bradley. "I'll take you, but you'd better give my friend his leg back first."

The Indian shook his head and held tight to it. "Don't worry," I told Drummer. "After he talks to Mr. Bradley, we'll get it back."

"We'd better!" Drummer grabbed his crutches and followed the procession around the side of the big house, where we found Aunt Belle whispering to Mr. Bradley. I figured she was telling him we were going to be a family, 'cause he gave her a giant kiss, which I interrupted with a pat on the shoulder, a huge smile and a handshake for Mr. Bradley. "I'm really happy!" The Indian pushed me in the back to get my attention. "Oh! This Indian wants to ask you questions about how you made Drummer's leg. I'll translate."

The other Indians joined us, and the *berdache* passed the leg from one to the other.

"Grab it from them, Daniel, before they take off with it!" Drummer whispered.

It was a bit of an effort to get the leg away from the Indian, but he finally released it and turned to Mr. Bradley. "What wood you use? What tools?"

"Come, I'll show you."

I loped along beside the small wiry man, feeling pleased as punch to be linked to him. In the shed where the tools were kept, he distributed different instruments amongst the Indians—adze, saw, drill and sandpaper—and the Indians nodded and grunted in response to his explanations as to the use of each tool.

He finished and started to put away the tools, but the *berdache* stopped him. "We take to island."

"Sorry," Donald Bradley said. "You can't do that. These tools belong to me. I need them for my work."

"Indians don't understand ownership, sir. They believe everything is shared. It's kinda hard to explain it to them."

"Tell them a carpenter without tools is a lion without teeth."

They seemed to understand and returned the tools.

"How's it going?"

Drummer was on a horse for the first time, and we were riding down the lane to the sugar maple, where we would watch the sun set over the lake. "It's a little lopsided," he said, "but I'll figure it out."

We reined in a distance from the Queen Tree. Her blazing red leaves were gently lecturing the waves, and her children were answering back with contented laps onto the shore. As the sun slipped down behind the Indians' island, it changed from gold to red to red-gold before slipping so low it left only a halo above the shadowed trees, and then it was gone.

I leaned on the pommel of the saddle. "It's been quite a day."

"It has that."

We were quiet, watching the sun's final decision to slip down into the lake.

"Will you be leaving with Belle and Mr. Bradley?"

"Not for a while. You can come with us if you want. I already asked Aunt Belle."

"Thanks, but I think I'll stay here. Major Cameron says the army has to pay me in land, considerin' I was injured and all. When she goes back to York, Dacana's gonna fight for it for me."

"What'll you do with the land?"

"They say I can rent it to them till I'm old enough to manage it myself. Meanwhile, they've invited me to stay with them, either here or, when the war's over, in York."

"At least we'll see each other."

"'Course we will."

We turned the horses and loped back to the farm where we knew dinner would be waiting. "Do ya think the Lieutenant will go to the island with the Indians?" Drummer asked.

"He seemed pretty interested."

"Ya think he would dress like that *berdache*?"

"Who knows? Maybe. Maybe it would make him happier."

CHAPTER 27
NOVEMBER 1813

▼

Daniel

Annie handed the platter down the table. "Some voyageurs passed through and told us there'd been a big battle at Chateauguay."

Major Cameron served himself some chicken, passed on the platter and took the bowl of roasted parsnips. "What did he tell you? Did we hold the Americans back?"

"It was Black Henri who talked to them."

We all looked at Black Henri, who was serving himself from the bowl of potatoes. "He said they had a smart leader named Salaberry and beat back de Americans at Chateauguay, then dey marched to Chrysler Farm to help de troops dere."

With a mouthful of chicken, I asked, "And what happened there?"

Black Henri didn't stop serving himself huge portions of everything that landed in front of him. "Dey fought British-style in an open field. De lines of the British, dey never broke. It was their kind of battle. The Americans, dey are better at de guerilla stuff."

Dacana got up to clear the table. "Shows the difference between the two countries—order against original thinking."

"We're original thinkers!" I protested.

"Of course we are," Dacana soothed. "But we want order in our armies and our government and to have it we choose to be ruled by a hierarchy. In America, the government and army are ruled by the people."

"Well, we're lucky to be here and away from it all," Aunt Belle said. "Why don't we—" Her words were interrupted by a knock on the door.

The Indian servant opened it, and I couldn't believe my eyes! "Joseph!" Mr. Bradley leaned away to let me climb out from my place on the bench. I ran to my friend and flung myself at him. "This is Joseph! I told you about him, Belle, he's the man who looked after me in Sandwich when Mother and Papa were busy, which was most of the time. I haven't seen him since we left Amherstburg." I looked back at Joseph and saw he still wore his hair shaved at the sides and straight up in the middle, reminding me of who he had become. "When he went to fight with Tecumseh, he changed his name to Deep River."

"We must talk," Joseph said.

"You'd best see what he wants," Aunt Belle said. "Seems he's come a long way to speak to you."

I went outside with him, and we both crouched down to have our talk. "How did you get here? Why did you come?"

He pulled a sac from his belt and handed it to me. I opened it, put my hand in and pulled out three carvings: a circle in a square, a star in a circle and a square in a star. I looked up at Joseph. "Mr. Wickam?"

"He died night of summer full moon. His lady was dead many months. He was too sad to live more. His house your house now. Lawyer man sent me." He handed me an official piece of paper.

I opened it but didn't see what I was reading. I knew the circle of Mr. and Mrs. Wickam's lives was not broken like so many who had been killed in the last two years, so my sadness was not so desperate, but it was hard to handle the finish of a closed circle. "How did the lawyer find you?"

"I go to Sandwich after they bury Tecumseh. Lawyer told me find you."

"Tecumseh's dead?"

He grunted and nodded his head. "Killed in battle at Moraviantown. Now the Indians separate. Some make peace with Americans. Some stay to fight with Matthew Elliott. Many go west. No hope for Indians."

"What will you do?"

"Fight with Elliott." He sounded as sad as he did when he had long hair and was drinking rum.

We talked for a long time. When I told him about Mother, he put his hand on my shoulder, and he grunted with approval at the news that I now had a new family, but it made me feel terrible that things were working out for me but not for him, nor for any of the Indians for that matter. To change the subject, I looked again at the piece of paper he gave me. "I don't know what to do about this. I guess Mr. Bradley and Aunt Belle can help me figure it out."

"The house wait for you."

"And Prophet? Do you know what happened to my dog?"

He shook his head.

I was sure that old hound was all right. Probably some neighbour took him. He was too smart to just go off and die. I refused to believe otherwise.

Joseph stood up. "I go now."

I didn't want him to leave. "The Indians from the island are having a big ceremony at the sugar maple. Won't you stay?"

He shook his head, gave me a sad smile and turned away. I watched his tired back disappear into the darkened lane. How could he walk away from our years together? I guess if he stayed he would have to be Joseph again, and he didn't want that.

I went back into the house and told the waiting faces the news of Tecumseh's death and the scattering of the Indians he had brought together.

"That's a serious blow for the British," Major Cameron said. "Were it not for the Indians, we would have been overrun by the Americans a year ago."

"Does it mean we'll be beaten?" Drummer asked as he snuck a piece of meat to Bruno under the table.

"No, but it will make things much harder for the British and the militia," he answered.

"He also brought these." I pulled out the carvings and the paper, handing the paper to Aunt Belle. "The Wickams were my friends, and they didn't have any children of their own."

Aunt Belle passed the paper around. Drummer, who couldn't read, demanded to know what it said.

"It says Mr. Wickam has left his house, all his possessions and a little bit of money to Daniel," Dacana said. "He must have loved you a lot, Daniel." She smiled at me.

"I guess so," I answered. "But I think Joseph loved me too, and he just walked away." I played with Mr. Wickam's carving. "Which doesn't exactly make me feel warm and confident." I was sitting on the bench between Aunt Belle and Donald Bradley and smiled up at them. Maybe I looked a little desperate, 'cause they both put their arms around me.

"When the war is over, we'll go to Sandwich and settle your affairs before returning to York. How does that sound?" Mr. Bradley asked.

"Do you think the war will be over?"

"We hope so," he answered.

Three days ago, the Indians began arriving in their canoes and set up wigwams in the area around the sugar maple. Then the celebrations started, and Drummer and I spent as much time as possible down there 'cause it was like a carnival of wonders. There was a fierce game of lacrosse with lots of body checking and the promise of many bruises. The ball they used was wood wrapped in deerskin. Because there was betting on the outcome, the sidelines were as exciting as the game, what with the yelling and cheering.

The next day was different for me because we were going to include the burial of Mother's ashes in the final celebration so all my friends were there, wandering around enjoying the festivities before we gathered later in the day.

Although my heart was not in it, I joined Drummer in pushing through a crowd of men to watch an Indian on his knees with four moccasins in a line in front of him. He lifted each one to show there was a bullet under one but not under the others. Another Indian placed bets with cowrie shells and then nodded his head, giving the kneeling Indian permission to start moving the four moccasins back and forth and around and about at a disturbing speed. He stopped and looked up at the man who had bet.

"It's under the left one," Drummer whispered. The Indian seemed to agree with my friend and pointed to the left moccasin, which the kneeling Indian lifted to show that they were both wrong. He lifted the slipper beside it to expose the bullet and then swept up the cowrie shells and put them in a sack at his waist.

"It's good you didn't bet," I teased Drummer.

"This is not fun! Let's try that game over there."

An Indian stood on a line holding a large rounded stone. On either side of him, the players were in position, each prepared to throw a spear. There was a countdown, and the Indian threw the stone at the same time as the players flung their spears.

"What're they doing?" Drummer asked.

"From the way that guy was whooping, it looks like the spear that lands closest to where the stone landed was the winner."

"Let's try it!"

"I don't feel much like it."

"Aw, c'mon, Daniel. You can't mope all day!"

Before I could answer, the drums and flutes called everyone to the sugar maple. The games were forgotten, and we all gathered into a large U with the great tree closing the circle.

All my friends joined Drummer and me in the circle, and like the Indians we let the beat of the drums sink into our bones and moved in place as the shaman danced into the circle. He swooped down as though picking something up and then opened his arms to throw the imaginary bundle into the air. "He is dancing the dance of fallen leaves, giving thanks to the sun and the moon for good harvest," Dacana explained.

The drums beat faster while the flutes repeated the same message over and over again and the shaman dipped and turned and rose and fell and we were all pulled out of ourselves and into the rhythm, becoming one.

Aunt Belle tapped my shoulder, pulling me back into myself. "It's time, Daniel."

Mr. Bradley held the box with the ashes and lifted the lid so I could put Mr. Wickam's carvings on top. I knew the ashes weren't really Mother's, that Mr. Bradley and Lieutenant Mackenzie had just scooped up some ashes from the area, but perhaps there was a bit of her there, enough to say goodbye.

The drums had slowed and the flutes were whispering gentle comfort as we all walked forward to the prepared hole at the base of the sugar maple. I was in front with the box. Aunt Belle and Mr. Bradley were right behind me, and my other friends followed so that we were inside the circle surrounded by Indians. The shaman stood by the small grave and took the box from me, which he placed into the hole and then covered with birchbark. An assistant threw dirt on top.

"Winter comes soon," the shaman said. "It is the silent time when the Great Tree mixes new knowledge with the old and sends the souls of sadness to the Gitchie Manitou on the wings of the West Wind, where they will be free. Your mother's soul is at rest now."

The beat increased and we backed into the group, becoming part of the circle again.

It felt like my muscles and bones had turned to jelly. Were it not for Mr. Bradley's strong arm, I might have collapsed and turned into nothing more than a lifeless puddle of skin, but he held on and the drum beat at memories of mother, both good and bad, and the worst part was I didn't know how I should feel.

I wished I had my mirror.

CHAPTER 28
DECEMBER 1813

▼

Matthew Elliott

Roundin' up stray Indians and trying to get them settled with enough food for the winter was an exhaustin' undertaking, I kin tell ya. First I had to get the military to give us the land and then find enough food to see them through the winter; no easy task, seein' as there was about 2,000 men, women and children, but when the Indians finally had their huts covered with bark and their bellies satisfied, I felt damned pleased with myself, which was a big mistake. New orders arrived and the army wanted us on the move again, but I was sure as hell not goin' anywhere before spending a few days at home with my Sarah. I put the orders inside my coat and headed out in spite of the approaching storm.

My horse was strugglin' in the snow, and I had ta bend into the freezing wind. My nostrils were glued together, forcin' me to breathe through the scarf tied around my mouth, and the effort dampened the scarf and was so strenuous I struggled to inhale. My eyes teared. The sight of our house was more than a relief and a comfort; it was my salvation.

I dropped down on the settee in front of the blazin' fire. The children were runnin' back and forth making a terrible racket, and the reverberations were too much for my old nerves. "Sarah!" I called. "Can't you do something about these children? I can't bear the noise." My Sarah came out of the kitchen, saw my head flung back in exhaustion, picked up the children and deposited them with the only servant we'd been able to keep.

"What's happened, Matthew?"

"There's news. Our fields in Amherstburg have been burned and the house vandalized, and I've been ordered to lead my Indians to Fort George. The British are goin' to try to take it back."

She collapsed into the chair beside me and took my hand. "Everything is gone?"

"Everything."

She took a big breath that swallowed the approachin' tears. "Well, we're lucky to have this house in Burlington."

"I suppose so." I shut my eyes.

Could be I nodded off, because Sarah's voice made me jerk. "Can't someone else lead the Indians to Fort George?"

"I'll go, Pa," Boy said from the door of the kitchen.

"I'm so damned tired, I'd let you go, Son, but the Indians won't go without me. I've bin around so long I think I've become a damned talisman or something."

"You're too old for this, Matthew."

"That is very true, my dear." I didn't mention that our need for money might only be satisfied if we defeated the Americans.

We plodded along, the Indians and me, silent black shadows in the blinding snow; I and some chiefs on horses, the rest on snowshoes, all of us bundled in bearskins. The wind sharpened every flake of snow, each flake piercing the skin and drivin' away thought.

Colonel John Murray came back to us. "Our troops can attack Fort George, we'll not need you there. If we're successful, the plan is to cross the river and attack Fort Niagara. Take your men and make camp downriver across from Lewiston. We'll signal when you are to cross and attack." I grunted in agreement, not unhappy to avoid a scuffle at Niagara.

"And Elliott, when the time comes, you must keep control of your Indians. No rape or plundering or useless murdering."

"I'm no Tecumseh, but I'll do my best."

There was mumbling amongst the Indians. I looked at where they were pointing.

"My God!" The Colonel groaned. "They've set Newark on fire!" He turned his horse. "Stay with our plan, Elliott. We'll contact you when we know more."

We pitched teepees in the woods but did not dare light fires. For warmth, many men squeezed in together. I left Round Head in charge and rode to Newark to see what was happening.

The whole town was on fire. Flames screamed into the freezin' air—red, yellow, orange—and they spread black soot everywhere. Black-faced women moaned as they pulled their screaming children away from the danger of collapsin' houses, and soldiers dashed from one place to another pulling one person from disaster as another was crushed by a burning beam. Hell could not be worse than this.

My horse bucked and whinnied, wantin' to flee the scene, forcing me to cling to the reins when I dismounted to try to help. I tied a scarf around my face and stumbled through the smoke, almost trippin' over an old man sitting on the ground watching his house burn. Holdin' tight to my frightened horse's reins, I pulled the old man to his feet but didn't know what to do with him. Tears were rollin' down his cheeks and he cried between strugglin' breaths, "Memories, burned memories, memories all burned, nothing left but the cinders of memories. All gone, all gone."

An army wagon pulled up, and I put the old boy in with the load of freezing victims and then charged through the smoke toward the cries of an old woman who lay shiverin' in her bed that'd bin plunked outside her burning house. "When they saw I couldn't walk, they carried my bed outside and burned the house and everything in it," she cried. "I've nothing, nothing in this whole world. What will I do?"

I pulled the blankets up to her chin. "Someone will be along soon, ma'am. They'll take you to shelter."

Across the road, a mother clutched her three children in a blanket and leaned against the warm chimney, the only part of her house still standing.

I led them to the wagon, and as they climbed in, I asked the driver where he would take them. "The Americans evacuated Fort George before they set fire to the town. We'll take them there."

Hundreds of people were left homeless, almost all women and children. "Where are your men?" I asked a woman as I helped her into a cart.

"Those who aren't prisoners of the Americans are fighting with the British," she told me.

The old man was right. All the houses, two churches, the library, the courthouse, the jail, all burned to the ground—memories in cinders.

I returned to my warriors and, followin' orders, we crossed the river to await the signal. I called Round Head to my teepee. "Can we control our warriors?"

"Now a different time," Round Head said. "No hope, only anger."

"That's what I'm afraid of. Kin you do anything, Round Head?"

He shook his head. "You must speak to them."

Sure and I'd call them from their hidin' places in the woods and make a grand speech that would alert the Americans. "I'll do my best."

I travelled from group to group and told them to control themselves, that they were warriors and not animals. They listened quietly but made no promises. It was the best I can do.

A thousand soldiers released from the prison when Fort Niagara was taken joined my 500 warriors, and we marched together to Lewiston. I had lost control and was washed forward on a cloud of revenge for the burning of Newark. 'Twas a dash into Lewiston by furious prophets believin' in an eye for an eye. My Indians were infected by the disease of revenge and were on a rampage—stripping houses, killing and scalping even women and children if they interfered.

I was one man. I could run from one place to another fightin' disaster, but the germ had wormed its way into the souls of the men and there was not a hope in hell of controlling it.

You would think that when it was over and there was time to review the horror, soldiers and warriors would have been hangin' their heads with guilt, but it was not the case. They were like animals lickin' their chops, and who was it that would be blamed? Oh, to be back in my little cottage with my Sarah.

Days of skirmishes and then we were on to Buffalo and more savagery. Fleeing citizens were randomly murdered and scalped. Soldiers burned every building, and Buffalo was ours. The fighting was over for 1813, it being too damned cold to go on.

We didn't even station an occupying force there; we just went home, leaving burned fields, ruined houses and homeless citizens behind us. Ah! The exhilaration of war!

CHAPTER 28
DECEMBER 1813/JANUARY 1814

▼

Daniel

On Christmas morning, Drummer and I woke extra early, and Bruno, not wanting to be left out, yipped and danced around our feet. There was a little ice on top of the water in the washbasin, but it couldn't dampen our spirits, and we didn't even try to be quiet as we washed up, 'cause it was important that Lieutenant Mackenzie and Mr. Bradley wake up to share the day.

In their bunks on the opposite side of the room, each man was awake and smiling—Donald Bradley with his hands behind his head and Lieutenant Mackenzie with his cheek squashed into a pillow exposing only one half-opened eye.

"Merry Christmas!" we chirped as we dried our faces.

"Merry Christmas!" they replied with early-morning voices.

"Aren't you getting up now?" Christmas wouldn't really start until we were all together.

"You boys go on over to the big house. We'll be right along," Donald Bradley suggested.

"Promise you won't go back to sleep!" I insisted.

"Go on with you! We'll be over after we wash up."

I started for the door, but Drummer grabbed my shoulder. "What about your present?" Each of us had drawn a name out of a hat. Drummer had gotten Major Cameron, and I had gotten Aunt Belle.

"I almost forgot!" I returned to my bed and from beneath it pulled out my trunk, in which I'd hidden the rolled birchbark tied with a red ribbon. "Let's go!"

There'd been a fresh snowfall, and the bright sun made the new flakes sparkle like millions of diamonds. Footprints going from the ladies' cabin to the big house, tiny hollows in the vast expanse of untouched snow, showed how small and unimportant we were to Mother Nature. She'd covered earth with a white blanket and, with a gentle wind, whispered a lullaby of memories. I loved this time of year: It was so clean and pure, and it was too cold for war.

Annie must have wakened extra early, as it took four hours to fire up the coals for the bake oven and the fragrance of the mincemeat pies was already teasing our nostrils while we ate our breakfast.

"When you've finished eating, I want you boys to decorate the garland Dacana and I wove into a ball," Annie said to Drummer and me. "Then we'll hang it from the beam in the big room." She turned to Major Cameron and Lieutenant Mackenzie. "You two bring in wood for the fire while Black Henri does some shovelling and cut greens to decorate the place."

Father Joe, the travelling priest, who had arrived in his sleigh the previous day, snuck a finger into Annie's plum-pudding batter. "Still the little dictator, are you, Annie?"

Annie slapped his hand. "It's policing that's needed when we have the likes of you in our kitchen!" Her affectionate tone said they were old friends.

"Looks like he's well fed wherever he goes!" Drummer whispered. The priest had bright red cheeks, glasses perched on the end of his nose and ears that look as though they'd so often been tucked forward under his winter toque that they were permanently bent in the wrong direction. He was dressed in a long cassock that did not disguise the size of the belly underneath. His smile wrinkled his eyes and made him seem more like a naughty boy than a Catholic priest. He saw us staring at him and winked as he stole another taste.

Breakfast was cleared, and Drummer and I remained at the long oak table stuffing nuts, berries, peppercorns and ribbons into the garland. "Don't stick everything in the same place, Drummer!" I told my friend. "We're supposed to decorate the whole ball."

"What's this ball for, anyway?" he asked.

Annie turned from her chopping. "We've always made one at Christmas, but this year it's even more important because Belle and Donald will get married under it, so you'd better make a good job of it!"

"When will we give out our presents?" I asked. Mr. Bradley had drawn my name, and the present sat on the table in the living room with all the others. I couldn't wait to see what was in it.

"Soon's Dacana gets up."

"Is she sick?"

"A little peaked, but she'll be up soon." Annie waved a wooden spoon at us. "There'll be no presents until that garland's hung."

Finally we were all sitting around the low table in the big room. The garland was hung, and we could smell the turkey Black Henri had shot cooking in the kitchen fire and the bread baking in the bake oven.

"Dacana should get the first present," Aunt Belle insisted. "She's our hostess, and we are all very grateful." She handed a soft present to Dacana who opened the side closest to her and peeked and then looked up at Aunt Belle with a surprised smile.

"How did you know?"

"Annie and I've known for a number of weeks now, and Annie had the wool tucked away in anticipation of the possibility."

Drummer looked as confused as I was. "Known what?" I asked. "What's the present?"

Dacana pulled aside the wrapping and produced a baby's blanket, which dumbfounded us all for a moment before we realized what it meant, but then the adults jumped up and congratulated Dacana and Major Cameron, the men with awkward handshakes and the women with hugs. Drummer and I followed a little more cautiously, unsure whether it was quite right to be talking about such things. Bruno felt the excitement and jumped up on everyone.

"How come the blanket's pink?" Drummer asked. "Could be yer having a boy."

"No," Dacana answered. "It's a girl. I'm sure. Perhaps later I'll have a boy, but my first child will be a girl who will carry the story of our country in her blood."

Drummer and I look confused.

"My mother was part Indian, part English," Dacana explained. "My father was a French Canadian voyageur, so I have the blood of this big country in my veins, and I will pass it and the memories that go with it to my daughter, who will also have the Scottish blood of her father." She rubbed her husband's knee.

"That's why her parents called her Dacana," Annie added. "'Tis the letters of Canada mixed up."

"An anagram," Lieutenant Mackenzie explained.

She sure suited the name, being of a grand size just like the country and having Indian eyes but light skin.

The present opening continued, and it seemed to me the gifts told more about the person who gave than the one who got. When a present was opened, the giver looked really anxious until he or she saw the expression on the receiver's face, and then the giver got a warm glow that felt even better than the delight of receiving a present. I understood this, because the chess set carved for me by Mr. Bradley was a wondrous present, and I knew that time and love was put into each beautiful piece, but when Aunt Belle cried upon reading the poem I wrote her, I almost wept with the pleasure of it.

With the fire blazing, sipping mugs of warmed cider, we gathered in various groups throughout the room: Lieutenant Mackenzie was teaching Drummer and me the moves of each carved chess piece; Dacana and Major Cameron were overseeing the final touches of our banquet; and Father Joe was off in a corner talking to Aunt Belle and Mr. Bradley. There seemed to be a little bit of disagreement, as Father Joe's tone was one of protest and Aunt Belle's one of soothing explanation. Mr. Bradley was not talking a lot. Finally they seemed to agree, and Father Joe clapped his hands to get our attention. "Bundle up, everyone. It seems the wedding ceremony is to take place at the sugar maple."

We all mumbled approval. Of course they should be married there. Why didn't we think of it before?

Black Henri and Lieutenant Mackenzie attached the horses to two sleighs and put bells on their harnesses. We climbed into the various seats, covered our laps with bearskin blankets and set off through the silent forest where each branch of every evergreen happily held a layer of snow. The sleighs' runners sliced through the crisp white blanket with a silvery sound. Bruno dashed along beside us, and I snuggled happily between Aunt Belle and Mr. Bradley.

"Look," I yelled, pointing at a birchbark dome at the base of the sugar maple, "there's somebody camped at the tree!"

"It's the shaman," Lieutenant Mackenzie said from the seat in front of us.

The horses were pulled up in front of the tree, and we got down more quietly than we would have if the hut hadn't been there. There was a fire burning in front, and the shaman crawled out of the shelter. Dacana went to him, exchanged greetings and explaining that "our friends"—she pointed to Aunt Belle and Mr. Bradley—"are here to get married."

The shaman grunted. "I will get my drum and my pipe." He turned to crawl back into the hut.

"No, no," Dacana said gently. "Our shaman will marry them." She gestured toward Father Joe.

"I will help!" the shaman insisted.

"Looks like the shaman is going to participate in your ceremony!" I whispered to Aunt Belle and Mr. Bradley.

They laughed and seemed to think it was a wonderful idea.

"Gather round," Father Joseph commanded.

Aunt Belle took Mr. Bradley's arm, and they stood in front of the priest with rest of us in a semicircle behind them. Father Joe's back was to the huge trunk of the sugar maple, and we were under the naked strength of its bare branches.

"We'll start with the Lord's prayer."

"Our Father," we all began, but we were interrupted by the shaman, who carried a birchbark container of warmed water.

"First they must wash their hands," he insisted.

"I'm sorry about this," Dacana said, "but he insists you wash your hands before the ceremony starts."

Father Joe rolled his eyes. Aunt Belle and Mr. Bradley shrugged their shoulders, took off their gloves and dipped their hands into the proffered bowl. The shaman prayed aloud as they did it.

"He's saying that you are washing away past evils, past memories and past loves and now are ready to stand before the Great Spirit, the source of life," Dacana translated.

Aunt Belle looked at Mr. Bradley with moist eyes.

"As I was saying," Father Joe interrupted, "we'll start with the Lord's prayer."

Again we began, "Our Father, who art in heaven—" While we were reciting, the shaman crawled into his hut and came out with a drum that he began to pound to the rhythm of our words.

"This is not the first time I've had to deal with a heathen invasion," Father Joe announced at the end of the prayer. "Experience tells me we'd best get on with the important part. Join hands, Belle and Donald. Now, Mr. Bradley, repeat after me. I, Donald Bradley, take you, Belle Fontaine, to be my lawful wedded wife, to have and to hold from this day forward, for better or worse, richer or poorer, in sickness and in health, until death do us part."

As Mr. Bradley looked into Aunt Belle's eyes and repeated the words with real sincerity, the shaman played his flute. By the time Aunt Belle had finished her vows, the Indian was dancing and drumming and blowing on the flute, and we were all laughing and clapping at the unexpected festiveness of the occasion. Even Father Joe was grinning as he said, "I now pronounce you husband and wife!" and we all whooped and joined the Indian in his high-stepping dance.

It was getting dark as we returned to the house. Aunt Belle and Mr. Bradley's arms met around my shoulder.

"We're a family now," Aunt Belle said. "We can leave for York any time."

I shut my eyes and let my head fall onto her shoulder with the pleasure of it.

"First there's the meeting Major Cameron has been insisting upon," Mr. Bradley reminded us.

"Father, will you say grace?" Dacana asked.

"With pleasure, my dear," the priest answered.

We all bowed our heads and let him bless the meal.

His blessing was nothing but words and words alone were never enough, but it was evening, and the sugar maple, the sunset, the lake and the stars were all quiet, so we would have to show our appreciation of this wonderful day the only way we could, even though it was only words.

"Amen!" everyone said in unison.

We passed the platters down the table and never stopped talking and laughing as we served ourselves turkey, lake trout, roast potatoes, onions and carrots.

"Do you feel different, Belle, now that you're attached to a man for the rest of your life?" Annie teased.

"Get away with you. Your teasing won't bother an old dame like me! I love this man." Aunt Belle kissed Mr. Bradley on the cheek.

He took her hand. "You're Belle Bradley now. It has a fine ring to it, don't you think?"

I had not thought of that, but it seemed to me to be a very good thing, 'cause it meant she'd be a different person than when she was Belle Fontaine—not that I didn't love the old Belle, but I knew her name carried sly memories for many of the men in York. After they were married for a while, Aunt Belle would be able to look in a mirror and be comfortable with both halves of herself.

A month passed. The ice on the lake was thick and the snow was deep, making it a good time for us to leave, so we all gathered around the kitchen table for the meeting that Dacana and Major Cameron had called.

"I've talked to you all separately, and I believe I know what each of you want for the near future." He turned first to Lieutenant Mackenzie. "You've said you'd like to go over to the island and study the Indian medicines." Mackenzie nodded his head. The Major looked at Drummer. "And you think you'd like to stay here with me?"

"Yup," Drummer agreed.

"Belle and Donald want to go back to York with Daniel, who wants to return to school."

Everybody agreed with his statements.

"Dacana and I suggest we form a company, one that could fulfill everyone's wishes." He turned to his wife. "Why don't you explain, since it was really your idea."

Dacana shook her head and smiled. "You explain, and I'll interrupt if necessary."

He looked down the table. "Lieutenant Mackenzie and Drummer will receive land as half-pay soldiers. I suggest they purchase the parcels adjoining this farm and make the land their investment in the new company. Daniel has inherited land in Sandwich that he could sell and invest the money in our venture. The apothecary and the medicine factory have to be rebuilt after the fire, and Donald Bradley could be in charge of the reconstruction. Annie and Black Henri would continue the work they've always done with the herbs and medicines, and Annie will have to take over for a while when Dacana's baby comes."

"But how can a company mix farming and medicine and an apothecary?" I asked.

"Aha!" Dacana said. "That's the crux of the idea. The land of Drummer and Lieutenant Mackenzie will not be farmed in the usual way. It will be an experimental farm where we can test medicines for animals and perhaps even have an animal hospital."

"That's where I want to work!" Drummer clapped his hands. "I 'member when Bruno got sick and the shaman gave him something that cured him.

Lieutenant Mackenzie can find out what it is, and I'll treat the animals with it." He looked around, a little embarrassed at his outburst. "'Course, I'll need a lot of learnin' first."

"Do you think you could take over the rebuilding, Donald?" Dacana asked Mr. Bradley.

"I'd like to take it on. It will mean a good income for Belle and me and let us provide a good home for Daniel."

"What'll we call the company?" I asked.

We threw around many names and finally decided on Castor, the French word for beaver, because that animal was the source of Dacana's wealth, her father having been a partner in the North West Company.

"I'm afraid we'll all have to go down to York to have the papers drawn up," Major Cameron told us. "We'll make Dacana president and I'll be vice-president. She will preside over the undertakings in York, leaving me with our own place here where I'll continue to grow crops and see to the experimental farm that one day Drummer may run. Is everyone in agreement?"

We all nodded our heads, and I could tell the others were as excited as I was.

"I've only one change I'll have to insist on," Dacana said. "You must be the president, my dear," she insisted to the Major, and when he shook his head she held her hand up. "It's not because you're a man that I'm suggesting this, it's because you are a Protestant and I'm Catholic. I can see the way the politics of the country are developing, and I predict there will be a compact of Protestant families that will dominate our world."

"But we're not interested in politics!" Major Cameron insisted.

"No, we're not, but we are interested in commerce and prevailing prejudices could interfere, so why not avoid them if we can?"

"She's right," Aunt Belle told him. "Can you imagine Bishop Strachan working with a crowd of Catholics?"

"The government has already allotted four times as much land for church construction to the Anglicans and Presbyterians as they have to the Catholics." Mr. Bradley added. "Which is a sure sign Dacana has logic behind her ideas."

"I'd not thought of that," Major Cameron confessed. "So be it. I shall be president."

"What do you think of that, Drummer?" I said. "We're shareholders in a company, and we're still kids."

"Damned good, I'd say!" He turned to Major Cameron. "I'm real excited about this farm. Maybe when our animal farm becomes famous, I'll be rich and I'll marry Dacana's baby."

"Who said you get to marry her? Maybe I will!" I protested.

"Now, now, you two, the child isn't even born yet." Dacana smiled and stroked her belly.

It was perfect day to be leaving. The sun was shining and there was no wind. Major Cameron was lending us the one-seated sleigh and a pair of horses to return to York.

"Dacana, Annie and Black Henri will be following you in a few days," he said as he watched the three of us climb onto the seat on which there were two fur blankets, one to sit on and the other to cover us. Mr. Bradley took the reins; I was in the middle between him and Aunt Belle, who was making sure we were all tucked in. Everyone was out to say goodbye.

"I'll see you when you come to York, Drummer," I said to my friend, who was leaning up against the sleigh.

"Jist a minute before you leave, I want to give you back your mirror." He pulled it out from underneath his red coat. "It really helped, Daniel, but I figure you need to have it back."

I leaned down and took it from him, secretly pleased to have the gift returned but a little insulted at the same time. "Thanks, Drummer, but why do you think I need it?"

"It helps with pain, don't it?" His tone suggested that the answer was so logical the question needn't have been asked, and I guessed he was right: My pain was just as invisible as his.

"Thanks!" There was a croak in my voice as I shook his hand.

"We'd best be off so we can take advantage of this beautiful day," Mr. Bradley said. He clucked at the horses and off we went to a chorus of goodbyes and vigorous hand-waving.

The snow-laden evergreens seemed to smile at us as we whisked down the lane toward the lake. Mr. Bradley pulled the horses to a slow trot as we passed the sugar maple, and we all turned our heads toward the Queen as we passed. Winter showed the strength of her elegant branches that curved up toward the sky and then down in a dance before stretching back up to smile at the sun.

"What're you saying to the tree?" I asked Aunt Belle.

"Not so much saying things, more like I'm sharing my remembrances of the last few months and hope the tree will store them lest I forget the wonderful things that have happened here."

"And you, Mr. Bradley?"

"I'm remembering the wedding. It wasn't exactly your standard ceremony, and that difference will be what brings smiles to our eyes and warmth to our hearts every time we think of it."

"What were you thinking, Daniel?" Aunt Belle asked.

"Thoughts were jumping around in my head like incomplete sentences. I remembered my deep-down misery disappeared when I slept under the tree, but before I could think about that it came to me that I'll probably always be a little bit sad and from there my mind jumped to you and Mr. Bradley and how comfortable it is to be with you, then from there I started looking at the future and then we were past the tree and I didn't say goodbye."

"You don't say goodbye to the sugar maple, you take it with you in your heart." Aunt Belle squeezed me to her.

The sleigh slid smoothly along the lake, taking us York and our new life.

CHAPTER 29
APRIL/MAY 1814

▼

Matthew Elliott

The big lake granted me an easy trip back from York by keepin' her surface smooth as silk, and I thanked God for small blessings 'cause there was little else in this world that was tranquil. Sarah was at the water to meet me, offerin' a hand to pull me up to the dock—an assistance I confess to have needed, as I was feelin' weak as a declawed lion.

"Did you have any luck, Matthew?" she asked me as we walked arm in arm to our little house up the lake.

"I'm afraid not, my Sarah. There just isn't any food available. In the area around the Thames, the mills are gone, the horses have been stolen, the livestock's bin killed and the whole damned area is burned to the ground, and in York there's not a business nor public building left standing. Amherstburg is occupied and the whole damned country is on the brink of starvation."

We sloshed along the muddy street, passing glassy-eyed citizens who trudged along with great effort and little strength, all tryin' to find something to buy that would salve their hunger. The 103rd regiment stationed in the hills and my 2,000 Indians encamped outside the village were also sufferin' from empty stomachs, and they were all creatin' big sad crowds on the streets of this small town. I could hardly look at them.

A drunken soldier staggered out of the tavern and knocked us off balance. I collapsed on the ground with my Sarah on top.

The man seemed to have enough sobriety to realize what he'd done. "I'm sorry, forgive me." He helped us both up and stood staring and weaving as we wiped ourselves off.

"What the fekin' hell do you think you're doing?" I yelled at him.

Sarah wiped me down and said, "It's all right, soldier. It was an accident."

"Accident?" I yelled. "Sure isn't the man a goddamned drunk? The accident is the hours he spent in the tavern."

The swaying soldier thought about my accusation for an unusually long minute. "I am drunk, sir, because I have no food in my stomach, there being none available hereabouts." He began to stagger away and yelled over his shoulder, "At least I haven't deserted."

Sarah grabbed my arm and pulled me toward the house. "Since you've been gone, I've seen a lot more of that, and it's hard to blame the soldiers. They've not been paid and are suffering from ague as well as dysentery. Many have deserted." She was bearing more of my weight than I should have permitted, but there was naught I could do about it. When we passed the tavern, she asked, "Whom did you see in York?"

"The top man, Lieutenant General Gordon Drummond. He's tryin' hard to bring some order to the chaos by passin' a bunch of laws, but I'm not sure it'll help." My voice was weak, an old man's growl.

"What kind of laws?"

"Outlawin' the distillation of grain 'cause all the wheat and oats and barley are needed for food. Confiscatin' the property of traitors and makin' the militia sign up for longer periods."

"That's all fine, Matthew, but what about food now? Can't the government buy food from somewhere?"

"That's another problem. The army's got only paper money in denominations of 25 pounds. A poor farmer owed 20 pounds doesn't get paid, and if he's owed 40 pounds he's paid only 25. Worse than that, the Americans have been spreading counterfeit bills, so the few farmers who have grain ta sell won't accept anything but gold." I leaned into my wife. "I'm not feelin' so good, my Sarah."

"Matthew, there's an officer at the door. You need to sign the papers for some corn they're delivering to the Indians."

I couldn't bring myself to move from my chair. "Tell him to take 'em to someone else in the Indian Department. Tell him I'm sick."

My Sarah dealt with the soldier at the door and came back to me. "Let me take you to bed."

"My throat hurts and my bones ache. Maybe if I got some sleep, I'd be able to pull myself together."

"He'll not leave his bed again."

"Shh, doctor, he might hear."

I was there and then I was not. The devil, Pain, would not release me. It dragged me back to battle after battle. I could smell the blood and feces and burn and smoke and I was there, unthinking, killing, wounding and screaming. *"Stop," Love said gently. "Look, Matthew." She showed me the empty battlefield and the trampled grass that began again to unfurl and greet the sun. "But the soldiers that bent it will not be back." She kissed my forehead. "You, me, those men, we are single teardrops in the universe of the Great Spirit."*

Sarah bent over me, washing my limbs with soap and a moist cloth.

"Are you makin' sure I'll be clean to meet my maker, Sarah my love?"

"Hush, Matthew."

She held up my arm to wash, and I stared at my aged nails full of bumps and waves.

"Do I smell a fire?"

"It's a beautiful day, and Boy's cooking out in the back."

I shut my eyes. The fragrance of burned pine branches took me back again to Love. *I'm sittin' cross-legged in front of the fire and inhalin' the fragrance of the burn. Love is cleanin' the soil out from under my nails while gently tryin' to explain the Indian way. "We are one family. We walk the same earth, drink from the same rivers, sleep under the same sky. Just as we cannot sell the water or the clouds, we cannot sell the earth because we do not own it." Tecumseh has a bullet hole in his neck; he hears her words, drops his head to his chin, turns away from us and disappears into the woods.*

"Matthew, wake up. Are you crying?"

I opened my eyes. Where was I? I stared at the beams across the ceiling. There was a spider making a web, *weaving strands that bound Boy and Sarah and the babes together and another strand around the throat of Alexander. Young Daniel was crawling on top of the strands; his knees sank in the spaces, but he kept going.*

The web appeared and disappeared. "Am I with you, my Sarah? I'm not sure if I'm alive dreamin' I'm dead or dead dreamin' I'm alive"

"You're here, Matthew, with me."

"I'm so very, very tired. Give me a kiss, my Sarah, and let me sleep."

Sarah's Diary

Matthew did not awaken from his sleep.

I washed his old, wrinkled body and prepared him for burial. Death had released the tension from his muscles, and it seemed as though his depleted body had exhaled the detritus of life. I prayed he was at peace and wept for him and for me and for the loss of our quiet love, one based on gratitude but, sadly, lacking lust.

Matthew and others complained so vehemently that Procter was finally brought before a court martial and found guilty. He was publicly reprimanded and suspended without rank or pay for six months.

After that, Matthew Elliott, my rough-edged husband who did not suffer fools lightly, was returned to favour, and his admirers were able to negotiate a better pension for me.

I'll go back to Amherstburg. I know the house has been ransacked and needs many repairs, but I can now afford to fix it all up.

Boy will come with me. I can't help it.

AUTHOR'S NOTE

▼

The war of 1812-14 in North America would never have happened had Napoleon not declared war on Britain.

To maintain mastery of the sea, Britain blockaded European ports, preventing ships from delivering their cargo to the continent. To achieve their goal, they captured and boarded hundreds of American vessels on the high seas. Their embargo had a dire effect on the economy of neutral America, but that was unimportant to Britain, which considered the United States a new, raw country of little consequence.

The British further enraged America by enacting the Orders in Council, which permitted the Royal Navy to stop American merchant ships, or ships of any neutral country, on the high seas in order to search for deserters, remove them and press them into British service. The citizens of the United States considered this action lawless and an infringement of their liberty.

James Madison became president in 1809 and in the election of 1810 a number of "war hawks" arrived in Washington. These men believed they should show strength in dealing with Great Britain, and as they took over leadership positions in Washington, they promulgated the dream that the whole continent—including the fertile lands and giant forest acreage still held by the English—should be under the American flag.

Anger with the British was not limited to the east coast. Westward expansion took frontiersmen into Indian territory in Kentucky and Ohio, and when the Indians fought to protect their land, it was put forth that British agents were arming the Indians and aiding them in their battles—a charge that was not entirely exaggerated.

A Shawnee chief named Tecumseh attempted to stem the invasion and protect Indian lands by forming a confederacy of Indian tribes, one strong enough to resist the invasion of the white man. Tecumseh's brother, a medicine man known as the Prophet, was a great orator, and the two formed a powerful union able to persuade warring tribes to unite against the encroachment of the white men.

In 1811, Governor William Henry Harrison of Indiana Territory marched with an army of 1,000 men to the Prophet's town of Tippecanoe, where a battle took place. History books vary in the reportage of this battle. Some say the Prophet attacked Harrison and others say it was Harrison and his men who attacked the town of Tippecanoe. Whatever the case, the Indians were routed and the town was put to the torch. Tecumseh, who had been on a trip to the south, returned to find his town in ashes and his warriors scattered. He had no choice but to join the English against the "Long Knives."

By 1811, the war hawks called for an invasion of British North America. Henry Clay, the Speaker of the House and a brilliant orator, beat the drums of war.

Congress, having ordered the creation of a volunteer army of 50,000 men in February 1812, declared war on Great Britain on June 18 of the same year. On June 23, Britain revoked the Orders in Council, but it was too late.

The war hawks did not win over the whole nation, especially the New England states, whose citizens refused to volunteer for military service. Massachusetts demonstrated its anger by hanging the Stars and Stripes at half-mast.

When war began, there were 7,000 men in the regular American armed forces, and old men who lacked experience and were generally incompetent commanded them.

After my story, there was one more great battle on Canadian soil, the bloodiest in the war. Having failed to take Montreal and Kingston, the Americans decided to invade the Niagara Peninsula, and the battle took place at Lundy's Lane. The outcome left no winners, just hundreds upon hundreds of dead and wounded. Each side has claimed victory in that battle. Winfield Scott has been acclaimed a hero in America for his defeat of Lieutenant General Drummond, and Canadians have boasted that no ground was taken or lost. It is the way of politicians and historians to slant such outcomes in their favour, making one realize that the moral reality of war is not fixed by the soldiers who fought but by the opinions formed through the propaganda of those in control.

After the battle of Lundy's Lane, the only American presence in Canada was the occupation of Amherstburg and 15 acres of ground around Fort Erie. The war continued, but not on Canadian soil.

With Napoleon defeated, the British were able to send 16,000 men to join the battle. It was they who burned Washington in August, but they achieved little else, retreating after a naval defeat on Lake Champlain in September.

The Treaty of Ghent was signed on December 24, 1814, stating that the two countries would return to their prewar status (*status quo ante bellum*). Unfortunately, the news did not arrive fast enough for the 2,000 British soldiers who lost their lives when defeated at the battle of New Orleans.

Because they defeated the British at Plattsburgh and New Orleans, the Americans believed they won the war. Canadians celebrated the win because they drove the Americans off their land. The British deemed themselves winners because they saved a colony. The true losers were the Indians, as the Americans refuted the Treaty of Greenville, which had granted the Indians the land north of the Ohio. The British, even though they had promised the Indians that the father across the ocean would never desert them, shamefully agreed to the American demands.